Dea

Deadly Circle

A Headland Mystery

DC Poolie

Deadly Circle/DC Poolie

Foreword

The co-authors, Dave and Cliff, were inspired to write this book after fairly recently becoming friends and discovering that they both had long held ambitions to write a crime novel.

Singularly, this would never have happened. However, collectively they have not only produced this book, but have also become the best of friends forging an enjoyable writing partnership.

The inspiration for this book was a historical area of Hartlepool, called the Headland, and its colourful characters.

Table of Contents

	page
Chapter 1	7
Chapter 2	22
Chapter 3	36
Chapter 4	43
Chapter 5	52
Chapter 6	67
Chapter 7	79
Chapter 8	93
Chapter 9	137
Chapter 10	144
Chapter 11	161
Chapter 12	177
Chapter 13	192
Chapter 14	200
Chapter 15	210
Chapter 16	226
Chapter 17	235
Chapter 18	252

Deadly Circle/DC Poolie

Confusion was etched across his young face. He turned this way and that struggling to find the person he had recently been so dependent on. He thought he could see her long blond hair in the mirror, but it wasn't enough to stifle the growing fear and panic that was welling up within. He had no idea of what was going on. He thought, like on every other day since they had come to this place that the three of them were going to the park to play and feed the ducks. That comforting routine was interrupted when these 2 strangers stepped out in front of them and blocked their way.

Now he was sitting in the back of a large and unfamiliar car. The smiling dark-haired lady, the lady stranger, had buckled up his seat belt and told him to sit there like a very good boy. He didn't know what to do. It wasn't right! The kind blond haired lady was now nowhere to be seen. He needed her.

She had helped them when mummy and daddy never came home. She had held them and comforted them. She had fed them and told them stories at bedtime. She had come to him when he woke up screaming and upset. She hadn't told him off, or smacked him, when he wet the bed. He instinctively knew that the blond lady was good for him but now there was this other dark-haired stranger maybe taking her place.

His attention was diverted when the door on the other side of the car opened, and he felt a rush of cold air hitting the left side of his face. He saw his baby brother, already strapped into the baby seat, looming towards him held in the strong arms of the man stranger who was grunting and muttering as he attempted to fix the baby seat in place. Seeing his little brother, a whole new emotion replaced his fear, and he reached out his hand towards him. His brother gurgled and smiled as their hands touched.

As if by magic the strangers were now already in the front seats both craning their necks to look at the 2 boys.

'We are going to take you to your new home. You will have lots of toys and a garden to play in,' said the dark-haired lady. 'We are your new mummy and daddy,' she added with a friendly smile. The baby just continued gurgling contented that he was with his bigger brother.

For a second, he relaxed, hopeful that maybe this wasn't such a bad day. Then he glanced at the man who was also smiling but there was something in the way the man was looking at him that brought back an overwhelming feeling of dread.

As the car drove off the lady kept talking reassuringly to the boys, but he wasn't listening. He now could see the lovely blond lady, his comfort blanket, waving in the rear-view mirror. As she grew smaller in the mirror and started to disappear completely, he felt a growing panic grabbing him and a warm trickle ran down his thigh.

Deadly Circle/DC Poolie

Chapter 1

Troy smiled inside when he pulled up outside the football ground in the black chauffeur driven BMW 7 series. It seemed no time at all since he had turned up here as a 15-year-old with dreams of winning a pro contract with his local club. Now he was back as a 32-year-old ex-international footballer to sign again for Hartlepool.

He was returning to his hometown club and his mission was to help them avoid another relegation battle. Although the earlier part of summer had brought a lot of rain, the sun was shining down on the seaside town and there wasn't a cloud in the sky. Troy was thankful that there was still the customary coastal breeze which would make that day, and the rest of summer training, pass without the high temperatures making things too uncomfortable.

Nothing much had changed in the years since he'd been away. The stadium still looked shabby, and the entrance and turnstiles were just as he remembered them. For a moment he had second thoughts and wondered if he was making the right move to come back.

His agent had assured him that he could get him a good club in a higher league or even in America. Maybe he was right, but Troy felt he owed the club that had given him his chance in football, and this just seemed the right time.

Deadly Circle/DC Poolie

Any remaining doubts evaporated when a familiar face came into view. Charlie Green the club's groundsman who had been with the club as long as anyone could remember ambled towards him. The big beaming smile that Troy remembered so well stretched across the old guy's face.

In fact, Charlie Green, long-time supporter and former player of Hartlepool United, was something of a local legend in the town. His 62 years had mostly been spent helping or playing for his hometown club.

When his 6-year playing career was prematurely ended by a bad knee injury, he had maintained his contact with the club by being a general odd job man around the ground. Back in those days football contracts didn't guarantee a life of retired luxury, particularly if they ended prematurely.

Eventually, he was rewarded with the full-time post of groundsman, a job he took on with his usual energy and enthusiasm. In a comparatively short space of time, he had the inside of the ground looking its best for years.

The playing surface was immaculate and was his pride and joy. No one was allowed on that pitch without Charlie's permission. His work did not go unnoticed, and he had regularly won the award for the best playing surface in League 2.

When they, unfortunately, were relegated from the football league he ruled the roost in the Conference too. Charlie and his team of volunteers were certainly indispensable to a football club where finance was always tight.

Of late Charlie had had to battle with sadness and loneliness in his private life. Charlie met his late wife, Meg, at a football match when she would come along to watch the games with her father. They had been together for almost 35 years before she was taken ill and died suddenly from a brain tumour.

Having this job at the club helped him to get over the massive loss and hole in his life, but he still missed her terribly and was glad he had the football club to keep him occupied. They had one child a boy Jason, now aged 23. He was a talented footballer who had moved to the USA when he had got the chance of a 3-year contract with a professional team in California.

Charlie always understood why his son took up the offer, but sometimes he did wish he was a lot closer to home. Because of COVID and financial constraints Charlie had yet to visit Jason. He hoped he would be going over there soon but his 'trip fund' wasn't even at half of its projected target. It really had been a long time since he had been able to hold someone he loved in his arms and in those dark, quiet times at home Charlie felt bereft.

He still lived in the same house he and his wife had lived in all their married life. It was located on the Headland area of the town, overlooking the North Sea. The house was still testimony to their life together with the same furniture, chosen by Meg and always tastefully done so, and the numerous framed pictures of them as a family. Charlie regularly stood for a long time in front of different ones remembering, in great detail, the circumstances of each photo.

He would naturally feel sad, but it was also cathartic for him. He would even smile at the various iterations of facial hair which he sported over the years. Meg must have really loved him to put up with some of them. The only ones she

9

vetoed were the goatee and the narrow moustache which Meg described as Hitleresque.

Nowadays, he rarely had any facial hair. If he did it was a traditional moustache meticulously trimmed just as Meg had preferred.

He had his faithful border collie Jess to keep him company and he would take Jess everyday to the football club. While he worked away on his pitch Jess sat on the side-line watching him, but like everyone else Jess knew not to go onto that pitch unless he was called.

'Good to see you back Troy,' said Charlie.

'Glad to see you again my friend. How's the pitch these days?' Troy replied.

It really helped Troy to see such a friendly and familiar face. He tried to remember when he had last seen Charlie or even spoken to him. Somehow Charlie no longer looked his full 5'10" as age had probably done something internally to his bones. His fair hair had been on the wane the last time they had met but fortunately, certainly to Troy's mind, Charlie had finally done away with his Bobby Charlton comb over settling for a trim and neat style which matched the bald area in the middle. Charlie's energy and wonderful nature were still there to be seen on that very friendly face and in his bright and lively green eyes. He obviously had kept himself fit over the years but like with many of a certain age, there was a distinct paunch starting to protrude over his waistband.

'Best part about this club at the moment Troy. Not the happiest place just now,' Charlie turned and looked wistfully towards the old buildings as he said this.

10

Deadly Circle/DC Poolie

'A few good results will help lift everyone's spirits I'm sure,' Troy said following Charlie's gaze.

Troy made his way over to the small block of buildings which were made up of

the home and away dressing rooms, a treatment room and the manager's office. The manager he was meeting was someone Troy had known at one of his previous clubs. Bob Scott had been towards the end of his own career when they had spent a short time together at Aston Villa. Troy's memory of him as a teammate was sketchy but he was certain that he remembered him as somewhat grumpy and unsociable. So, it was quite a surprise when Bob Scott rang him in person to ask if he would be interested in rejoining Hartlepool United FC.

The meeting in the boardroom did not take long as Troy had already decided, along with his absentee agent, Paul Hughes, who was on honeymoon with his new bride that it was a move he wanted to make and that the pre-agreed contract was more than acceptable. The third person involved in the meeting was club chairman, Sidney Hackett, whose long-term commitment to the club had been the backbone of its recent resurrection.

The only shock for Troy was the personality transplant which his ex-teammate seemed to have had. He was cheerful and enthusiastic about the team and what he thought Troy could bring to the side. To conclude the negotiations representatives of the local press and the club's social media were invited into the boardroom to take the customary pictures and to hear a short statement read out by Bob Scott on behalf of the club. To the disappointment of the reporters from the local newspapers there was to be no Q and A session.

11

Deadly Circle/DC Poolie

As a fans-based club it had been decided that any preliminary information and interaction would come through the club's social media team. In other words, Steve and Daisy from the local 6th form college who, as well as helping the club they both supported and loved, were gaining credits towards their media 'A' level.

Various photographs were taken including one where the three protagonists were standing under a Hartlepool United banner with Troy and the chairman holding up a club shirt with Troy's name and new squad number on it. Finally, after a handshake and a hearty man hug from his new Gaffer, Troy stepped outside and met up again with Charlie Green.

'Everything go ok then Troy?' Charlie asked.

'Straight forward as I expected. I've already got the keys to my new digs in my hands and now just need to find my way there.'

'What address is that then?' the old guy enquired.

'48 Waterside Apartments,' replied Troy.

The surprised expression on Charlie's face did not go unnoticed by Troy but he let it pass without comment and together they walked towards the BMW, and it's immaculately dressed driver who was waiting beside it.

When they pulled up outside the apartments Troy understood that surprised look. Very expensive looking apartments right on the marina front overlooked a row of luxury yachts which were moored a short distance from the front entrance to the apartments.

As they stepped away from the car Troy did a full 360. This would have looked comical to any onlooker, as Charlie mirrored Troy's circular action but a fraction of a second behind his footballer friend.

'Wow!' Troy exclaimed. 'When did this all happen?' He couldn't contain his surprise.

'I know,' replied Charlie, 'Hartlepool is certainly redeveloping itself nicely. Of course,' he was now looking across the marina to the north, 'that's where my heart lies.'

He was staring at the peninsula known as the Headland, an area surrounded by the North Sea with a certain eclectic beauty to it. The historical old houses, many painted in subtle pastel shades, looked majestic in the fading light, framing the coastline, strong and permanent.

'That place, and its people, got me through COVID.' The affection in his voice was clear.

They were just about to use the bigger of the 2 keys Troy had been given to enter the building by the secure main entrance door when they heard a rather strange voice.

'Excuse me. Can I help you?'

Standing behind them was a rather strange looking man. As well as being painfully thin with a mop of longish, unkempt, greasy hair this man obviously took no pride in his appearance. His clothes were ill fitting and stained.

'Christ!' thought Troy, 'How can you walk around outside, amongst normal people, looking like that?'

Fortunately, Charlie interjected and explained they were looking for number 48. 'My friend here will be living there,' he added.

'Ah yes,' replied the man, 'You must be from the football club. I'm the janitor.' He smiled showing the most uneven and discoloured teeth Troy had ever seen.

'It's on the 5th floor to the right.' He seemed pleased with himself and was obviously waiting for some form of approbation.

'Thanks,' said Troy.

'Yes, thanks,' echoed Charlie. They turned back towards the main door and used the key to enter the block of apartments.

'God! He really gave me the creeps,' Troy confided in Charlie once in the lift. 'Hope I don't meet him on a dark night,' he laughed.

'Come on Troy give the man a break. We can't all look and dress like George Clooney.'

Troy's degree of surprise about this area of Hartlepool and the apartment block went up several notches when the door to no. 48 was opened. He was confronted by a penthouse apartment which was unbelievably sumptuous. He looked around in disbelief because it was far more than he could ever have expected.

'You are obviously well in the gaffer's good books Troy,' smiled Charlie.

'As long as I don't get the bill for this place, I'm well pleased,' Troy laughed.

They both heard a familiar ding and Charlie reached into his jacket pocket to pull out his smartphone.

'That was quick,' said Charlie smiling, 'Those kids deserve to get top grades in their exam.'

'What do you mean?' Troy asked totally unaware of what Charlie was talking about.

Charlie sat down on the sofa and beckoned Troy to join him. 'Your signing has already been released on the club's

Deadly Circle/DC Poolie

Instagram account. There is a glowing biography about you as a person and a player and they've posted a few pics too.' Charlie looked at one picture with particular scrutiny, 'Scratch that comment about them deserving top grades.'

Troy leaned in but couldn't see anything wrong with the picture, 'Looks fine to me.'

'Come on Troy. They need to learn the art of picture composition. Don't you think it would have been better if you and Bob had been holding the shirt? I mean you two are the same height and build and poor old Sid looks like a hobbit between the two of you. He is almost having to hold the shirt aloft to have it level.'

'I see what you mean but maybe with Bob and I both being just over 6 foot tall and having similar shortish brown hair they thought it'd be clearer to people which one of us is the newly signed player. Even a league 2 team wouldn't be desperate enough to sign an overweight 70-year-old.'

'I guess,' said Charlie a little deflated that his argument had been shot down. 'Your girlish highlights don't stand out too much and not everyone who will see the picture in the newspapers would know what a has been like you looks like.'

'Same old Charlie,' laughed Troy playfully hitting Charlie on the shoulder. He knew Charlie would never say such a thing to hurt anyone, yet alone Troy. Humour had always been his default tactic, 'Let's read that bio.' And with that he took the phone from Charlie.

Charlie watched as Troy read the text. He hadn't seen Troy for ages but still could read Troy's mood from his very expressive face.

Deadly Circle/DC Poolie

'What's wrong?' he asked knowing that Troy wasn't completely happy with the bio.

Troy paused for a few seconds, 'Well they are factually correct when it comes to my career, but this makes me look like a saint.'

Charlie took back his phone and read. 'Well, you have done a lot for charity over the years,' he commented. 'You always give 100 percent and you have been loyal to every team you've played for.'

'Maybe so. What about the drink problems I had at Villa?'

'Two things my friend. Firstly, you battled and overcame them. And only a very few people actually were ever aware because it didn't really affect your game. Secondly, you are, contrary to popular opinion, a very self-critical person who has always battled with self-confidence issues. Do you remember when you first arrived here? You were so conflicted. An obvious football talent with a great future but you were so hard on yourself.'

Troy looked fondly at Charlie and placed his hand affectionately on Charlie's arm.

'Yes, I do remember. People thought I was arrogant or a spoilt brat. Only you, and then dear Meg, saw the truth and helped me by getting me to talk things through. Gradually, I gained more confidence and more control.'

Charlie stiffened slightly at the mention of his beloved wife. He still would get very emotional when he heard her name. Or even thought of her in fact.

'I still have those demons. Sometimes I wonder if I'm bipolar.'

Deadly Circle/DC Poolie

'Don't be silly,' Charlie chastised his younger friend. 'Any woman currently in your life?'

'Not since the end of last season when someone I loved dumped me,' Troy mused. 'Can't blame her. I think I have genuine commitment issues. You and Meg are the only people who have ever got really close to me. Looking back on things I never even seemed to have the sort of relationship with my parents that my friends had with theirs.'

Charlie spent the next ten minutes trying to lighten the conversation. Finally, he got up.

'Training is in the morning at 10 at the university complex. Do you know where it is?' Charlie enquired.

'Yes, I'll be there,' replied Troy. 'I'm looking forward to meeting my new teammates.'

Troy sensed something in Charlie's expression but couldn't decide what it meant so he just let it go. After Charlie had hugged him goodbye and left, Troy sat down on the expensive L-shaped scarlet leather sofa shutting his eyes looking to settle himself into his new surroundings.

Ten minutes later, hardly a surprise to anyone who knew Troy, he was wide awake and now wandering around the apartment again, but this time with the critical eye of someone who was going to use it as a home and not a holiday rental.

Essentially it was a modern, highly specked and open planned 2-bedroom apartment. The colour scheme was bright and monotone but, more importantly for Troy, not the ubiquitous magnolia. Any colour accents were found in the primary coloured, but also very clean looking, furniture. The 65" smart TV was attached to the feature wall.

'That will be perfect for film nights and my PlayStation,' Troy thought to himself. Next to the spacious living and cooking area there was a family bathroom. As was the current trend this bathroom was, in fact, bath-less with a massive walk-in shower instead. The 2 bedrooms were of a similar size but there was no difficulty for Troy in deciding which one would be his. The one with the sea view and the en-suite clearly stood out.

Opening the bi-fold doors, Troy stepped out onto the balcony, and he surprised himself when he let out an audible gasp. He hadn't expected this. The panoramic view from the 5th floor of the building was breath-taking. Any sea view is desirable but, to a boy who grew up in the area, this one encapsulated the essence of the region.

He sat down on one of the 2 rattan chairs and stared southwards towards Teesside. Some picky people would complain about the industrial area near Middlesbrough ruining the view, or the wind farm sitting proudly on top of the waves being an eyesore, but to Troy this was home. His home.

There was a slight chill in the air, so Troy got up to go inside. As he did, he caught a glimpse of a different part of the Marina. One which seemed to act as a fly trap to the people of Hartlepool, an area of waterside bars and restaurants. Troy's expression changed. Most would have thought such a neighbouring development would be an added benefit to what was an excellent place to live. Troy's face, as he shut the patio doors, showed that he was now anything but happy.

Deadly Circle/DC Poolie

I looked over at my brother sleeping in his cot. I had heard my new foster mummy say how cute and innocent he looked when he was asleep. I must admit he looked at peace and I envied him. It was still in the summer holidays, and I hadn't really met anyone since we had arrived. Mummy, that is what she wanted me to call her, didn't work and was always checking up on us but Father was only in the house first thing in the morning and then came home just before we had tea.

Mummy said it was up to me whether I wanted to have my own room or not. She was more than happy when I told her I'd rather share with my brother, at least for a while, until we both settled in. I could tell Father wasn't so pleased. In fact, he hardly ever seemed pleased, or smiled.

I was feeling quite happy as we had had chicken nuggets, my favourite, for tea and I had done everything they said I should do before bedtime. Quietly, so as not to wake him in his cot, I cleaned my teeth and changed into my pyjamas. Now I was waiting for mummy to come and tuck me into bed. She always used to do that. I could have done it myself, but I think it made her feel like my real mummy. I still cry at night when I think of her. I miss her so much: her hair cascading onto my face as she kissed me goodnight and her smell. I will never forget her smell or the warmth I felt when she held me close.

The door opened and in walked mummy, alone. I never used to see Father until mummy had gone. I was beginning to like her, but she did seem very quiet and shy. She never really said much. I think it was because she was afraid of waking the baby, which was silly because once asleep, he never stirred until much later.

'Do you need anything?' she asked me, just like every night. I thanked her, shaking my head and looked at the glass of water on the bedside table. She followed my gaze and said, 'Remember only drink a little if you are thirsty. We don't want any more accidents and you've done so well recently'. She smoothed out my duvet kissing me on the forehead and turned around to leave. 'Father will be up soon. Sleep well sweet Prince.'

As I heard the door close, I pondered on whether that made her a Queen? Or maybe my real mummy was? I liked that idea.

Laying there on my back, I heard footsteps on the stairs. These were much heavier so it must be Father. The door opened and his, now familiar, silhouette moved across the room. Normally he used to stand quite formally by the side of the bed, and we would exchange a few words before he disappeared. I didn't mind that because he didn't act as friendly as my real daddy used to. This time though he came around to the other side of the bed, away from the cot, and sat down so that he was right next to me.

'I am going to tell you a secret,' he said. 'It is something all boys learn and is something we never share with the girls. Would you like that?' His voice sounded different, like he was out of breath from running.

I didn't have a chance to reply before he continued, 'All boys and their fathers, when they are your age, do something special together. Only they can do it because girls are *different.' His voice became even quieter and seemed to shake a little bit.*

He slid his hand under my duvet and moved it across my body until it held my willy.

'This is how we are different,' he continued. And with that he took my hand and placed it on top of his trousers. He then moved it up and down forcing it to hold on to something hard under his trousers.

'That is how I am different to women,' he said excitedly. 'When mummy is at bingo tomorrow, I will tell you more about this secret.' He then removed his hand from under the duvet and placed mine back to where it was before.

'Now be a good boy and get to sleep. Remember this is going to be a boys' secret. You mustn't tell mummy or anyone else. Do you understand?'

I nodded and he left the room.

In the dark I lay there feeling confused but also quite happy. I could tell that father was finally pleased with me and we were going to share a secret. I felt sorry for mummy that she couldn't share in the fun.

Chapter 2

Troy turned up at the local university training centre a little early as he didn't want to make a bad impression on his first day. As the marina wasn't too far from the training centre Troy had decided to walk. He thought it would help him to feel back in step, in this case quite literally, with his hometown.

During the walk he did, however, make a mental note to sort out a new car now that his driving ban was over. He didn't fancy that walk every day in the cold of winter. At the centre he was quite impressed with the G5 pitches and equipment.

Most English football clubs have, over the years, improved both the methods of training and their facilities but very few teams have such state-of-the-art training pitches available.

Troy is a down to earth, grass roots footballer and most of all he was looking forward to getting the ball out and meeting his new teammates.

'After all football is a team sport.'

That was the mantra of his old PE teacher and Troy had always been governed by this doctrine.

After a few light exercises and drills, run by the first team coach, Harry Garside, they were set up for a 9 a side game on the full-size artificial pitch. Although not the most sensitive of people even Troy was starting to sense a cool atmosphere amongst the squad, which mainly seemed to be centred around him.

'Maybe,' he thought, 'It's just them waiting to see what I'm like and it's up to me to convince them that I'm here to do what I can do to help the team avoid relegation.'

Two players, Goalkeeper Brad Picken and a young reserve midfield player Tony Marsh, made the effort to come over to shake Troy's hand and welcome him to the club. Even so, Troy was still left with the impression that there was something not being said. It was hard for him to think otherwise as the rest of the players seemed to be avoiding eye contact, or any other type of contact for that matter, with him.

The game started and Troy began slowly to feel his way into the game and his allotted team. Slowly it struck Troy that they were waiting for him to show them something of his talents. So, when the next was ball played up to him he turned and pushed the ball through the defender's legs firing it into the top corner of the goal. 'That should impress them,' he thought.

Evidently this proved not to be the case because when he turned to look at his new teammates there was a lot of whispering behind hands and head shaking. The defender in question, Billy Brook, looked red faced and angry as he faced up to Troy.

'Do that again and you'll be in hospital when you wake up,' he shouted.

After that the game deteriorated into a series of less than welcoming challenges on Troy and he was quite relieved when the whistle blew to end the game.

Troy walked off the field with Brad and Tony who, seemingly, were the only two welcoming people in the squad.

23

Deadly Circle/DC Poolie

'Are all the training games as lively as that?' Troy asked the pair.

'Not usually but some of the lads think you are getting special treatment from the club, and it is causing some resentment,' was their reply.

Troy wasn't sure what to make of that comment but decided to let it go for now.

In fact, on reflection, he would have to agree to some extent. He was well impressed with his luxurious marina apartment and was probably on higher wages than the other lads, but he had dropped down from the premier league to league 2 when he could have earned more by moving to other teams at a higher level. Maybe if things turn out as he hoped over the next couple of months the players' opinions of him may improve. Certainly, the upcoming run of fixtures could decide the club's future and confirm the success of Troy's signing.

'Or maybe it would prove the doubters right,' Troy thought negatively to himself.

His first game would most likely be the home game against Doncaster Rovers, a big game for Troy and the team with a lot resting on the result. After that a 2nd round FA Cup game against non-league team Whitby Town and the ensuing fixtures against Salford and Stockport County could make Troy's return to his old club a lot more comfortable.

Charlie Green the kit man/groundsman met him as he was leaving the building to return to his apartment.

'How did that go Troy?' Charlie asked.

'Could have gone better I reckon. Early days though I suppose,' Troy replied.

24

Deadly Circle/DC Poolie

'Any plans for tonight lad?' the old guy enquired.

'Not really Charlie. I may have a wander around the marina to see what's about.'

'Watch what you are doing round there Troy. Not always the best place to be out on your own.'

'Who knows I might not be on my own for long,' grinned Troy.

Deadly Circle/DC Poolie

The first game v AFC Wimbledon H   0-0

Pre-season went by without much improvement in the dressing room atmosphere. So, it was no surprise that Troy wasn't really in a very positive mood before the first home match with Wimbledon. He cut a very lonely figure sitting there in the pre match build up. He left the changing room, head slightly bowed, and walked towards the pitch.

However, when Troy emerged from the tunnel and jogged onto the pitch for that first home game of the season, he had not realised how much he would be affected by these few steps. Since he had last played here, he had graced all the major football stadia in England and quite a few in Europe too.

Although he had never played for England, he had played in Cup semi-finals, and even in one final, on the hallowed turf at Wembley. Now towards the twilight of his career he had returned home. Home to Hartlepool, a smallish town isolated on the northern side of the river Tees and to the south of the much larger cities of Sunderland and Newcastle. Home to Victoria Park, an ageing stadium with a capacity of under 8,000, more than 10 times smaller than that of Wembley, but on a Saturday afternoon one which becomes the heartbeat of the town.

This is a town with an identity. An identity which is unknown to virtually everyone else in the country, but it's that very anonymity which pushes the people of Hartlepool to have such a strong pride in its identity.

People from this town don't support the other larger and more successful teams relatively close by like Middlesbrough or go slightly further north to the 'Stadium of Shite' or even to the home of the black and white deckchairs in Geordieland. Apart from the pot hunters you find everywhere, who follow Man United, Liverpool or even worse a cockney side like Chelsea, the population are loyal 'Pools fans who would follow their team into oblivion if it were needed.

Recently their resolve had been tested when they were relegated from the Football league but even then, they had resolutely followed the side until, through the play offs, they had made it back to 'where they belong'.

Troy felt the surge of extra noise and excitement from the fans when he appeared. Initially, he fought the urge to drink in the atmosphere, but he knew that he needed to try and feed off it if he were to succeed. He stopped briefly to give a short wave to each of the stands.

What he saw in those moments impressed him greatly. The stands were virtually full to the rafters with fans who themselves were overflowing with hope and expectations. From the main stand came most of the chanting. These more vocal fans, who had chosen to position themselves next to the away fans to be able to taunt them, knew their job was to take the role of a 12th team member trying to give their team an edge.

As he waved in their direction the chant 'Troy Harvey, he is one of our own' reached his ears and someone threw a blue flare, matching the team's colours, onto the pitch.

Troy recognised the effect of a rise in his adrenaline levels. He needed to calm down if he were to make these fans, his people, happy. He needed to kick a ball and warm up.

Sadly, the passion of excited fans and the fire in the bellies of pumped-up players doesn't guarantee success and that first game of the season passed by literally without incident, ending in a 0-0 draw. Troy knew in himself that he had not played well, and he could tell that his teammates were beginning to wonder just why he had been brought in and what he could give to the team to move them forward.

On top of that Troy was starting to feel very angry and frustrated with his own continued lack of form. Only the gaffer, Bob Scott, seemed to be on his side. Though telling the rest of the team Troy was the only player putting enough effort in was never going to improve his popularity in the dressing room.

Troy's lack of form and the thought of going back alone to his waterside apartment were only leading him in one direction. That same unhappiness and feeling of being generally unsettled in life had taken him to a bad place once before much earlier in his career.

Charlie Green watched Troy make his way across the car park to his pre-booked taxi with a shake of his head. He knew trouble could be on the way for his friend if he didn't step in soon.

Game 2 v Blackburn Rovers (caribou cup)   0-3

The second game of Troy's return was a home cup tie against a higher league team in Blackburn Rovers. A comprehensive 3-0 home defeat was the result. Only the performance of young midfielder Tony Marsh gave Troy any satisfaction in the game. He himself had once again struggled in the match and was having a hard time finding any real level of confidence and self-belief.

Deadly Circle/DC Poolie

'Maybe a couple of drinks and some female company would help,' he thought. 'Just an hour round the marina bars. What harm could that do?'

Charlie met him coming out of the dressing room and could tell straight away he was not a happy man.

'No point dwelling on that game,' Charlie said. 'We weren't expected to win against them, and it's the league games which matter really.'

'Maybe,' Troy replied, 'but I expect more from myself and it's just not happening at the moment.'

Game 3 v Newport County (A) 1-1

There was the usual buzz of chatter between the squad as they boarded the coach for the long journey down to Newport. None of this banter included Troy who was still finding himself very much the outsider. He settled into a seat and put his headphones on not expecting any company at all.

'Mind if I sit here Troy?' It was young Tony Marsh asking.

'Not at all kid. Don't think I'm very good company at the moment though.'

'Are you sure you want to sit with the most unpopular guy in the squad?' Troy added.

'I'm not sure that's true Troy. It's just a couple of guys who seem to rule the roost in this team.'

Troy enjoyed the journey more than he'd expected. His new friend and ally talked football more or less all the way to Newport, asking Troy's advice on all different parts of the game and about his career so far.

29

Deadly Circle/DC Poolie

In the changing room Troy was extra pleased when the manager read out the side and young Tony was in the team to make his league debut. Manager Bob Scott had decided to change his team shape to include Tony Marsh. By doing so striker Jimmy Dunne was demoted to the bench. Not something he appreciated at all. He muttered something barely audible but loud enough for Troy to hear. It was clear he blamed Troy's seeming influence with the gaffer and this assertion was reinforced, he surmised, after seeing Tony and him getting on so well on the coach journey.

Troy decided to challenge Dunne over this and told him he had never talked team selection with the manager. But he was wasting his time. Dunne had already made up his mind and nothing was going to persuade him otherwise.

The game kicked off and was even scrappier than any of the games so far. This was mostly due to a short sharp thunderstorm which had swept across South Wales, hitting Newport, an hour before kick off. The result being that the pitch was quite boggy with lots of small pools of water, despite the efforts of the ground staff, which slowed the ball making fluid play difficult. In fact, it was touch and go whether to play the match at all and there had to be a pitch inspection before kick off.

Troy felt he was playing marginally better than in the other games, having adapted to the conditions quicker than most. Having Tony Marsh in the team alongside him was giving him something else to think about and they already had built up some intuitive interplay.

Troy thought to himself, 'It's like we have an instant understanding of how the other thinks on the pitch. It's a sort

Deadly Circle/DC Poolie

of telepathy.' He was particularly enjoying talking him through the game and he already could tell that Tony could really play and had every chance of having a good career.

The game was going along well with neither side looking likely to score and both seemed to have settled for one point. That was until centre back Billy Brook knocked a back pass to his keeper which fell fatally short, due to one of the pools of water. The Newport striker nipped in and slotted the ball into the goal past Brad Picken.

Just when it looked like another loss for the team Troy managed to find young Tony in the penalty area and he smashed the ball into the roof of the net. The goal seemed to lift everyone, the players and the few supporters who had made the long journey.

With just a few minutes left in the game the referee awarded the team a penalty and a big chance to claim a first win of the season. Regular penalty taker Jimmy Dunne was not in the team and manager Bob Scott screamed from the touchline for Troy to step up and take the kick.

Troy had never been keen on taking penalties but felt, as an experienced player, he should take the responsibility. He hit the ball really well low to the keepers left but the Newport keeper guessed right and tipped the ball on to the post and it came back into his hands. Troy heard the groans from the players and the small band of supporters behind the goal.

The final whistle blew almost straight after, and Troy knew he had thrown away the chance of a first victory for the team.

Deadly Circle/DC Poolie

Deadly Circle/DC Poolie

'Come and sit here my darling.' As she said this with a warm smile, she patted the cushion next to her on the sofa. She was wearing a pretty light blue dress, one she said was Father's favourite, and her hair was up in tight dark bun. 'You know I'm really starting to worry,' she continued as I limped across the living room to take my allocated place, 'When I was young, I hated Sunday evenings.'

She leant forward to be closer to me as she started this story. 'I wasn't very good at school and thought the teachers disliked me because of my poor grades. Every Sunday before I went to bed, I had to watch Antiques Roadshow with my parents. They used to talk to me about the programme because it was one of their favourites. I think they were hoping they might see something like one of their possessions which might earn them lots of money.' I looked at her not quite sure why she was telling me this.

'They didn't realise how nervous this programme made me feel because I knew when I woke up the following morning I would have to go to school. I dreaded Sunday evenings, particularly Antiques Roadshow, and my parents never even noticed.'

There was obviously a point to this, but I still didn't know what it was. I was just about to ask her to explain when her tone changed and she sat upright, her gaze fixed on me.

'What is wrong with Fridays? Why am I forever having to patch you up on a Thursday, either physically or emotionally? If it's not you falling off your bike racing other

33

Deadly Circle/DC Poolie

boys down Symonds Hill like last month or twisting your ankle jumping off your father's shed roof, like today, then it is the one day I find you moping in your room and can hardly get a word out of you. Tell me darling is there something I need to know? Something you aren't telling me?'

I looked at her. I could see the love and desperation in her eyes, but I couldn't tell her the truth. I couldn't!

In my mind I looked back over the last 4 years and thought about 'our special secret' as Father always referred to it. I couldn't tell her that it was Father who had insisted on me asking for my own room.

'We don't want to spoil the baby's sleep,' he had argued. I couldn't tell her of our special bond, our special ritual, our ongoing secret 'It is just something shared by all fathers and sons. It is not for mothers and sisters. It will help you become a better man.' I remember him saying this quite often in the beginning. I couldn't her tell her that the ritual always started with father sitting in the bedroom chair, his legs flared wide open and his hand on his groin as I took all my clothes off. All that is except my white underpants. I couldn't share with her that part 2 of the ritual was me standing close in front of him 'as tall as you can' while he pulled my pants down and then started to massage me.

'Make sure you have bathed beforehand and cleaned very carefully down below. Real men are always clean down there.' This he would tell me every Thursday night when he came to the room to say good night. I couldn't express to her how confused I was when he would then get met to undo his trousers. As they fell to the floor, I got to know that he too would be wearing white underpants. His message was clear.

34

Deadly Circle/DC Poolie

We needed to take our time and not to rush things. 'That is how real men treat ladies, by taking time and respecting their need for pleasure too.'

I was expected to massage him as he had massaged me.

He gave me a clear step by step instruction on how to make him 'very happy'. I nodded enthusiastically when he told me this hoping I wouldn't let him or myself down. I was pleased that my, usually grumpy, Father would be so excited and content with me. When Father relaxed, after it was all over, he would say something like, 'Well done boy. Your training is going well.' I didn't really understand it all, but I thought I would given time and I was pleased that Father and I were spending time together. Even if it did seem always to be doing this.

I think it was when Father invited me to the shed one evening that I started to have negative feelings about our relationship.

'We need to move to the final step of your training,' he told me. 'And I've set up the back of the shed as a man cave.'

The look on his face was one of pure excitement and I could see that he was very pleased with himself. I, too, felt pleasure but a pleasure, not for myself, but for being included in someone else's joy.

That first Friday we entered the shed together. I was worried about my brother being alone in the house, but father just smiled saying he will sleep right through and be very safe.

It was only later did I realise that the 'special Friday cocoa' was spiked with melatonin. Inside I initially thought it silly to have come to the shed as we were doing the same things as always.

Deadly Circle/DC Poolie

But I was wrong. We weren't just going to do the same things. Now he wanted me to use my mouth as well as my hands. I hated it. I felt that I was choking. I found it hard to breath properly and if I gagged Father would become very angry and tell me off.

He would say, 'You are spoiling our ritual. You will never satisfy a woman if you can't do this.'

And I did get better at it for him. Because the week following such an outburst was difficult for everyone in the house due to his uncontrolled temper. And I blamed myself for that.

I started to hate Fridays and I really hated that shed. The one I jumped off hoping to end up in hospital away from my father. I couldn't tell mummy any of that.

'I'm sorry mummy I really am. I like Fridays. We have Art and PE on the same day at school. Everyone is happy, even the teachers, because the weekend is coming, and I like it because you enjoy yourself with your friends at the Bingo.'

She pulled me towards her hugging me closely.

'I really do hope that is the truth,' she said finally. 'But I will be watching. If I think that there really is a problem, then I will have to tell father.' I held on to her extremely tightly hoping she wouldn't feel my body tense up.

Inwardly I was imploring her, 'Please don't do that. Don't ever do that!'

36

Chapter 3

After that match Charlie had his work cut out to keep Troy's spirits up. It was even harder after matches where he had to resort to texting to support Troy as his form continued to fail.

Doncaster Rovers (H) August 20th

Hartlepool 1 – Doncaster Rovers 2

Charlie Boy - 19.30

CB- *Where are you? How are you doing?*

> **TH-** In the tapas bar. Need something to eat with my many Pints of Estrella Damm.

CB- *Are you alone? You shouldn't be.*

> **TH-** At the moment yes but the night is young.

CB- *You played better today. Your dummy made our goal.*

> **TH-** Yes but OPTA says I only had 15 touches!!! And I got 5/10 on the bloody BBC sport app.

CB- *That can be from people who weren't even at the game. So, means SFA!!*

> **TH-** That may be so but even my teammates don't like me and freeze me out both on and off the bloody pitch!!!

CB- *Stay there. Don't move. I could do with a pint.*

Deadly Circle/DC Poolie

TH- Ok, Charlie. I will order you some patatas bravas.

Deadly Circle/DC Poolie

Salford (A) August 27th

Salford 3 – Hartlepool 0

One week on and Troy's demeanour after the game meant that Charlie needed to text Troy again.

Charlie Boy – 20.05

CB- *What happened to you? I didn't even see you get off the coach.*

TH- I honestly couldn't stomach the whinging.

CB- *What do you mean?*

TH- 3 hours sitting in front of bloody Billy Brook would even get under the skin of a saint.

CB- *He can be loud and opinionated. Everyone knows what he is like. You shouldn't let him get to you.*

TH- Even worse when everything that comes out of his loud, massive mouth are really thinly veiled criticisms of 'a questionable recruitment plan'. Felt like decking him.

CB- *But you didn't. Don't let him get to you. Fancy some company? I'm at a bit of a loose end and could pop over.*

TH- Perhaps I do Charlie but, no offence, ideally someone who has slightly different plumbing to you. I still have some energy to work off.

CB- *Take care Troy. There are some devious gold diggers out there.*

39

Deadly Circle/DC Poolie

Stockport County (H) September 3rd

Hartlepool 0 – Stockport County 0

If things had been simmering up until now the first home game of September was when things really boiled over. Charlie was distraught about what had taken place and started texting Troy as soon as he could.

Charlie Boy - 19.51

CB- *The boss is really pissed Troy.*

        TH- Well so am I. He can go fuck himself.

CB- *You shouldn't have left the ground before the match finished.*

        TH- Well, I wouldn't have if he hadn't have subbed me. It was so wrong.

CB- *Come on Troy. You're a professional. Everyone gets subbed sometimes.*

        TH- I know Charlie but I was having my best game yet. Some manager if he couldn't see that. The fans all could.

CB- *He felt that others who had been on the bench all season needed a chance.*

        TH- Now you are making me sound like some prima donna. I don't need this Charlie!!

CB- *No Troy. You know I don't think that of you. I know what sort of person you are. It's been a tough start to the season for you.*

Deadly Circle/DC Poolie

TH- Sorry Charlie. Not in a good frame of mind to talk bloody football. Got to go. There's a lovely you lady with her hand on my crotch. She is feeling neglected and I'm a real gent.

Deadly Circle/DC Poolie

'Oh no!' My heart was pounding, and I was covered in sweat. 'This can't be happening!' I thought, my imagination now running at 200mph. 'This can't be the next step.'

As I stood there looking down my mind wandered back to the previous Friday.

As usual He was sitting in his chair waiting for me to undress. This I did quickly, no longer with any desire to please Him or enjoy our special secret, and with my eyes shut. For weeks now I had shown increasing reluctance, not that He seemed to notice, and just tried to get it over with as soon as possible. I tried not to recoil as he touched my body but tonight, I was aware of something different happening to me. My father seemed to realise this at the same time as me because, instead of being silent, as normal, during this part of the ritual, he made a noise. It sounded like he was disappointed in some way. I fought the urge to open my eyes and knew his next action would be to pull off my pants.

He habitually did this slowly while he touched himself with the other hand but this time, I felt 2 hands struggling to get them down to my ankles. I became perplexed because I usually then felt him massaging me and then touching me down below. I had grown to dislike everything about these evenings, but I didn't like this change in routine either and it worried me.

'Already!' he exclaimed. 'I knew it had to happen sometime soon.'

I couldn't bear it any longer and opened my eyes expecting to see Him right up next to my body. He wasn't *though. He was sitting back in his chair with his hands down by side and was looking, without blinking, at my naked body. His face was contorted and looked like mummy did when she ate something sour like lemons.*

I followed his gaze and was shocked to see my willy not limply hanging as usual but much bigger and pointing towards Father. In fact, it looked just like father's willy did on these evenings. I didn't understand what was happening and my focus turned from it back towards him.

'You are becoming a man,' he finally exclaimed. 'My work with you is done.'

He did not look happy at all. In fact, he said the last part with a note of anger. With that he stood up and left the shed. I didn't know what to do standing there with no clothes on and my willy doing something I had never seen before.

Although I was both frightened as to what was going on with my body, I was also elated at the thought that I wasn't going to have to complete the disgusting ritual that night. I suddenly felt cold. I looked around the shed beyond the ritual area, past the old tools, hardly ever used, towards the door. It was wide open, and a cool draught was coming in. I pulled my pants up and noticed that everything down below had returned to normal. I carefully picked up my other clothes and got dressed. After that I shut the door and stayed in the shed because I didn't want to bump into father, especially not in the mood he now seemed to be in. As I sat there waiting to see the lights of mummy's friend's car my thoughts turned to the following week.

What would He do? 'Maybe nothing,' I hoped.

43

Deadly Circle/DC Poolie

For the whole week my father didn't say a word to me except when mother was about.

He no longer came to wish me goodnight.

'He is old enough to say good night downstairs. He doesn't need mollycoddling,' he told mummy. As Friday approached, I started to become anxious that things hadn't changed at all and that I would have to continue meeting Him. This fear grew on Thursday evening when, while upstairs doing my homework, I heard his heavy footsteps coming up the stairs.

'Please don't let him come in here,' I pleaded holding my hands as if in prayer. The footsteps came closer, and my breathing almost stopped expecting to see the handle of the door turn. It didn't though and I heard Him go by my door and then they stopped.

'Oh no!' My heart was pounding, and I was covered in sweat. 'This can't be happening!' I thought with my imagination now running at 200mph. 'This can't be the next step.'

I kept on looking down watching as Father led my little brother by the hand into the shed. Tomorrow would be Friday, bingo night!

Chapter 4

Alan Tubbs, the janitor at the Marina Apartments, scruffy as ever, struggled to contain his curiosity when he heard the sirens and saw the blue police lights heading in the direction of the marina. He scurried out of his ground floor flat and was surprised to see a crowd already gathered outside. Two PCs were trying to keep people back from the front of the apartments. Pushing his way to the front of the crowd he found a screen blocking the view of whatever was causing all the fuss.

'I'm the janitor here,' he said to the nearest PC. 'Can I help in any way?'

'No thank you sir,' the PC replied. 'Just step back away from the barrier please.'

Tubbs, being the nosey arrogant type, did not like being kept in the dark and his facial expressions made that obvious. Annoyed, he turned away and walked briskly back to the entrance of the apartments.

The lead police car pulled up by the roadside close to the edge of the growing crowd. DS Mark Cross and DC Angela Hart, his young colleague, stepped out from the car. They made their way through the crowd to the PC standing alongside the screen. DS Cross flashed his ID card to the PC and made his way to the back of the barrier.

45

Deadly Circle/DC Poolie

The scene that met him was a shock, even to an experienced officer like Cross.

He turned to DC Hart, 'Be prepared. This is not a pretty sight,' he said. DC Hart breathed in deeply and slowly moved behind the screen. What confronted her behind the screen almost made her baulk.

A naked female body was impaled on the spiked metal railing and there was an ever-growing pool of blood on the paved area, which had been laid in a herringbone fashion, around the front of the apartments. Angela Hart had seen quite a view gruesome sights, especially when she was working traffic, and this shouldn't have affected her as much as it did.

She looked at the contorted and ruptured body and couldn't help but feel incredibly sorry that someone so young and pretty had had their life cut short in such a violent manner. On top of that, as she steeled herself for a closer examination, this poor woman lying in front of her had been stripped of all dignity with the grotesquely ornate spike jutting at least nine inches out of her chest in such a manner that both of her breasts lay at a ten to two clock face angle on either side.

It looked like some macabre performance art piece at the Tate Modern. As she turned to look at DS Cross, she briefly wondered who could have done such a horrible thing. She didn't dwell on that thought as she knew the answer. Almost anyone.

Hart was relieved that the dry spell had continued. This meant that any important forensic evidence would not have been compromised. She looked at Cross who was pulling at his tie, freeing it a little from the shirt's top button which he then undid.

Deadly Circle/DC Poolie

Although it was still quite early this area was sheltered and already becoming quite warm. Hart could imagine it being a real sun trap for the residents.

'Thank God the body was found early in the morning,' she thought. She dreaded to think what would have happened to this body if it were left undiscovered at this time of year. Hart shuddered at the thought of insects invading this poor girl's body or carnivorous animals feasting on her.

'Who reported this crime, Officer?' DS Cross asked. He didn't have the empathy of DC Hart. He had absorbed what he needed from the scene, and he would now have to wait, impatiently, for the forensic evidence to give him some scientific support in his sole mission. To find the bastard who had done this. It was this balance in personalities that made Cross and Hart such a dynamic team. At least that was what Hart hoped.

'It was an anonymous tip off called into the station,' replied the PC.

'Do we have access to the 4 apartments directly above?'

'Yes, we do sir. It's only one of the top penthouse apartments where we have still to speak to the occupier.'

'Any key holder we can get hold of?'

'The janitor is around somewhere sir. He should be able to help.'

'Find him for me and let's find out if he knows anything.'

Tubbs was delighted when the same PC, who he thought had brushed him aside, came knocking on his door to say DS Cross would like to speak to him.

He was asked the name of the occupier of the penthouse and if he knew whether he was in or out.

'Troy Harvey, the footballer, is living there now. Haven't seen or heard anything of him today.'

He picked up the set of master keys and set off towards the lift with DS Cross and DC Hart followed by two young, uniformed police constables, who positioned themselves either side of the apartment door.

After some heavy knocking on the door, which got no response, DS Cross asked the janitor to open the door. He unlocked the door to the penthouse and went to follow the two police officers into the apartment.

'Thanks for your help, sir. We will contact you if we need you again,' DS Cross said, as he shuffled the janitor back out onto the landing and closed the door. The two officers walked into the open plan living area, and both made a sharp intake of breath. Furniture was overturned, a glass coffee table was smashed into pieces and blood was splattered on the walls and carpets. A trail of blood led out through the french doors onto the balcony where the patio plants and furniture were strewn around.

'Looks like this could be our scene of crime,' Cross said wryly.

'Best get ourselves some white suits, gloves and over shoes.'

Cross turned and spoke somewhat bluntly to one of the uniformed police constables who had come up with Hart and Cross and now were standing silently in the doorway of the apartment awaiting instruction.

Deadly Circle/DC Poolie

'Two sets of scenes of crime wear should be some in the incident van outside,' said Cross, without any semblance of manners.

DC Hart looked across at the young constable and nodded with a smile. Even the lower ranks at the station were well aware of DS Cross and his reputation. He soon returned with two sets of the protective clothing and handed them over to DC Hart. Hart took them acknowledging and appreciating the effort. Cross, of course, ignored the PC.

'Right, you two. Stand there on guard. Don't let anyone in, not even the SOCO team. Not until I or DC Hart say so,' Cross was wagging a finger as he continued. 'Got it?'

Both the uniformed officers nodded and then turned so that they could face anyone who would be approaching the apartment.

Suitably dressed in their Scene of Crime Suits they stepped again into the open plan penthouse. Hart was imagining the penthouse in pristine condition and couldn't help but be a little envious of the footballer who lived here in such a prime location with furnishings which, had seemingly come straight out of the centre pages of Ideal Home. Her professionalism kicked in and her mind turned back to looking at the apartment as a crime scene.

'Looks like our footballer friend could do with a cleaner don't you think?' Cross stated in a dead pan voice. He wasn't well known for having a sense of humor, so Hart forced a weak smile.

'I was more wondering where he is now sir,' was her reply.

Deadly Circle/DC Poolie

They both looked towards what they assumed was the master bedroom door, which was closed. DS Cross pushed open the door and the answer to the DC's question lay before them.

A naked man, presumably Troy Harvey, lay spread-eagled across the bed. His arms hanging down towards the floor. They both instantly noticed the bloodied knuckles and scratches on his back and face.

'Is he still alive sir?' DC Hart asked as the senior officer checked for a pulse.

'Yes, he is. Unconscious but still breathing. Call an ambulance and a medic. That will be our best chance to find out what's gone on here and to keep him alive.'

'Next we will need a proper identification as we are assuming this is the occupant of the apartment, Troy Harvey,' Cross stated.

Angela Hart turned and walked to the wall where there was a picture of a footballer receiving his FA Cup medal.

'I think we have the answer here sir,' she said, looking at the picture, 'I thought I recognised him from the local paper and this picture confirms it.'

The ambulance crew were there in minutes and were getting Troy onto a stretcher when DS Cross asked, 'What are his chances then boys? At the moment he is the only one who may be able to tell us what's happened here.'

'Seems like he is under the influence of drink or drugs,' the ambulance man replied. 'Won't know for certain until the doctor has checked him over.'

Deadly Circle/DC Poolie

'Be sure to let me know when he regains consciousness. He is a suspect in this case. In fact, at the moment, he's our only suspect.'

The medical crew wheeled Troy out into the corridor and headed for the lift. Tubbs, the janitor, was hovering around trying his best to find out what he could. He got little change out of the medics who had come across this type of person many times before.

Walking alongside the gurney, he bombarded them with questions about the man they were lifting into the ambulance. But to the janitor's annoyance they refused to answer, and he headed back amongst the crowd to listen to any gossip or rumours he could.

He was even more disappointed when nobody there took any notice of him despite wearing his Janitor's lanyard. His ears pricked up when just behind him he heard someone making a phone call.

'Is that the 'Pools media department?' he heard the voice say. 'Just thought you'd like to know Troy Harvey has been taken away in an ambulance with a police car following.'

There was a pause and then the voice continued, 'Yes, I'm sure it was him. I was standing right next to the ambulance when he was put in it. Just like I was I was standing right behind the goal when he missed that penalty. I think you also ought to know that there is rumour of a dead body under his apartment. Think he might be in need of some help.'

The janitor smiled to himself and mused 'I think he is beyond help from what I've seen. Good riddance to bad rubbish.'

Deadly Circle/DC Poolie

Meanwhile the two detectives and the team of Scene of Crime Officers all in their white SOC suits began a meticulous search of Troy's penthouse apartment. Samples of blood and hair were taken bagged and labelled. All potentially to be used as evidence in the court case which was undoubtedly to follow.

It was the next morning before DS Cross was informed that his suspect had regained consciousness and was due to be released from hospital. Police officers, who had been stationed at the hospital all night were ready, as ordered, to bring Troy straight to the station for questioning.

Deadly Circle/DC Poolie

The middle-aged man in the uniform stepped inside the room and I followed.

'This will be your home for the next few days son till the powers that be decide where they are going to put you. You will be fine here as long as you behave yourself and obey the rules. I will be back soon to check that you are ok and settled in'.

He stepped outside the room and the heavy door slammed shut behind him and I heard the key turn in the lock. I fell back on the bed and pulled the rough grey blanket high over my head.

'How did this all happen, what did I do wrong?' I sobbed. 'I was just trying to protect my young brother from the abuse I had suffered these last years, surely that was the right thing to do.'

My mind went back to those times in the potting shed. At first, I was happy that I was pleasing Father and that we had that special secret that only boys and their fathers should know. Only as I got older did I start to think that this was not right. I felt then that I was being lied to and used somehow.

When I sensed Father's growing interest in my younger brother, I realised I had to do something about this to make it stop.

I remember that Friday night so well. Mummy had gone to her usual night at the local bingo hall. My little brother was playing contentedly with his toys in his room. I knew Father would go down beforehand to set things up and that would my chance. I still wasn't really sure what I was going to do. I plucked up the courage and made my way down to the potting shed. Inside I looked around for something to use. I eventually came across something I was sure would be suitable and hid myself away behind an old bookcase, now being used to store gardening equipment.

It seemed an age before I heard the backdoor of the house close and his heavy footsteps on the gravel path which led down to the shed.

The old, shed door creaked open and I heard the click of the light switch. Luckily, I had thought ahead and removed the lightbulb so the shed would remain in what seemed an almost impenetrable darkness.

'Are you in here hiding Billy? You shouldn't be in here.' Father said, as he moved further into the dark shed. I sensed him edging slowly through the gloom and he, bit by bit, got closer to the bookcase, my rather fragile hiding place. When he was very close, I saw my chance and cracked the garden spade I'd found down hard on Father's head. As he collapsed his head smashed into some old building bricks piled in the corner and he lay motionless on the potting shed floor.

I dropped the garden spade and sprinted sobbing back into the house where I ran to my brother in his room. I put my arm around him, as much for my benefit as his, and took him into the living room. When mummy returned home, we were sitting silently clinging to one another on the sofa.

Deadly Circle/DC Poolie

Chapter 5

It had been a relatively quiet day so far and desk sergeant George Younger, who had been nursing a hangover since returning from yesterday's match, was very grateful for that. Aside from old Mrs Walton making her, almost daily, visit to the station requesting help to find her problematic pussy, George had been left very much alone with his glass of water and blisters of paracetamol.

So it was in a very unprofessional stance, leaning head bowed almost touching the counter which stood between him and any member of the public, that the 3 men found him.

'Damn!' thought George as he realised that he wasn't alone. 'We really must get the door seen to.' Ordinarily there is a sort of warning sound created by the door opening.

'We are here to see Troy Harvey,' stated a meticulously dressed elderly man. 'We understand that he is being transferred here from the hospital.'

George was a little taken aback as it was only 24 hours earlier that he had seen Mr Harvey get unceremoniously subbed during the 0-0 draw with Stockport. George, as a Hartlepool fan, hadn't really made his mind up about this new 'super' signing but hadn't been surprised when the manager had taken him off.

That thought was literally running through his mind when his focus transferred from the silver haired gentleman to the people who were accompanying him. Now George was really surprised as one of the men was in fact Bob Scott, the Hartlepool manager, who had taken that very decision. He also recognised the diminutive and slightly rotund figure of the club's chairman, Sidney Hackett.

'I am Arthur Broadbent, Mr Harvey's solicitor,' the first man continued. 'He has the right of representation and that is why I'm here. Mr. Scott and Mr. Hackett have come in their various capacities as his employers and Mr Scott,' now Arthur Broadbent was pointing towards Bob Scott's hand, 'has brought in some training clothes for Mr Harvey to wear. We understand he was only wearing a Scene of Crime suit when he went to the hospital.'

George explained that, as Desk Sergeant, he hadn't been made aware of the situation and he asked them to be seated as he made a phone call.

'Apparently the car transporting Mr Harvey will be here in five minutes. He is to be questioned regarding the incident at the Marina in interview room 2.' George felt happier now he knew what was going on. 'Would you like me to take the bag in so that Troy, I mean Mr Harvey, can get changed before the interview?'

Arthur Broadbent smiled a condescending smile and shook his head. 'As his solicitor and legal advisor, I want to have 5 minutes with my client before the interview. He can get changed then.' Arthur turned to the others and told them to go back to the ground.

'The police won't allow more than one of us in with Troy and I will keep you informed.' With that he took the bag with the clothes from Bob Scott and returned to his chair. Realising

56

that, despite being a little off hand, he was correct the others turned for the door.

Fifteen minutes later Arthur was standing outside interview room 2 still with the sports bag in his hand. Down the corridor he could see Troy approaching. Behind him were two uniformed officers. Being more a corporate representative of the club than a football fan Arthur had never seen Troy close up. He tried not to show it, but initial signs were more than a little worrying. He knew from the little information he had gleaned that Troy would look the worse for wear and he expected the unkempt hair and a bleary-eyed visage but, even when wearing a SOCO suit, Troy was exhibiting some very incriminating signs: bloodied knuckles and a giant scratch on his face.

Arthur stopped the two policemen in their tracks and told them that he and his client needed privacy for Mr Harvey to change and also for him to be able to talk to his client before the interview. They had been briefed that this would be the case and nodded their assent. Arthur introduced himself to Troy and gestured for him to enter the room. Arthur followed him and shut the door firmly behind him. Inside he glanced around to make sure all recording equipment was turned off. Even if such recordings proved to be inadmissible, he knew of cases where such evidence had given the police a route to pursue.

He gave Troy the bag of training clothes.

'Get out of that paper suit and put these on,' he instructed Troy. 'There is some clean training gear from the club, and we stopped off at Matalan for some underwear. Not very designer I know but needs must,' he grinned.

57

Deadly Circle/DC Poolie

Arthur was a prim and proper person by nature, almost prudish. Only three women had seen him naked: the midwife who delivered him; his mother and his wife, Sylvia. Even with Sylvia Arthur was very much a lights off type of man. Should he need to use public facilities, and that wasn't often, Arthur would prefer a cubicle but in those extreme cases when one wasn't available, he would wait for an end urinal where he would pointedly stand at a 45-degree angle.

Given this nature Arthur had to force himself to watch Troy take off the SOCO suit. Naked underneath Arthur could see more evidence of scratches and bruising on Troy's torso. Arthur, having seen what he needed to, turned away and glanced up at the clock. They had 10 minutes until the agreed start of the interview.

'Troy, a few ground rules first,' Arthur leaned towards Troy who was in the chair next to him. 'You may call me Arthur in private, but we will stick to the more formal Mr Broadbent and Mr Harvey during interviews or when we are not with people who are on our side.'

Troy looked at Arthur and nodded. Arthur could see that Troy was back in control of his faculties but there was still some haziness in his eyes and something else, fear.

'What can you tell me about last night Troy? Did you kill her? I need to know what you know if you want me to help.'

Troy listened and absorbed the words.

'I don't know. I can't remember anything after being in the bar at the marina.'

Troy tried to focus on Arthur's face as he spoke. His future could be at the mercy of this man's ability to help him. Outwardly, Troy could see that Arthur was an extremely competent and intelligent man who, Troy hoped, was excellent at his job. But was he committed to the cause? Troy wasn't so sure but at that moment in time he had no other option.

'I think based on that and given the speedy set up of this interview,' Arthur finally had started to speak again, 'it is in your best interests to reply, 'No comment' to all their questions.'

'Won't that make me look guilty?' Troy sounded worried.

'No, that is your right. Better than saying something you change at a later date.'

'Okay, I guess that does make sense.'

Troy was still mulling this over as the door opened and in walked 2 plain clothed police officers. They took their seats opposite Arthur and Troy. Troy looked at each of them as they introduced themselves onto the recording.

'This recording is taking place at 4.45pm on Sunday September 4th and present are Mr Troy Harvey, and his solicitor Mr Arthur Broadbent. Also present are Detective Sergeant Mark Cross, (Troy saw in that moment a 30 something man in a blue suit with a grey tie, dark haired but already starting to show a receding hairline, in fairly good shape but signs of a belly forming. Most worryingly he didn't see any warmth in this policeman) and Detective Constable Angela Hart.' (Troy instantly warmed to her. She was dressed formally as all women had to do in this profession but there was a softness in the way she looked and presented herself. She had shortish, almost blond hair with blue eyes that showed an innate kindness. Troy had to reel himself in. This was someone who could do him harm, not a possible date or conquest.)

59

Deadly Circle/DC Poolie

'At this moment in time,' Mark Cross continued, 'we are treating you as a witness and maybe even as a victim.' This comment surprised Troy and he glanced towards Arthur who was steadfastly staring at Mark Cross. 'There are obviously some contradictory things we need to clear up but the traces of Rohypnol in your body suggest we need to be open at this stage.' He sat back in his chair looking at Troy and then at Arthur. He seemed quite pleased with himself.

'Now Mr Harvey what can you tell us about last night?' It was Angela Hart who spoke now in a soft, almost confiding tone.

Troy glanced once again at Arthur. This time Arthur tilted his head slightly and almost imperceptibly shook his head. He was telling Troy to keep to their plan.

'No comment,' Troy almost stuttered as these words came out.

'Really is that the way you want to play this?' Mark Cross couldn't contain his sudden anger. 'We are trying to give you a chance to explain what seems to be a very compromising crime scene with you, save the Rohypnol in your system, being very much implicated in the crime.' His voice became more and more agitated throughout that outburst.

'My client is struggling to recollect what happened to him and doesn't want to commit himself to a statement which he might later, when he has had time to recover both his memory and capacities, contradict.' Arthur was bristling as he said this. The air of authority and confidence was clear.

'You mean when he has had time to concoct a story,' Mark Cross was all but snarling.

'Do you remember meeting the girl?'

'No comment.'

Angela tried to get the interview back on track, but Troy was doing what his solicitor advised and he continued to do this to all of her follow up questions.

Both sides were becoming increasingly frustrated. The police due to this line of answering and Arthur because he couldn't understand why they were still asking the same questions knowing the answer wouldn't change.

At that moment there was a knock on the door and a young female police officer entered holding a file. She handed it to Mark Cross.

'Interview paused at 17.36,' he announced. As he read the 2 sheets of paper inside the file, a smile formed on his face. Troy sensed that whatever was written on it was not good news. Not good for Troy that was. Mark passed the sheets to Angela. She quickly absorbed the information and looked directly at Troy.

'Interview recommenced,' Mark Cross looked like the cat who had found the cream. Not only found it but devoured it.

'Can you explain Mr Harvey why we found a plastic bag of Rohypnol in your toilet cistern? Don't bother with your 'no comment' reply. We think we know. You used it on your victim and then took a small amount yourself to throw us off your track and make us think you might be a victim.'

Troy felt like someone had kicked him in the stomach and stirred it up like a cement mixer. He looked pleadingly at his solicitor but before any action or response could be made Mark Cross spoke again. 'In accordance with the laws of this country we can keep you in custody for 24 hours. We are going to exercise this right, and we still have 21 hours left of that 24. Tomorrow morning you will be formally questioned again. But this time as a suspect.' Troy was now struggling to control his breathing and he stared unblinkingly at the floor trying to regain his composure.

'We need a sample of your DNA. It would not be in your best interest to decline this request,' Cross continued. Troy looked at Arthur Broadbent who shrugged his shoulders as if to say they will get it anyway.

'Mr Broadbent, out of courtesy I will allow you 10 minutes with your client and then he will be taken to the cells.' With that he and Angela Hart stood up and left the interview room.

'What's going on?' Troy asked Arthur. 'I've never even been near the toilet cistern, nor do I have any idea how to get hold of Rohypnol.'

'I've got to be honest Troy,' Arthur replied. 'It's not looking good. I've tried to buy you some time with the 'no comment' tactic but this new evidence on top of everything else does seem to point at you. Try to get some rest. Maybe you will remember something that will help our defence.'

Troy looked shell-shocked and was unable to speak.

'See you in the morning Troy,' Arthur was now standing up and almost out the door. He didn't even look back as the uniformed policemen came in to the room to escort Troy to the cells.

. . . .

Deadly Circle/DC Poolie

The following morning came eventually for Troy. The time since he had left the interview room had seemed almost to stand still and Troy couldn't remember ever wishing time to pass more quickly.

'Was hell worse than purgatory or was it the other way around?' he had thought to himself. Whatever the answer was Troy had never felt in a darker place. During those agonisingly slow hours he cycled through many emotional states: confusion as to how this was happening; frustration for not being able to remember anything after going to the bar area; loneliness and isolation in the cell with no one seemingly able to dig him out of this hole and a sense of fear and dread for what was to come. That last emotion dominated throughout the night, and he barely slept on the functional but really uncomfortable mattress. The feeling of loneliness made him almost rejoice in the hourly patrol by the policeman on duty who slid open the viewing panel in the door to check that all was safe and well in the cell.

Feeling, and sensing, he looked like shit, he was grateful when handed toiletries in the morning and was escorted to the shower. The shower was a good one with a powerful stream of hot water. This has a restorative effect on Troy, and as he returned to his cell, he resolved to take whatever would come that day head on, with a positive attitude.

At 9.30 the door opened and in stepped Arthur Broadbent. Today he was in a different, yet still expensive, dark grey pin striped suit and a similar coloured tie, almost black.

Deadly Circle/DC Poolie

'I hope that isn't a sign of how serious things are for me,' Troy thought. 'He wouldn't look incorrectly dressed at a funeral.'

Despite these negative musings Troy steeled himself and forced a smile.

'How are you today, Troy? Did they treat you well? Have you remembered any more of that evening?'

Arthur's questions hit Troy like bullets from an automatic weapon not allowing him to answer before the next question hit.

Troy took his time and replied 'Not too bad but very worried. Yes, they have been very professional and not a fucking thing. Do you think my memory of that night will ever return?'

Arthur shrugged, 'Amnesia can be temporary in such cases, I think. What we need is a game plan. The club and I are right behind you.'

Troy listened and nodded his thanks.

'I think today we need to be as open and honest as we can be. This won't be hard because you can't remember anything anyway.' Arthur stared at Troy to make sure he was taking this in.

The next 20 minutes passed quite quickly with Arthur asking Troy to tell him what he could remember before the blackout. At 10am they were ushered into the same interview room where the two detectives were already seated. This time Tory noticed a few differences to the room. There was a TV set up in the corner and Cross and Hart seemed to have a pile of folders lying on the desk in front of them.

After the formalities Mark Cross got straight to the point.

Deadly Circle/DC Poolie

'Mr Harvey did you take this young lady,' with that he pushed an autopsy photo of a brunette in front of Troy, 'to your apartment and eventually kill her by throwing her off your balcony?'

He sat back waiting for a reply.

'I don't know. I'm sure I couldn't do that. I can't remember,' Troy stumbled over these short phrases and pulled at his hair in a semi frenzied way.

'Have you ever met this woman?' Cross continued. He clearly had a line of questioning planned.

'I don't recognise her at all,' Troy replied, clearing his throat. 'I suppose if she is local then it is possible.'

Cross didn't seem to be listening to Troy at all. He turned and nodded towards PC Hart who, on cue, switched on the TV and and pressed play. A video started on the big screen TV. A man and a woman were entering the apartment block.

'It must be the CCTV from the entrance,' Troy realised.

The man was wearing a hoodie and the picture was, at best, grainy.

As they watched the woman, already unsteady on her feet, lean into what seemed a very 'in control' male. Arthur, who had been silent up until now spoke up.

'Surely you can't expect anyone to say categorically that the man on the video is definitely Mr Harvey. That could be about 15 percent of the male population and as for the woman her face is constantly turned into the body of the unknown man.' Arthur looked very authoritative and a little pleased with himself.

'That's as maybe,' Angela Hart spoke now, 'What we do know for certain is that clothes identical to the ones worn by the lady here were found scattered, some covered in blood and ripped, in Mr Harvey's apartment. A hoodie, jogging bottoms and various undergarments were also found in the washing machine having been through a full wash cycle.'

There was a pause and the detectives both looked, almost unblinkingly, at Troy.

'I can't explain any of this,' Troy said. He wanted to try to defend himself but had nothing to offer. Arthur made a gesture basically telling Troy to stop talking.

Cross now took his turn. 'Mr Harvey can you explain why your DNA was found on the victim in many locations? The more incriminating being under her fingernails.' Troy looked like he had been poleaxed and shook his head. 'Or why her DNA was on you?' Troy's mind went back to the hospital where he had been subjected to a full examination.

Troy didn't know what to say. He just stared ahead, his eyes looking almost empty.

The detective one-two continued with PC Hart back leading the questions. She held up a double-sided piece of paper.

'This is a blood report from the hospital Mr Harvey,' she spoke these words pointedly but in a very controlled manner. 'It shows that the level of Rohypnol in your system was 4 times less than that in the victim. That leads us to believe, combined with the discovery of the date rape drug in your cistern, that this was self-administered after the murder and done so with a view to putting us off your track.'

Cross now jumped in, 'Most criminals aren't as clever as they think they are. They don't understand how technologically advanced our forensic investigation can be.'

Deadly Circle/DC Poolie

'Does this evidence jog anything in your memory Mr Harvey?' Hart was dovetailing beautifully with her sergeant.

Troy shook his head just as Arthur spoke, 'My client has told you all he knows.'

'Well then,' Cross was gathering the evidence back together, 'We have presented our evidence to the Crown Prosecution Service, and they have advised us that we can charge you with murder. The victim will be known as Miss X until we have a formal identification.'

Troy's head dropped in disbelief. This was the worst-case scenario he had worried about all night.

'You will be escorted now back to the cells until a remand hearing takes place,' Cross looked victorious.

Arthur Broadbent stood up and shook Troy's hand.

'Don't worry Troy, we won't desert you,' he said. 'Someone in the office will always be there to represent you.'

As he walked out leaving Troy with the police officers Troy thought to himself, 'Yeah but not you.'

Deadly Circle/DC Poolie

The blow to Father's head had been fatal and I found myself incarcerated by the time I was barely 12 years old. My time in various youth offender and detention centres dragged by until eventually I was transferred to an adult prison in the Midlands. A period of my life which I will try forever to forget about, but I knew what I had done and why.

Long ago, I had accepted my sentence and reconciled myself to it and looked forward to the time when I could meet up again with my brother and find out how his life had turned out. Although our adoptive mother had always been loving and kind to us both, I always knew I had only one blood relative, and it was that which had got me through all those years inside.

If I learned anything at all in those early institutions, it was that you must look after yourself whatever the cost or your life would be hell.

At 15 I was transferred to the young offender's institute in Wetherby and those lessons learned became even more valuable.

Ray (Razor) Lucketti was the 'boy' who, because of his lack of fear and violent demeanour, reigned supreme in Wetherby and wasted no time at all in letting me know. On my first night he and two of his sidekicks paid a visit to my room. I took a good beating that night just to make sure that I was aware of how things were run. I was reasonably fit having worked out most days whilst I'd been locked up, so my revenge wasn't long in coming. After a verbal set-to with Razor's main henchman, I flattened him in the near empty shower block and news of this soon reached the man himself. To my surprise I seemed to pick up a degree of respect from this and Razor and his Squad left me alone from then on.

When I was transferred, at 18, to the adult jail to serve out the rest of my sentence the same rules applied but this time there was an even higher level of violence. Every week some poor soul or some undeserving bastard got stuck with a Shiv. Consequently, I felt I had no choice but to play their game or perish in that dog-eat-dog world. Razor Lucketti had been transferred to the same jail the year before and it didn't take long for the two of us to team up. It would be hard to say that we became good friends. It was more a case of allying ourselves to each other knowing that we would have each other's back and because of our history we trusted each other to do just that.

When my release eventually came around, I knew I was a very different person to the boy who was incarcerated all those years ago. People knew now that any slight, perceived insult or rebuff would be answered in a violent and blunt way.

Chapter 6

Charlie Green sat staring out of the café window across at the Magistrates Court. His face looked grey, and his shoulders were slumped like he had the weight of the world on them.

From his left a mug appeared followed by a hand, a sleeve and them an arm. No more images came into his peripheral vision, but the angle lowered down and down until the mug sat in front of him. 'English Breakfast tea, milk and 2 sugars.'

The voice, rather shaky and obviously southern in origin, came from Barry Barnes who in turn sat in the chair opposite Charlie and placed his latte macchiato on a beer mat.

'I think they must get these from the pub next door,' he added. 'I suppose it would cut the overheads a little.'

Charlie, who had entered the café on sufferance and in a foul mood, particularly with Barry, couldn't help but grin. He wasn't one for holding grudges, even if the person in question was an annoying cockney.

'Why did you ask me here?' Charlie decided he couldn't stay silent for long.

'Firstly, to apologise and then, as I know you are his friend, to plan our next step.'

Charlie looked dumbfounded at the man opposite. Was this articulate, and already quite amusing young man really the same man, the Solicitor, who had got tongue tied, seemed ill prepared and out of his depth in court less than an hour before? The same man who had allowed Charlie's friend, Troy, to be denied bail and remanded in custody. Because this man hadn't done his job properly Troy was now going to jail. Charlie's neck tensed as his level of frustration and anger rose once more.

Sensing a change in atmosphere Barry quickly continued.

'I really screwed up in there and I know I did not represent Mr Harvey appropriately. I really am sorry.'

'Screwed up is an understatement,' growled Charlie, who surprised even himself by the venom in his voice.

'It was my first time ever in front of a judge. You see I only passed my exams and qualified this year.' Barry's voice was getting higher again just like it had been the whole time in court. 'Mr Broadbent only told me this morning that I'd be taking over from him. He said I'd get bail easily and that the Crown wouldn't seek for Mr Harvey to be remanded in custody. I didn't know what to do when the Prosecutor became aggressive. I just froze. It was like my brain stopped working.'

'I was wondering if you actually had a brain.' Charlie was starting to feel sorry for the kid and his anger turned towards Arthur Broadbent.

'And the evidence seemed so damning.' Barry just needed, it seemed quite obvious to Charlie, to get this off his chest as he was still reeling from what had happened to him professionally in court.

'I know Barry. May I call you Barry?'

Barry nodded, relieved that Charlie's anger with him had seemingly subsided.

Deadly Circle/DC Poolie

'CCTV, DNA and the primary crime scene.' he stopped remembering how the Prosecutor had piece by piece submitted the evidence. 'It was like a leaking dam of evidence was swamping me and I couldn't see how, or if, I could do anything to counteract the flow.'

'To be honest Barry your performance, or lack of one, was a bit like watching a train crash in slow motion.' Charlie said the next sentence after sighing and putting his head in his hands muffling what was normally a strong and confident voice, 'But I did think might he still get bail until my evidence sunk his hopes, or that of my phone anyway. If I had deleted my text history with Troy, like he had, they wouldn't have been able to portray Troy as a habitual sexual predator and used the safety of the women in Hartlepool as a reason to oppose his bail. I mean he is a young man with normal needs. But he is most definitely not a sex fiend. They twisted what was in those texts and with that his hopes of bail went under. Like the Titanic, quickly and without trace.'

'Well, that's one thing we have in common,' smiled Barry. 'We both use water metaphors.'

'Yes, I think we are starting to get on swimmingly,' Charlie laughed, but stopped when he took a swig of his tea. 'Bloody hell that's hot! You didn't ask for much milk then.'

They sat drinking their respective drinks for a few minutes. During that time Charlie silently cursed himself again.

Barry, sensing Charlie needed a pick me up, spoke once more. 'What is done is done. But I don't think Mr Harvey got a fair shake today and I'm going to ask Mr Broadbent if I can work exclusively on this case until we have another try for bail.'

Deadly Circle/DC Poolie

'Can we have another bail hearing?' Charlie had perked up.

'Yes, everyone is entitled to that. But we need to be better prepared. Maybe find some loopholes in the evidence to present next time. We may need more than the two of us. There is a lot of ground to cover.'

'I think I know just the people.' Charlie couldn't contain his excitement. 'Meet me outside Verrills Fish and Chip shop on the Headland tomorrow at 2pm. It's my half day.'

'One more thing,' Charlie added.

'What is that?' Barry replied.

'You are going to have to find another drink to have with these guys. It will be hard enough to get them working with a Southerner. But one who drinks macchiatos? No chance!'

He finished his tea and got up 'See you tomorrow.' He turned and headed towards the door.

'What have I let myself in for?' Barry asked himself silently. He then grinned as he sensed that working with Charlie was going to be something out of the ordinary and maybe fun.

He picked up his coffee, took a sip and grimaced, 'These bloody macchiatos go cold quickly. Maybe I do need to find another drink?'

Deadly Circle/DC Poolie

'Why you ungrateful little bastard! Don't you know what I've done for you? What I've given up and suffered for you?'

I was back behind the cashier's window at Ocean Beach Pleasure Park licking my wounds, both physical and mental, wistfully looking out across the road towards the North Sea. Every wave that lapped up on the shore seemed to bring back yet another flashback, a whole sequence of failure and futility.

'Can you give me change for the slot machines?' asked some snotty, acne pocked kid who was staring at me waving a crumpled £5 note. I felt like asking him why he wasn't at school because he didn't look a day over 15 and certainly not old enough to play those machines.

I glanced over in the direction of the manager's office and remembered the company policy *'If there aren't any police about and there is plausible deniability then give the little scrotes the ammunition to fuel their gambling addiction.'* As my eyes had unquestionably been in receipt of a beating and therefore, I could argue blurred vision, I gave the little weasel his change in pound coins. *'Don't give them any excuse not to spend the maximum of money here by giving them small change.'* These were the wise words of my manager and the full extent of my induction training.

As the youth wondered off to the machines my mind again started to take me back into the past. I finally left prison and was installed at a halfway house. Actually, aside from the do-gooders and constant monitoring, it was better than what I had expected. I had my own room, a comfortable bed and even *an en-suite bathroom with shower. I kept my head down and got a job, not exactly a vocational experience, valeting cars at a dealership whose owner was a friend of my parole officer.*

I knew if I kept my head down for 6 months then I would be free to start my quest, to reunite us. Little did I know that those 6 months were to be the happiest of my adult life so far. As soon as I could I set off to where we had lived with mummy and that vile old brute. I thought I would find you both living in the same house and that I would be welcomed back, at least by you, as a returning hero. How different it was. The beautiful house now over 20 years on was being used as flats for asylum seekers. When I did find someone who spoke good enough English to ask about my family nobody there even knew that it used to be just one house. I tried the neighbours but the whole street had become an area of buy to let. Not one person remembered you or mummy. I didn't know what to do next. I had nowhere to live and no job. This wasn't what was meant to be. I decided to try the local shops to see if i could find someone who remembered them. The local newsagent's wife was stood behind the counter bereft of customers, so I went in and asked for a copy of the local rag.

'I'm looking for a flat or a house to buy in this area. Do you know of any?' I asked.

'There is a section inside that paper of places for sale. But it's mostly rentals around here these days,' she replied.

'Seems a nice, quiet area around here.' I wanted to keep the conversation going.

'Not too bad but there are a lot of foreigners around now though. Not like it was in the old days.' She seemed more than happy to chat.

Deadly Circle/DC Poolie

'Not too much excitement then?' I pushed her further.

'None at all really. Can't think of the last big news story round here and we have had this shop 25yrs at least,' she said, turning to rearrange the sweet jars. I smiled to myself remembering how mummy used to buy me milk bottles as a treat.

Focussing on the task at hand I chortled, 'Not a crime hotspot then?'

'Well, we did have a murder in the street. 20 odd years ago it must be now. A young kid walloped his foster dad over the head with a garden spade. Not sure why. Plenty of gossip theories circulating at the time though.'

'Oh dear!' Now we were on topic, 'Sounds dramatic. What happened to the rest of the family? Did they feel able to keep living in the area?' I felt I was on to something at last.

'There was only a wife and a young baby as far as I recall. I think something happened to the wife but i'm not sure.' She seemed a bit disappointed in this gap in her knowledge. 'I bet they have the local newspapers from that time on record at the library. It's open until 5pm today.'

I thanked her and strode outside with a reawakened purpose.

I found the central library on the High Street and there I explained that I was trying to reconnect with the surviving members of my family whose life changed so dramatically on that evening so many years ago. I wanted to be seen as a returning relative not a convicted killer. They might be more inclined to help me. Five minutes later the sweet old man, who had willingly taken on the task of helping me, looked up from his laptop and his whole demeanour changed.

Deadly Circle/DC Poolie

'I know who you are,' he hissed (remembering that we were still in a library.). 'It says here that when your mother took her life after the trial that there was no one to grieve or mourn at the funeral as both parents had no other family.' He glared at me as he continued sarcastically 'No coincidence is it then that the killer was released a few months ago and he was your age?'

That was like a series of punches to the solar plexus. Had mummy really killed herself because of me? That thought sapped me of all my energy. It wasn't her fault. She thought she was helping us by providing a loving home. For a split second I just looked at him. I wanted to yell back at him and tell the real story. I wanted to ask what had happened to my little brother, but I was too ashamed and humiliated so I turned around and walked out of the library knowing that everyone there was looking at me. I could sense their hatred. I still needed to find out about my brother though. So, after a night in a cheap B&B, I went to the council offices. After waiting for what seemed an age, I was directed to the second floor and given the name of someone who might be able to help me.

This time I mentioned the nature of the abuse. I needed to get this person on my side as, after all, it was my last resort. Mrs Benson, that was her name, tutted as she listened to my story.

After I finished, she leant forward and said, 'I'm sorry I don't have access to such records, but I can tell you that your brother will have been put back into the Care System and maybe even adopted again.' My stomach turned when I heard this. 'Anyway, I know that you won't be able to see the files as

Deadly Circle/DC Poolie

they are confidential. He is over 18 and may decide to come looking for you. So, fingers crossed eh.'

I got up in a semi daze. Suddenly I found myself outside in the park opposite thinking, 'What do I do now?'

From that time until now my life has just been a series of fuck ups bouncing from one failure to the next. I have been fired from half of my jobs because of my attitude and the rest were so dead end and boring that I quit them after a few months at most. I lurched from one seedy bedsit to another sometimes doing a runner when the rent was due.

I think my description must have been circulated around all the letting agencies in the Northeast as I sometimes had doors slammed in my face before I could even explain what I wanted. No money, no decent job equalled no long-term relationships.

If I say so myself, I can scrub up quite nicely and I'm in good shape as I've been quite active physically. So, when I can be bothered, I can have my pick of the girls. Eventually though I can't disguise the damage done to me mentally by Father, the various state institutions and their inmates and I get dumped. I still can't take the lead role in the bedroom and, although some of my sex partners, have found this cute in the short term, they soon get bored by my passive nature and later frustrated by my inability to initiate sex.

'Are you sure you aren't gay?' was an allegation that more than a couple of them had thrown at me.

My focus shifted from the boy, who was getting irritated by his lack of success on the slot machines, to the TV on the wall in the corner. As usual it was showing Sky Sports News. Had it not been for that channel I wouldn't look like a car

78

crash victim, nor would I be in the foul mood in which I found myself.

The previous week on a rainy, quiet day I had found myself watching the back end of a piece about a Newcastle footballer who was moving to another football club in the Northeast, Hartlepool. I wasn't really engaged but something about the little bit I heard piqued my interest, so I waited for the inevitable repeat of the report.

'It has to be him!' I thought. 'He comes from the right town. He is the right age and was adopted as a boy and, most importantly, he looks a lot like me.' I realised that subconsciously it had been the pictures and not the story that I had noticed earlier. I couldn't believe it. I had found him.

A week later, armed with another piece of information gleaned from a 3rd viewing of the story, I was on the Quayside in Newcastle waiting outside the hotel where Newcastle was having an end of season big bash.

I hadn't really worked out my plan but decided that I would approach him after the celebrations when he would be more relaxed. As the night drew on, I was surprised how busy the area was even at that time and I was worried I wouldn't be able to spot him or follow him. Finally, people started to emerge, but I couldn't see him. I panicked for a while thinking he might have decided to take a room there.

Lots of alcohol is usually consumed on these occasions, I assumed, so I was more than hopeful that he wasn't driving. On the other side of the pedestrian area there were quite a lot of large cars arriving. Maybe drivers to take them home? At that moment I saw him coming out of the hotel dressed in a lounge suit and with a gorgeous blond hanging on to his arm.

Deadly Circle/DC Poolie

'This is it I thought. I have to get to him before he reaches the cars.' I quickened my step but still found myself having to catch them up from behind.

'Roy!' I shouted. 'It's me.' He didn't look around. I wasn't going to get there in time.

'Roy!' I was even louder this time and grabbed the right arm of the woman as it was the only part of them, I could reach. She screamed and her shoulder bag fell to the floor as she did so.

Roy turned around and put himself between her and me. I was about to explain things as his right fist hit me square on the nose. I sensed blood spurting everywhere as I fell to the floor. As I landed, I felt a flurry of kicks landing on my torso and head. I curled myself up into the foetus position just as I used to do when this had happened to me in the various institutions in the past. As quickly as the attack had started it had now come to an end. I could feel his hot breath on my face as he bent down to pick up the bag.

'You are lucky that there are witnesses and I don't want to upset the lady any more you worthless piece of shit!'

Within seconds I heard the sound of car doors shutting and one car driving away.

'Oi, you fuck off or you'll get some more.'

'Yeah, if you don't we will call the police.' The other drivers were now getting involved. Even with my head ringing and pain emanating from the whole of my body I knew I had to get out of there, so I pulled myself to my feet and looked for the solace of any darkened area to drag myself off to.

Deadly Circle/DC Poolie

This time it was a tenner that brought me back to reality. I smiled, not sympathetically, and gave the poor loser his change.

'Why you ungrateful little bastard! Don't you know what I've done for you? What I've given up and suffered for you?' I mused with an evil smile. 'You are going to suffer now Roy! Hartlepool here I come.' I had lost so many years of freedom for him and now he was going see the side of me that I had learnt inside. A side which up until now I had usually been able to suppress. One that hits back.

Chapter 7

Junior Solicitor Barry Barnes checked his appearance in the mirror. Freshly shaved and with wavy fair hair brushed as neat as he could get it. His rather slight physique fitted quite well into a classic solicitor's dark 3-piece suit. Underneath his crisp white shirt showcased his rather flamboyant yellow tie. This belied his actual rather quiet nature. He had always been someone who preferred not to stand out but to remain in the shadows. This manner of appearance was really to appease his mother who had repeatedly told him that he needed to dress to impress if he were ever to get on in life.

Satisfied, he made his way downstairs from his town centre flat to the carpark. He had thought about walking over to his afternoon meeting on the Headland but decided against it. His newly acquired VW car was just too much of a novelty for him. One of his life journey ambitions was to buy himself a brand-new car, and his recently found job at the Hartlepool solicitors allowed him to do just that. It had meant moving away from his home in the south, but he needed to get his foot in the door of his chosen career and this job had turned up.

Since his father had died when he was a teenager it had been just him and his mum. Well physically maybe but the legacy of his father lingered. It had been his father's wish for Barry to become a solicitor, just as he had been, and his mum had made it her life's work to make sure that this dream was to become a reality. Barry wasn't averse to the career but had no affinity with the formality that went hand in hand with such a job. He wanted to help people and was afraid of being too corporate. His mum, whose influence on him was very powerful, told him that this liberal bent was just a phase and that he needed to find work in a traditional solicitors. She was adamant that his goal was to become a partner. A position which his poor father was about to attain when he suffered that fatal heart attack.

Academically Barry had always been in the top 10% at school but he resisted his mother's wishes for him to study at the most prestigious universities offering Law. Instead of going to Oxford or Cambridge he infuriated his mother by electing to do his degree at Leeds University which, according to the Guardian, is ranked 9th in the country. Even during those years of study his mother wouldn't stop interfering with his career path and each summer organised an internship for Barry at the Solicitors where his father used to work. She also meddled in Barry's love life setting him up with, Alice, the rather plain daughter of one of the partners at the firm. Barry's mum had it all planned but there was one flaw in her great strategy. Barry is, and always will be, gay. After Barry sat his final exams, he bit the bullet and came out to his unsuspecting mother.

She had been so engrossed with steering his career and planning his future she hadn't really got to know him at all. To be fair Barry hadn't been sure himself until he was 16. His father's death had left him in an emotional turmoil. Because his mother had gone one step too far by setting Barry up with Alice it actually became Barry's escape route.

Deadly Circle/DC Poolie

There was no way Barry would become partner in a firm where he had hurt the daughter of one of its executive by dumping her. Reluctantly Barry's mother had to accept his decision to move north for work. However, she insisted on vetting any potential firm. Barry, happy enough to have cut some of the apron strings, ceded on this and that was how he found himself working for Arthur Broadbent.

The smell of the new car interior and the sound system belting out Bob Marley and the Wailers brought a smile to Barry's face as he set off for his Headland meeting. Although he had been living in Hartlepool for the last few months, he had never yet made his way over to the Headland. From his colleagues at work, he had gathered it was a part of the town that divided opinion.

On the short drive over to his meeting he began to understand why that was.

The drive began with the docks on one side of the road and a row of rather run-down basic housing on the other. A large red bricked building, which he later learned was the old library for the area, passed by on his left. This just seemed to him to be a typical working-class area of town. A row of shops a couple of cafes and pubs with nothing much to differentiate the place from lots of others. The outlook definitely picked up when Barry reached the end of the road. A glimpse of the North Sea caught his attention straight away. For someone who had always lived well away from the seaside there was something exciting about the salt air and the sound of waves crashing onto the shore.

He pulled into the car park behind the well-known Verrills fish and chip shop. The town square and gardens were close by, and the area was certainly looking a lot more attractive to the southern boy's eyes. He stepped out of his car and surveyed his surroundings. Well-kept public gardens and a highly impressive old church stood out. He looked around for Charlie and the group he was supposed to be meeting here and on spotting them he gave a wave and walked over to meet them.

Ten minutes later Barry was surveying a rather motley crew sitting in front of him, and he sighed inwardly. The five of them were seated around a large picnic table belonging to the fish and chip shop. Each one of them was tucking into a portion of chips, salt and vinegar naturally, with a large mug of tea to wash it down. At this establishment Barry couldn't have ordered a macchiato even if he wanted to. He realised that he couldn't avert his eyes from the person in the group who had insisted on having mushy peas with his chips. According to Charlie this was 'the one and only' Andy Chalmers.

'Thank God for that!' Barry thought as he looked Andy up and down. Even if he weren't eating his food still seated on his mobility scooter he still would have stood out. It had a taken a full five minutes to position that bloody thing at the right angle for Andy to still be able to reach his food and drink 'without having to lean too far and hurt my back'. For one thing he was, even on a very warm day, wearing a rather fetching, 'NOT', brown Russian fleecy hat with the ear protectors down.

'He wears that every single day of the year.' Charlie had whispered to Barry when he saw the look of disbelief on his face. 'It's so he can always plausibly deny whether he has heard something or someone. He can't half shift in that thing if he has annoyed someone,' Charlie smiled, as he looked at his friend. The sartorial elegance didn't stop there because, between that hat and the Dunlop green flash on his feet, Andy was dressed top to toe in a royal blue polyester track suit which was so old, it looked like a Jimmy Saville hand me down. Barry dreaded to think what could have caused the stains on the tracksuit, particularly the ones near his groin. Watching Andy shovel a hand full of chips covered in a disgusting green slush into his stubbled face, Barry winced. 'Has he never heard of a fork?'

Barry turned his attention to the two more normal ones. He used the phrase loosely.

Dave Stephens, at least, looked like he had seen a barber this year and knew what a razor was. Dave was undoubtedly the sensible one in the group. At just under 6 feet tall this handsome man with his short cut greying curly hair cut the most striking figure amongst the group.

He took pride in the fact that he had gained little weight over the years and believed that his hair made him look distinguished.

He chose to ignore Andy's more coarse observations such as, 'Oi Dave, I need to clean a really dirty saucepan. Lend me your hair.'

In truth even his wife, Kath, when touching his hair described it as a having the texture of a Brillo pad. Dave's face was a kind one with bright blue eyes and an almost perpetual smile. He also seemed to possess the brains of the group and seemed to know a fact about everything.

According to Dave, Verrills has always been the best fish and chip shop in Hartlepool although its quality wasn't quite as a good as when these three sexagenarians, or maybe even slightly older, were of school age.

The final member of this trio was Cliff Goodman. As Barry studied Cliff the show 'Last of the Summer Wine' came to mind.

'Is this the true circle of life?' Barry wondered. As kids you wouldn't be able to tell them apart, running around in shorts and having fun. Then the stresses or opportunities of adulthood that they had encountered made them all go in different directions and become the totally diverse people Barry saw in front of him. Finally, they gravitate towards one another. They remember each other as they used to be and accept the differences they have.

Cliff Goodman was the type of man everyone liked. He was good looking with the Paul Newman coloured eyes that ladies seemed to love. Always cheerful with a seemingly permanent smile on his face. At around 5ft 8ins he was the smallest of this merry band, but he took great pride in his appearance and was always very smartly turned out. He dressed most times as if on the way to the golf course and that smart casual look was him looking his scruffiest. He is the type of person who always is able to come up with some quip or put down in even the tensest of situations. Barry was soon to be on the receiving end of some of these comments from Cliff,

'Will you able to cope without there being jellied eels on the menu, Barry?'

'Are you alright eating outside this time of year? We know how soft you Southerners are.'

Deadly Circle/DC Poolie

Because his face seemed to always be smiling when he launched into the gentle taunting quips, Barry wasn't put out in the slightest. Instead, he saw it as some form of acceptance.

As there was total silence around the table, save the disgusting noises coming from Andy's open mouth as he ate, Barry seized the opportunity to address those assembled.

'Now I know Charlie has outlined the situation. Charlie and I want to help Troy Harvey in this difficult situation. But we can't do it alone. We need your help. Are you willing to help Charlie and me? I know you are all Hartlepool fans, but this is about helping an individual too.'

Andy stopped mid chomp and asked. 'Is there anything in this for us? Any reward?'

Charlie replied before Barry could speak. 'I can't promise you any money but I'm sure if we get Troy off and get him playing again then the club will be very grateful and generous. Maybe free season tickets? We could even get you a new club tracksuit Andy. God knows you could do with one.'

Andy looked a bit miffed when everyone, including Barry, nodded in agreement to that.

Dave then spoke for the group. 'I think we need to mull it over. Come with us on our walk.'

Barry looked at the passers-by. Because it was a surprisingly warm day the majority of the men were just wearing shorts and t-shirts. The women were either dressed similarly or wearing light summer dresses. Realising that he was grossly overdressed for a walk on such a day, Barry excused himself for a short while so that he could leave his jacket and waistcoat.

Deadly Circle/DC Poolie

Five minutes later the three regular walkers plus Charlie and Barry, now in shirtsleeves, set off on their daily walk along the Headland Seafront. Dave fired up his Bluetooth speaker which he carried around in his ever-present backpack. Mostly golden oldies, Barry noticed, and the people passing by all seemed to comment positively on the songs.

Barry could now see the attraction of this part of town. Plenty of others obviously had the same opinion of this area as there were a fair number of couples, numerous dog walkers or just people taking in the sea air. Even the industrial sites of Teesside across the bay could not detract from the view of the Cleveland hills in the distance. The 3 and 4 storey period houses, which they walked past along the seafront, gave the occupants a spectacular view across the North Sea.

Dave was enjoying showing Barry the hard to spot remains of the open-air swimming pool which was destroyed in a severe storm in the early 50's and had never been rebuilt.

'Are people over here always this friendly?' Barry asked.

'Not sure what you mean,' Charlie replied.

'Think I've said more 'good mornings' and 'hellos' in the last 30 minutes than in all of my time back home.'

'That's cockneys for you mate. Proper ignorant bastards, present company excepted of course,' Charlie laughed.

'No problem, Charlie. You're probably right anyway. There is certainly a different attitude and pace of life down there. I'm starting to like it up here more and more each day.'

The group made their way along the seafront chatting away amongst themselves and to people as they passed by.

They reached an impressive war memorial statue and gardens close by the lighthouse. An elderly gent had attracted a small crowd as he played a banjo and sang. He was obviously well known because everyone seemed to know his name and were asking for songs, they had obviously heard him play and sing before.

'Who is the old chap busking, is he a regular down here?' Barry enquired.

'He is on the front every day. He doesn't miss many at all and knows everyone and everyone seems to know him,' Dave replied.

'He is something of a local legend is Henry and he always has a story to tell. To tell the truth he is probably the most popular man on the headland,' added Dave.

'How are you today, Henry?' Andy asked.

'Fine thanks. Just though I'd come out and get some fresh air and play a few tunes on my old banjo.'

'As if you would have stayed in the house on a day like this. It would take a bad day for you to miss out,' chortled Andy.

'This is a friend of ours, Barry Barnes. He's a cockney but apart from that he is a good bloke.' Charlie laughed as he said it.

'Never mind son someone must be. What brings you up here to the promised land?' Henry enquired.

'Work Henry. I work as a solicitor in the town centre.'

'For fucks sake couldn't you get a proper job son? I've had my share of dealings with solicitors and most of them didn't go well.' Henry suddenly looked uninterested and turned around to play another tune.

Deadly Circle/DC Poolie

'Don't think he thought much of me,' Barry said to the group as they continued their walk along the promenade after leaving Henry.

'He is a top guy don't worry about that. He will be fine,' Andy chimed in. 'If you haven't been sworn at by Henry you haven't actually been on the headland.'

Barry eventually found himself with Charlie at the back of the group.

'Even if they agree to work with us do you really think these three can help?' he asked Charlie. 'I mean they don't really inspire confidence.'

'Don't judge a book by its cover,' was Charlie's measured response. 'They are all skilled in different ways. Andy hasn't worked in over 30 years. He has social security, and his doctors, believing that he can't walk more than 30 yards unassisted and that he has a glass back. Yet I've seen him sprint upstairs to the toilet when he has had three pints and was scared of peeing himself. Not to mention they still pay him when he goes on his yearly retreat to Ireland.'

'What about the others?' Barry asked.

'Well Dave is a planner and a thinker, and he has access to a company car from the Electrical Company where he used to work. Cliff, as you can see, can talk his way into and out of any situation with his charm and good looks.'

Barry looked satisfied with this summary.

'Here is the coffee wagon boys. Anyone wanting a drink?' Charlie asked.

Barry ordered his coffee, a flat white trying not to be too 'Southern Posh' and stood to the side as the others ordered their preference. He noticed that this little enterprise encouraged its customers with a free biscotti.

'That's a nice touch,' he thought as Andy, who surprisingly was last in line, ordered his drink.

'I've never heard of that one but, at that price, I have just got to try it. Especially as I'm not paying,' he grinned. 'Joyce, give me a macchiato please and I reckon one of your large double chocolate chip muffins would sit fine on top of that.'

Barry was just about to say something when he saw Charlie smirking but decided it was wiser to let it pass without comment.

Soon the four who had walked there were seated, albeit a little squashed together, on the solitary bench near the coffee van while Andy was munching away on his muffin facing them astride his scooter.

'Well,' Barry tentatively asked the group. 'Are you in?'

'Of course, we are,' Dave again spoke for the group. 'We always were going to help but we just wanted to check you out first. We can't let a 'Poolie' rot in jail without trying to help him. Particularly when he might help United get out of the mess they are in.'

'Poolie?' enquired Barry.

'Yeah, anybody from Hartlepool is a Poolie,' Cliff answered. 'He may have played crap so far this year, but he is still a good player and God knows we need him.'

Andy, who was wiping his mouth with vigour, added his consent. 'For a cockney you don't seem that bad even if you are a little tight. I mean the chips were alright, but you could have bought us some fish too.'

Deadly Circle/DC Poolie

Charlie looked at his friends fondly. He had thought they would help. But he wouldn't have bet his house on it.

Barry spoke again. This time more confidently, 'Well thanks guys. We really appreciate it. I know Troy will too. Charlie and I hoped you'd say yes. Accordingly, we have prepared a plan.'

They all looked at him expectantly.

'In my car, I assume we have to return that way, we have put together some folders for each of you. You will find,' he continued, 'pens and paper and a few pictures of Troy. We have also taken the liberty of providing you with some initial interview questions to get you in the swing of things.'

Charlie now took over. 'Knowing you as I do Barry asked me to assign potential roles for each of you. That way we can cover more ground in the short time available to us.'

'That makes sense,' Dave commented.

'Andy,' Charlie went on, 'You will base yourself around the marina area. It's flat and mobility scooter friendly. We need you to go to the bars and restaurants showing the picture to the staff and customers. Troy lives on the doorstep and we need a picture of his life in that marina area.'

Andy seemed almost gleeful, 'Food, drink and women. I think I can cope.'

'Cliff, we need you to do the same sort of thing but there is one snag.' Charlie looked almost apologetic.

'What is that?' Cliff's normal confidence sounded like it had disappeared.

'We want you to do that, but in West Hartlepool'.

To a man the three of them spat towards the ground.

'You poor sod,' Andy chuckled.

93

Deadly Circle/DC Poolie

'Dave, you have the most challenging job.' Barry thought he should step in. 'Charlie tells me you have access to a company car from your old place of work?'

'That's right,' Dave replied. 'They have a back-up car, which is rarely used, and me and the wife have been allowed to use it for weekend breaks in the past.'

'Great,' Barry leant forward. 'We need someone mobile who can do background checks on Troy, especially where he has played football in the past. Character witnesses and statements can be useful in court cases.'

Charlie and Barry started to stand up.

'Hold on,' said Cliff. 'If we are going to walk all the way back now, I vote we have another coffee first.'

'I fancy one of those muffins too,' Dave said, looking at the van to check their stock.

'I think we all do,' said Barry laughing, 'Even Andy I suspect.' He turned to where Andy's mobility scooter had been only to see it, out the corner of his eye, already parked at the back of the queue.

'Come on then,' Andy beckoned. 'You're paying.'

Deadly Circle/DC Poolie

I'm here!!

You've had playtime all your life little brother while I've had detention.

Not a fair balance considering what I did for you.

Now it's my turn to play and for you to feel your life turned upside down.

I've got my digs sorted out and I visited an ex-girlfriend in Darlington who's a hairdresser. It really is amazing what a few snips here and a little hair colouring there can do. I look so much like you now that we could be mistaken for brothers.

Oh, that's right we are.

Ding ding – playtime and freedom for me to have some fun.

Chapter 8

Dave had gone straight into action when he got back from that first walk with Barry and Charlie on the promenade. Knowing that Cliff and Andy were covering Hartlepool he decided to work back through Troy's career starting with his previous club first.

As a die-hard Hartlepool United fan, he knew that Troy was a summer signing from Newcastle United. That pleased Dave because it meant 2 things: firstly, that any trip in the company car wouldn't be too onerous because Newcastle was just up the road and secondly, he already had some contacts amongst Newcastle United fans.

His first job was to dig out his old contact book, a battered black A5 volume, with those indented pages with letters on them, so you could quickly jump to contacts beginning with a specific letter. Old school as it was it held information, be that phone numbers, email addresses and even fax numbers, for everyone Dave had ever needed to be in communication with. He had once experimented with Outlook on his laptop, but he soon realised that he just didn't trust it.

The first port of call was to phone Alex Bull the company rep for Tyneside. He was a Newcastle season ticket holder and had been since he was a kid. They had, in fact, talked earlier that year when it seemed on the cards that Troy would be heading down the coast. Alex had really sung the praises of Troy saying that Hartlepool would be getting a real player. This was something that Dave had believed at the time but in his few matches so far Troy certainly had not delivered performances anywhere near that level.

As Newcastle were playing away at Wolves that evening, a match being shown on TV, Dave decided not to call until half time. As it turned out this was a good decision because with the half time score being 1-1 Alex was in a fairly positive mood when he answered the phone. Had Dave waited until after the game then he might have met with a frostier response as Wolves ended up hammering Newcastle 4-1.

Meticulous Dave, not wanting to miss anything out, had drawn up a comprehensive list of questions for Alex and thankfully Alex was happy to share what he knew. Apparently, Troy, during his 18 months at the club, had kept his head down and, apart from the rumour of one violent incident after the season had finished, his record had been exemplary both on and off the pitch. When pushed Alex said that he didn't really know any details about the incident. Gossip, particularly non-playing gossip, was of no interest to him. He went on to suggest that Dave follow and contact @Talkingmagpies on twitter for more info. They run an unofficial Newcastle United social media platform for fans. Dave thought this was a great idea and as he already had a twitter account, to follow the club's away matches, it would only take seconds to do so. Alex went on to suggest that he'd let them know about Dave and the sincerity of his quest so that they then would follow him back allowing for more private communication via DMs.

Apparently disgusted by the team's performance at Wolverhampton, Dave was surprised when, at 10.30pm, just

97

before going to bed he received a DM from them asking how they could help. They, to be accurate, were a small team of younger fans, led by a guy called Alan Bate and it was Alan who was communicating with Dave that evening.

Twenty minutes, and numerous DMs, later Dave headed upstairs to join his wife, Kath, in bed. However, he wasn't going to be sleeping anytime soon because he was still processing all the information he had gleaned from Alan. According to Alan, one of the club's regular drivers, Sid Nugent, who was also an @Talkingmagpies source, had told them of a violent altercation between Troy and another man on the night of the team's award ceremonies. It had taken place right in front of the shocked drivers.

Seemingly, as the incident might have harmed the reputation of the club @Talkingmagpies had decided to sit on the story. Should Dave wish to pursue things then he'd find Sid Nugent, who was very much a creature of habit, in a café down the road from Newcastle's training ground. He would be needed between 3pm and 5pm to chauffeur the players around so 2pm would definitely be the time to chat to Sid.

'Road trip later this week then,' thought Dave to himself as he pulled back the duvet and snuggled into the crook of Kath's back. 'I think on my way to pick up the car I will drop by the apartments and chat with the janitor. In that job they see much more than people realise and neither Charlie nor Barry had mentioned him. Worth the detour I think.'

His thoughts were interrupted as Kath turned over and caught him square on the nose with her elbow. Dave turned as well to allow for a more comfortable spooning position.

Deadly Circle/DC Poolie

'I will take that as a hint.' Dave shut his eyes and started to plan the best route for Newcastle.

....

Andy lived in what he, rather tongue in cheek, called the Wild West frontier with the Badlands. His 2 up 2 down terrace on Mountbatten Drive was right at the start of the historic area called the Headland which, in the eyes of its inhabitants, was the only place that could truly call itself Hartlepool. Those who hailed from West Hartlepool, as it should really still be called, had hijacked the identity of the Headland and that certainly had left a lot of resentment east of the border. Andy, Dave and Cliff had often commented on how the street names this side of that invisible border all had the names of great military generals and even thought that an unofficial flag would be an apt 2 finger gesture directed at the local council who always seemed to represent more those living in the newer part of town.

Andy checked he had everything he needed: the photo of Troy; the stationery pack and a folder to keep it safe and together. He didn't really use the pannier on the scooter as he had Dave to do all the carrying for him. Before leaving the house, he checked himself in the mirror. He wanted to look smart today. Even Andy knew that if he were to get answers from the people he was going to speak to, and win their trust, he needed to make an effort to look the part, or at least the best part he could portray. He still had the brown Russian hat on. That was his signature look and would never change. It was even in his will, not that there was much to put in it, that he wanted to be cremated in it. He had had the material tested and it was safe to burn. His affection for the hat did not run to the Russians, who he hadn't trusted since his time on the merchant ships. He looked down at the now sparkly, green flash trainers with some pride.

'Dave has done a good job with the whitener there,' he thought to himself. 'I should get him to do my black dress trainers for the next funeral I have to attend. Everyone I know looks like they're at death's door.'

He then assessed the aesthetic of his new tracksuit. He smiled as he remembered Charlie being really pissed off with him after the walk.

'I think I need a bit of my reward up front,' he had demanded of Charlie. If there was one thing Andy had learned, it was that if you don't ask you don't get. And Andy was very good at asking. From Charlie's perspective it wasn't asking it was 'downright nagging'

'In the end,' he told Barry, 'I had to relent and gave Andy a brand-new Hartlepool tracksuit. I think he was hoping for some spending money but seemed quite happy with it anyway. Hope I'm not around when he finds out it is last year's model. Thank God they had one in extra small. He really is just bones and saggy skin.'

Andy thought, as he stared back at himself from the hall mirror, that he looked really quite dapper and that the deep blue set off his hat beautifully. It would look really cool with the hoodie up and give him even more protection against the cold when up over the hat.

The garden outside was an eclectic array of ornaments gathered over the decades of living there. He didn't want to touch anything as it reflected the warmth and love of his long-departed wife. He still choked a little when he thought of her lying on a lounger out there. The only thing she hadn't put in the garden was his mobility scooter which, for charging purposes, needed to be right next to the front door. He tapped the dial to check that it was fully charged. It wasn't that far to the marina, but he didn't want to have to get Dave to push it.

He chuckled remembering the one-time Dave had almost lost his cool with Andy. It had run out of power right down the bottom of the Headland, and it was only after Dave, red-faced, had pushed it up the hill with Andy on it, because he was 'too stressed to walk another inch', that they realised that the battery lead had somehow been disconnected and that it wasn't flat at all.

'It's all right Dave,' Andy had said almost heroically when the cable was reconnected. 'I can manage it from here. You're not looking too good. You'd better get home.' And with that he disappeared down the road.

For a mobility scooter the A179, the direct and fastest road, is best avoided. Not only is it full of traffic at most times of the day it also is the road the non-locals would use. For Andy non-locals were even farther down the evolutionary chain than those from West Hartlepool.

To that end Andy chose to drive along Lancaster Road past the Dunelm superstore, which apparently was Mrs Dave's shop of choice for all things bedroom. When she had said that to Andy he couldn't help but wonder how extensive their range of dildos and vibrators was. Since that day he couldn't look at her without some rather saucy images popping up in his mind.

He was now on Middleton Road. This was the bit he was dreading, the busy roundabout.

Deadly Circle/DC Poolie

'There should be a subway or something,' he thought as he approached it. He had one strategy, find a gap and go full pelt. He didn't have any protection against vehicular collisions. Mobility scooters don't even come with air bags.

He let a red Peugeot go by, thought he saw a gap, and floored it. From his right, even under his old hat and hoodie, he heard a loud toot and what he thought might have been the screeching of brakes. Fortunately, this time he didn't detect the sound of any metal on metal, or the feel of something colliding into him, so head down he continued.

With relief he found himself on the other side of the roundabout and now on the much quieter part of Middleton Road which led to the marina. On his right, across a stretch of water, he saw the Seaton Hi-Light Lighthouse and the Marina Arcade lay ahead.

'Now where shall I start?' he mused.

....

Charlie Green and Cliff Goodman met up outside the Victoria Park football ground knowing that their assigned mission was to check out the bars and restaurants around the centre of the town. Troy had been living in his plush penthouse apartment on the marina which was a short walk away. Charlie had known him long enough to be aware that Troy enjoyed the company of the ladies and was fond of a drink. Based on this he was hopeful of someone having some information about Troy's lifestyle away from football.

'Where shall we start then Cliff?' Charlie asked.

Deadly Circle/DC Poolie

Cliff thought for a while then replied. 'The weather is pretty good. I mean there are a few clouds but it's certainly not going to rain. We'll walk into town and call in the first bar we come to. I reckon that's just what Troy would do.'

Charlie cast an eye to the skies and then smiled, nodding in agreement.

As the pair made the short walk to the Main Street, where the popular bars were situated, Cliff looked at Charlie and asked, 'between you and me Charlie do you think Troy could be a murderer?'

'To be honest Cliff I'm not sure. All the signs seem to point to him having done it but I've known Troy since he first joined the football club as a kid and I have to believe that that young boy, and the man he has grown up to be, could not have done anything as bad as that.'

'Not exactly a full-on belief then Charlie.'

'It's difficult to be completely sure, but my gut feeling is that there are things we don't know yet about this whole affair. I count Troy as a good friend, even if we had lost touch for a while, and I'll do what I can to make sure the full story is known, and that Troy gets a fair hearing.'

The pair got to the first bar on the Main Street, The Golden Swan, stepped inside and made their way to the bar.

The buxom middle-aged barmaid spoke up. 'What can I get you lads?'

'Two pints of bitter please luv and take a drink for yourself.' Charlie flashed his best smile to the barmaid.

'Well thanks a lot.' she grinned 'It's a rarity these days to get a drink bought for me. The young 'uns wouldn't dream of it.'

103

Deadly Circle/DC Poolie

'You're welcome luv. You may be able to help us out.'

Charlie produced the photograph of Troy and asked if she had ever seen him in the bar by himself or with anyone else.

'Can't say I have,' she replied. 'He could have been in here weekends. It's bouncing in here then and hard to see who's in.'

'Can we leave a few flyers here?' Cliff asked the barmaid. He held up one that he had produced at home and then got Charlie to surreptitiously print off 100 in the club's office. It basically asked for information people could give to help Troy in his predicament. It had a picture of Troy, to get people's attention, and gave Charlie's mobile phone number.

'Course you can darling,' replied the barmaid. 'Although doubt you'll get any response. Not what you'd call community spirited, those that come in here. More likely to take them home if they've run out of bog paper.' Not particularly hopeful after that response, Cliff left the flyers anyway.

The next two or three bars gave similar answers. A couple of the barmen recognized Troy as a local footballer but said they couldn't remember him being in their bars at all.

'Not going too well so far is it,' Cliff commented. 'I'll be pissed before we find a bar where they recognize our man. Hopefully somebody may respond to a flyer.'

'In a way it's good that he hasn't been up to any bother in these bars. If he hasn't stood out, then he has been on good behaviour. Let's try another tack. Fancy something to eat, Chinese maybe? I know Troy is partial to a Chinese,' Charlie suggested.

Deadly Circle/DC Poolie

....

Dave had always been someone you could depend on. To anyone who met him it was clear that he had a heart of gold. These traits had been inherited from the two key women in his childhood years: his mother and, more significantly, his grandma who had been the matriarch of the family. Agnes, or Nessie as everyone called her, was a born and bred Headlander.

Having had to do what was needed to survive the depression and the years both during and after the Second World War Agnes had become a local hero. Her inherent compassion had saved many families from going under during these difficult times. Almost single-handedly, she had organised and overseen a lifesaving co-operative where skills and resources in the Headland community had been shared and redirected to ensure that no one in the community succumbed to the dangers they were confronting. Even more surprising was that she did most of this without a husband for she had been widowed at an early age with her husband dying of Tuberculosis – the dreaded TB.

Dave's mum, Hilda, was also a battler and she had always been determined to carry on the good work of her mother but in a manner that met her skill set. To that end she surprised nobody when she passed her nursing exams, finally rising to the position of matron at the University Hospital of Hartlepool. If that wasn't enough, during the years before the NHS was formed, she provided, on days when she wasn't working, health care and advice for her neighbours and anyone else in need from the area.

105

Deadly Circle/DC Poolie

Dave was what people would describe as a safe pair of hands. His wife, Kath, was grateful every day that she had chosen him over the brash and more outward going Tommy Wilkinson who was now, according to local gossip, on his 4th wife. Kath smiled with pride every time she looked at their daughter Eunice. Not only had genetics bestowed on her his piercing blue eyes and seemingly permanent warm smile but she also inherited his calm and caring nature. Dave is nobody's fool though for behind that smile there is someone who listens and processes. Outwardly he may seem to believe whatever people say but those who really know Dave know how shrewd, reflective and balanced he is.

Dave wasn't a risk taker either and that careful decision making had led him to working, from the day he left school until his last working day, at the small but friendly Middlesbrough Electricals. He was so popular there that tears flowed at his retirement do from both his work colleagues and customers alike. Since retiring Dave had virtually adopted Andy and Cliff. Even Charlie to some extent could, despite still working, be added to that list of people which Dave described as his "extended family".

However, it was a symbiotic relationship from which he also reaped a lot of benefits, especially during COVID. Dave was undoubtedly the linchpin of the group and the other 3 knew that they were in his debt. That was why they put up with his 'fun facts' and 'interestingly enough' interjections when they were out. Although they had learned to switch off when he went into lecturing mode, they missed both him and that mode when he occasionally had to cry off.

Deadly Circle/DC Poolie

That morning Dave set off to do his bit for "Operation Troy". Before collecting the firm's Mazda 6 for his research trips his first mission was to drop by the Marina Apartment Complex and chat to its janitor. The sun was shining brightly when Dave set of from his Headland home. He had decided to walk the 2 or 3 miles over to the marina although there was an early autumn chill in the air as he made his way.

Walking briskly, he was using this time to plan his way through his day. Always methodical in his approach to life and any problems coming his way he was very much looking forward to today and the interviews he had planned.

He approached the block of marina apartments and made his way to the entrance doors. A large sign on an inside wall gave directions to the various numbered doors. Dave knew that the janitor, a man named Alan Tubbs, lived alone in apartment number 1. He had heard a lot of accounts and rumours about the janitor but was determined, as in most things, to make his own judgement about the man.

Dave approached the door to number 1 and rang the bell. There was certainly no instant response. He was just about to leave when he was sure that he heard a sound from inside the flat. So having had no luck with the doorbell he knocked as loudly as he could. It took three attempts before he heard the key turn in the lock.

'What can I do for you?' Dave was asked.

'My name is Dave Stephens and I'd like to speak to Mr Tubbs the janitor, please. Is that you?'

'Yes, that's me. What is it you'd like to speak about?'

'Troy Harvey the footballer lives in these apartments. Obviously, you'll be aware of the trouble he is in at the moment,' Dave began. 'Some of my friends and I are trying to build a picture of his personality and movements.'

'My opinion of Troy Harvey is not likely to help his predicament,' Tubbs replied. 'A jumped up nobody trying to be something he is not.'

Dave sensed some real anger and bitterness in the janitor's tone.

'Can you just tell me what kind of resident you would say he was?' Dave asked although he felt he already knew the answer he was likely to get.

'I had no time for him at all. He was always noisy. He'd come in late from the bars usually with some dumb blonde on his arm or a bloody nose. It was always one of the two.'

'Would you usually be up and around at that late hour Mr Tubbs?' Dave was starting to get a measure of Alan Tubbs.

'I'm the janitor I'm around all kinds of hours.' Tubbs snapped back at Dave.

Dave soon realised he would not be getting any positive comments on Troy from this particular guy so thanked him for his time and made to leave. Normally a polite man who avoids confrontation Dave couldn't resist a parting shot at a man who needed bringing down a peg or two.

'I'm surprised, especially given the recent tragic events, that the front doors to the building were left open for every man and his wife to enter at will. I would have thought the residents association would need to look carefully at this situation and pay particular scrutiny to the man who is responsible for the health, safety and security of the people who live here. To me it seems at least negligent and is borderline reckless.' Dave stared directly at Tubbs as he said

108

this. He then turned his back to Tubbs and walked purposefully down the corridor.

As he made to leave the apartment block, he glanced again at the names board at the front entrance. He spotted the names of the couple who lived in the apartment directly below Troy's penthouse.

'Worth a try,' he thought as he hopped into the lift and headed up to get a second opinion on Troy's lifestyle. He rang the doorbell, and the door was opened almost immediately by a grey-haired elderly lady.

'Mrs Grieveson, is it? I wonder if I could have a word with you and your husband.'

'What about?' she asked.

'Troy Harvey,' Dave replied. 'I'm a friend of his.'

Just then an older man shuffled along the passageway tapping a white stick along the wall.

'Who is it, Gladys?' the man asked.

'Just someone asking about Troy the young man who lives upstairs.'

'Ask him in then Gladys. We don't get many visitors, you know that.'

'Alright Jim, I'll look after him. You get back in the room before you trip yourself up,' his wife replied.

Gladys Grieveson opened the door fully allowing Dave to enter and make his way into the sitting room. She explained that her husband Jim had lost his sight 10 years previously, but he got on with his life as best he could.

'I'm sure sometimes he forgets he is blind and wants to do everything as he used to.' she obviously felt that she needed to explain further.

109

Deadly Circle/DC Poolie

'I may be blind Gladys, but I can hear very well. Especially when you are talking about me,' Jim Grieveson shouted from his chair.

Dave could tell from that little exchange how close the pair were. Gladys just smiled and asked Dave to sit down.

'Can I get you a cup of tea? Sorry I didn't get your name,' Gladys asked.

'My fault, I should have said. My name is Dave Stephens, and with some friends, I am trying to find out the truth behind this trouble that Troy is involved in at the moment.'

Once he had explained the purpose of his visit, they seemed happy to share what they knew about Troy. They told Dave that Troy was always very helpful to them. He would call most days to see that they were both well and if there was anything they needed.

Gladys mentioned that she would often cook meals and take a plate upstairs to Troy.

'I don't think he is much of a cook, and it can't be healthy to eat out so much or rely on takeaways,' she said, feeling the need to explain her good deeds.

Yes, they had both heard him coming in late and quite often with 'company', but he was a good-looking, affluent single man enjoying himself and saw nothing unusual in that.

Jim even joked that he saw very little of Troy mainly because of being blind but was happy that his improved hearing allowed him to occasionally enjoy the sounds from the penthouse. They reminded him, he said, of his courting days with Gladys. This got him a swift kick across his ankle from his wife. Dave smiled at the antics, and obvious love, the pair were showing without embarrassment.

'I hope this is how people see me and Kath,' he thought.

'What about the night it all happened. Did you see or hear anything out of the ordinary then?' Dave asked.

Gladys thought for a while and then replied, 'Can't say I did. It was just a day like any other as far as I can remember.'

'What about you, Mr Grieveson, anything special that you remember?' Dave turned towards the old man to make sure his voice wasn't muffled.

'Call me Jim young man. No need for formalities here,' he replied. 'As you will know these new spec apartments are very well insulated and sound proofed so it's rare for the wife to hear anything from the other apartments but, since losing my sight, my sense of hearing has certainly gone up a few notches. There were a few loud voices and sounds like furniture being moved. It was nothing really out of the ordinary, so I thought no more of it. It could have been Troy's television because sometimes I can hear that.'

Gladys then spoke up, 'I do hope Troy is proved innocent of all this. I can't believe he did it. He seems a lovely man and I can't say a bad word against him.'

He thanked them with a genuine affection and walked away reflecting on the two very different opinions of Troy he had just heard. He knew which one he gave more credence to.

……..

Back in the, now busier, marina area Andy's stomach quickly gave him the answer to what he should do first. So, he

111

Deadly Circle/DC Poolie

headed to the other end of the long arcade of bars and restaurants until he was outside the Lock Gates. Cliff was always going on about the quality of food here, and the lovely waitresses too. Inside there were various types of seating, high, low, plush and functional, all arranged around tables set for either 2 or 4 people. Andy decided to sit at a table for 2 near the window where he had a clear view of his scooter.

'We aren't on the Headland now,' he thought to himself.

An overweight, middle-aged waiter appeared, much to Andy's disappointment. He looked past the waiter, over his shoulder, to the counter hoping to see some of Cliff's recommended 'eye candy' but there was no one else there. His interest picked up when the waiter said, 'Here is the menu. Suzie will be out in a minute to take your order.'

Andy was ravenous but he wasn't going to pay £7.99 for the full breakfast and 'That doesn't even include a drink'.

He surreptitiously pulled out, what Dave called, his 'Granny Purse'. There was actually over £200 in it, mostly in a secret side compartment. He carefully created a cash pile of coins totalling £5.99 and pushed it to the side of him.

Three minutes later a pretty brunette in her early 30s approached. As she got nearer Andy was taken by the subtle, yet very alluring, scent she must have been wearing.

'What can I get you?' She asked with a pleasant, natural smile.

'Well, as it's my birthday and I've promised myself a treat,' Andy replied, almost shyly. 'My late wife and I always had a special breakfast on our birthdays.' He decided not to lay it on anymore. Why use a trowel when a fine brush would do. 'I'd like your half breakfast please.'

Deadly Circle/DC Poolie

'Anything to drink?' Suzie asked. She caught him half glancing at the pile of coins as he replied.

'Just some tap water please.'

While he waited for the food, he watched people passing by, some looking admiringly at his scooter, and studied the general hubbub of the area.

As if on cue Suzie reappeared with what was clearly a full breakfast of double everything and two rounds of toast.

'Just a small gift from us on your birthday,' she said, as she placed a massive pot of tea and a mug by the side of the plate of food.

'Thank you so much.' Is what Andy said. 'Result!' Is what Andy thought.

Feeling both incredibly full and pleased with himself, a totally clean plate in front of him showing why, Andy remembered to show the photo of Troy to Suzie before he left. He explained that the man in the photo was a friend, who was in some trouble, and that any information they might have could help him.

'I told his solicitor I was coming here for my birthday breakfast, and he thought I could do some of his leg work for him.' He looked almost saintly, were it not for still having his Russian hat on indoors, as he said this. Suzie called Jamie, the podgy waiter, over and they looked at the picture together.

Five minutes later, after thanking Suzie and Jamie profusely, Andy was mounting his scooter having been given the following information: Yes, they knew who he was and what he had been charged with; no, he wasn't a regular as the players usually had breakfast at the ground, but he had eaten scrambled eggs on toast there 2 times, both on a Sunday and he

113

usually seemed quiet, maybe hungover. However, he did seem to like a chat with the waitresses in particular. Andy checked the notes he had taken to make sure he hadn't forgotten anything and then thought about his next step.

As it wasn't yet time for the bars to open for their lunchtime trade, he looked towards the car park and saw a parking attendant walking officiously amongst the cars. The car park was well known for having rip off prices. The abstemious drivers would have to pay these extortionate prices, but the vast majority chose to get there by taxi as Hartlepool wasn't famous for having a high number of designated drivers. There was no doubt that the car park was a real cash cow for whoever owned the land. Andy had seen the charges as he came in and was horrified by them. Or would have been had he had a car.

His efforts with the attendant and the few delivery drivers, who stopped nearby during this time, fell on stony ground. One driver knew who Troy was. The others didn't and moreover couldn't care less.

'I don't look a lot at faces just the car numbers.' This was one of the more intelligent answers he had got from the parking attendant.

At 11.30am most of the rest of the establishments came to life. Andy had decided to stay at this end and work his way down. His logic being that here he was nearer to Troy's apartment. Armed again with the photo, his pen and his notebook he entered every establishment which was now serving. Troy, it seemed, was very selective where he ate. Of all of the restaurants it was only the tapas bar that remembered him eating there. The story from there and seemingly every bar

114

was the same. Most places saw him at least once a week and he drank at most 2 drinks before leaving. Andy quickly surmised, by the short amount of time Troy had been in Hartlepool and the vast number of bars that it didn't mean that Troy only drank that amount each night he was out. He was often seen in the company of a female companion. In the words of one very opinionated barman, probably a Middlesbrough fan, 'They were attracted to him like flies around shit.'

There were a few accounts of him staggering out of the bar in the arms of a fly.

'Lucky shit,' thought Andy.

In the final bar they even described him leaving there on the night of the murder with a woman. Andy underlined this note as he took down the description, at best vague, of the woman.

'Damn!' He thought. 'I don't even know what the victim looked like. We need to find that out from Barry or Charlie.'

Andy was feeling knackered. He hadn't worked this hard since he had to trash his, normally tidy, house for a social security visit. He was on the verge of giving up when an unobtrusive entrance to the end unit drew his attention.

Outwardly it gave away nothing as to the nature of its business but what caught Andy's eye, as he caught his breath, was the seemingly odd nature of its clientele. It was all single men, of various ages and appearance, entering on their own. Not only did they go in on their own but each one of them gave a quick backwards glance before stepping purposefully through the darkened doorway. Suddenly, Andy felt rejuvenated and his interested piqued. In fact, it had reached Mount Everest levels of peaking.

115

Deadly Circle/DC Poolie

Having, again, parked his scooter just to the side of the establishment's entrance, Andy walked through the doors. Not only is the glass blackened but there is a black curtain to go through as well. What greeted Andy on the other side was, once more, unlike any of the other Marina venues. He found himself in a square, dimly lit room with small tables around its perimeter. At the far end was a bar but this one had no draught taps. Instead, there was just bottles on the shelves behind.

Not all the tables were occupied but those that were had those self-same single men, he had seen entering just before, sitting looking a little anxious and some had a wine or spirit glass in front of them. Andy knew where he was. It certainly looked more like a waiting, or holding, room than a drinking place and his suspicions were confirmed when a short-haired brunette collected one of the men and led him upstairs.

'This is going to be fun.' Andy was smiling at the very thought. He went and sat at an empty table. When the waitresses came over and asked him if he wanted a drink, he declined saying he was driving. Andy enjoyed the to and fro over the next 20 minutes commenting to himself on the lack of, or the apparent lack of, staying power of the middle-aged gent he had seen go upstairs when he had entered.

Finally, a wavy-haired blond in her twenties and very little else came over and spoke to him. 'Sir, unfortunately we have no lift but there is a special downstairs room for our more senior customers. My name is Sandra,' she continued. 'Would sir like to come with me to look at our special menu or maybe sir would prefer a slightly different flavour? We do, also, have some offers for the older client.'

116

Deadly Circle/DC Poolie

The code wasn't very subtle to someone of Andy's experience and age. 'Sandra you are just to my taste,' he said gallantly.

The room was surprisingly clean, given its busy nature, and there was a menu on the table to the side of the bed.

'If sir would like to take a minute to look at the menu.' Sandra obviously was one who stuck to the script.

Andy wasn't really listening. His eyes were scanning up and down looking for what he considered a bargain.

'I would like the frontal hand massage and relief,' he said ordering as if he were at the local Italian. £10 was the seniors' price. He considered that good value. That was less than a pack of fags for heaven's sake.

'Will sir be paying by cash or card? We do ask for payment up front.'

Andy took out the granny purse and extracted a £10 note. Sandra took the note and placed it in a safe in the corner. He noticed a card reader was in there too.

'The oldest profession wasn't lagging behind the newest technology,' he mused.

'Normally this is performed with the client naked,' she smiled.

Andy wasn't at all shy, but he would be in a bit of a hurry afterwards if he was to get home before dark. 'I will leave my hat and socks on if that is alright?'

'Whatever sir wants. I'm afraid the price doesn't include me undressing you.'

'No worries.' Andy replied already taking off the new hoodie. He was pleased that he had put on clean pants only 2 days ago. He hadn't even got to the stage of wearing them inside out.

Naked apart from those aforementioned items he turned to face her and asked, 'Where do you want me?'

Sandra, who was rubbing KY jelly onto her hands, looked up at smiled again.

'On your back on the bed you silly boy. I can see you've given many a young lady a very good time with that.' She said this staring directly at his manhood.

Andy almost swelled with pride at that compliment. 'The swelling will happen soon,' he thought.

Being Andy, he naturally tried his best to get his money's worth, but Sandra was both sexy and skilled.

As he started to get dressed, afterwards, he offered her the photo of Troy.

'Did this man ever visit the establishment?' he asked.

Sandra, who had fastidiously just washed and dried her hands stared intently at the photo. Her smile turned into a frown.

'Hold on! He looks like the one who went with Samantha a few weeks ago.' Andy watched as she became more and more agitated. 'The bastard roughed her up badly because he couldn't perform.'

She turned and looked fiercely at Andy. 'He's not a friend of yours, is he? Stay there!' she commanded, as she turned to leave the room.

'Where are you going?' Andy asked rather stunned by this weird turn of events.

Deadly Circle/DC Poolie

'I'm going to get Norman, the guy working on the door,' she replied, without looking back. 'He is desperate to find this guy and give him a good hiding. Samantha is his girlfriend.'

For a split-second Andy contemplated the concept of a prostitute having a boyfriend but then he came to his senses. He speedily finished dressing and exited through the concealed emergency door in the corner which he had noticed earlier.

'Surely it must be illegal to cover an emergency exit like that with a curtain,' he thought, as he shut the door behind him. He turned the corner at the back of the unit and set off to find his scooter.

. . . .

In West Hartlepool the Twisted Bamboo had built up a great reputation for its food and atmosphere and was now seen as definitely the place to be and be seen in locally. Certainly, a lot of money had gone into the refurbishment and top-quality furnishings and lighting had given the place a big city feels.

There had always been rumors about the people behind the venture and just where all this money had come from. Drug dealing, money laundering and Triad gangs were always being whispered about, but nothing was ever brought up in public.

A young Chinese waitress made her way over to their table to take their order.

'Are you ready to order please?' she asked.

'Can I just have a Chicken Curry with boiled rice please?' Charlie asked. 'What are you having then Cliff?'

'Think I'll have Crispy Duck for a starter and beef and red peppers for my main.'

'Does that come with rice?' Cliff enquired.

119

'It does sir. We do a Chef's special rice which I can recommend,' she said.

'Great I'll have that as well please. Anything you recommend is good enough for me.' Charlie cringed at the comment from his friend. 'He really is a chancer,' he mused.

They both enjoyed their meals. Even if Charlie grimaced a little at the bill Cliff assured him that it was well worth it. Of course, that's easy to say when you are not paying for the food.

They were just about ready to leave when Charlie produced the photograph of Troy and called the waitress over again.

'Do you recognize the man in this photograph? He might have been in here for a meal at some time,' Charlie said.

The waitress's expression seemed to say she did, although she said nothing at all. She turned sharply and, with the picture in hand, she disappeared through the back into the kitchen.

She reappeared after a few minutes and beckoned them to follow her right the way through the kitchen and out the back. Charlie went first following the waitress. His mind was running riot trying to work out what was going on. That made him oblivious to his surroundings. Cliff on the other hand was more meerkat like, looking around and absorbing everything he saw.

His curiosity was piqued in the kitchen where there seemed to be 2 types of people: those wearing aprons and hats scuttling to and fro with a clear purpose and another smaller group, all male, dressed in black and rather surprisingly wearing sunglasses. They seemed to be transferring fairly heavy sacks to a cupboard, or room, next to the freezer. The pair ended up standing outside in a darkened yard. The shadows from the tall buildings surrounding the restaurant made them think that it was already early evening.

It was a few minutes later when three of the biggest oriental men they had ever seen stepped out of the shadows. The three crowded around Cliff and Charlie getting practically nose to nose with the pair.

'The waitress out front tells us you've been asking questions. Our boss doesn't like people coming in here asking questions you see.'

Cliff was shaking as he replied. 'No problem. We were just trying to trace a friend of ours and we were hoping he might have been seen around here recently.'

'Is that so?' the biggest of the three began. 'We don't expect to see the pair of you around here asking questions again. Do you get our meaning?'

'And by the way if you do happen to meet up with your friend give him this. It's the bill that he didn't pay when he did a runner from here.' The smallest of the three giants chimed in.

'It will be much better for him if you find him before we do. Whatever amount that bill says he owes maybe he should pay double just for my boss's inconvenience. I'd also suggest you don't come back here until this is sorted.'

He then produced an 18" machete from his jacket and even in the poor light the weapon seemed to glisten. A joint shiver ran through both Cliff and Charlie. They both knew that this blade had never been used to julienne a carrot. Somebody's ears or fingers perhaps. As he waved the machete in the air the gate out into the even darker alley behind the restaurant opened and they were pushed out, almost falling over each other as the gate slammed behind them. Cliff didn't need to look back to confirm what he had seen going on in the background. Even in the extreme murk he had seen the self-same group of men dressed in black offloading, what he knew to be, more sacks from the back of a van and taking them into the restaurant through the delivery door.

The pair walked quickly away from the gate and were relieved when they were back on the Main Street. Once there they hurried as quickly as they could away from the Twisted Bamboo. Charlie glanced over his shoulder and swore himself off Chinese food for the foreseeable future. That resolve was made even stronger when Cliff told him what he had seen going on. So, it was true. The restaurant was a cover for drugs.

Before going their separate ways, Cliff and Charlie agreed to meet the next morning outside the McDonald's close to the centre of town. They did this with the idea of planning their next move.

…….

To any passer-by it would have been an entertaining cross between a slow motion all action chase and a piece of pure farce. Andy had successfully reached his scooter and set off back towards the Lock Gates end of the marina arcade. However, Norman, who obviously wasn't as dumb as he looked, had soon assessed the situation when confronted by the empty bedroom and was now on foot, but in pursuit, of the fleeing Andy.

Speed walking, at the best of times, looks rather silly to the non-participant but Norman, who was dressed formally, in a suit and tie, for his job, looked borderline slapstick as he tried to close in on the scooter. What made it even more surreal was that he was trying to do so without alerting the people around to what was going on. Andy, once realising what was happening, had opted initially for straight line speed and stuck to the car park road.

Unfortunately for him he was driving into the flow of the traffic and after a couple of near misses he elected to mount the pavement and take his chances with the less dangerous pedestrians. Norman, buoyed by Andy's tactic, was closing in. He could feel the sweat on his brow due to the exertion and nervous energy expended. His demeanour wasn't helped by the fact that people were starting to stare at him. Little did he realise that his face was also now extremely red and that the white shirt he was wearing, unfortunately now a size too small due to not following the washing instructions, made his bulbous neck spill out over the collar. In effect he looked like an angry tomato about to explode.

Andy didn't really have a plan. If anything, he was really hoping that Norman would run out of energy and give up the ghost. As he continued to weave left and then right, avoiding both tables and customers, Andy snuck a look behind and saw Norman was less than 5 yards behind.

'Bloody hell!' thought Andy. 'He must really love Samantha. Suzie, Sandra and Samantha. Do all women who work here must have a name beginning with S?'

By now he had passed the Lock Gates Cafe and was approaching the footbridge of the same name. Andy remembered that his nephew, Stephen, worked in a restaurant on the other side of the lock footbridge.

123

Deadly Circle/DC Poolie

'If I can get there,' he realised, 'I will be safe'.

Before he needed, or pretended to need, the scooter, he had spent many a twilight hour magnet fishing for the coins in the bowl held by the monkey statue. To most the statue was the representation of a monkey, which was hanged in Napoleonic times by the people of Hartlepool mistaking it for a French spy. But to Andy it had meant a bag of chips each evening at worst.

As he approached the footbridge across the lock, he realised that he had never driven across it before, and it suddenly seemed both narrower and much more bendy than he remembered. At that very moment, a few yards short of the footbridge, Norman made a grab for Andy's hoodie which had fallen onto his shoulders, Andy unexpectedly veered left leaving Norman grasping at fresh air. Without anything to slow him down he ran full pelt into the wooden strut which was, in essence, the left side of the entrance. There was an awful cracking sound as Norman's left knee impacted with the strut. The scream which then emanated from Norman would even have scared the monkey.

Having checked that nothing was broken he turned to see that, 20 yards away, Andy had already parked his scooter in front of the Marina Harbour Master's office and, scooter key in hand, was bounding up the stairs 2 at a time to the first floor where the Harbour Master had his office.

The Harbour Master in question, whose job seemingly was to spend most of his time on watch from his lofty position, was Andy's former neighbour, Tim Bentham.

'Hello Andy,' said Tim, who had thought he had seen the last of Andy when, after years of trying, he had finally sold his house and was able to move to pastures and neighbours new. 'What are you doing here?'

'Seeking sanctuary,'Andy thought to himself. But what he said was, 'just thought I'd pay you a visit as I was in the vicinity.'

'Nice to see you, Andy,' replied Tim, who out of habit, when Andy used to drop by daily, picked up a kettle and walked over with it to the sink. '2 tea bags, extra milk and 5 sugars as usual?' he asked.

'Of course,' said Andy. 'That's just how I like it,' he added as he looked down at Norman, who finally having accepted defeat, had stopped glaring up at Andy. Instead, he had now turned and was limping rather badly and slowly back in the direction of the brothel.

'Tim, is that tea ready yet?' Andy smiled as he sat down in Tim's comfy lookout chair.

....

The following morning Charlie arrived at the McDonald's five minutes early with Cliff arriving 10 minutes later.

'Did you sleep well last night?' Charlie enquired, 'After our run in with those Triad guys yesterday I mean.'

'Yes, I was fine thanks. We can't let those boys get to us. We have a big job on our hands in helping Troy,' a determined Cliff replied.

The pair made their way into the restaurant and sat at a table near the window.

Deadly Circle/DC Poolie

'What do you fancy for your breakfast then?' Cliff asked, 'We must have burned up some calories between us the speed we moved away from that Chinese place yesterday.'

'Nothing like having a machete waved in a person's face to quicken up their movements,' Charlie replied with a grin. 'A bacon bun and a large hot coffee with two sugars would be perfect. And much appreciated thank you.'

'Your wish is my command sir. I'll be back as soon as possible. You just sit there and enjoy the view.'

Cliff wandered over to the counter and ordered their breakfast food and drinks, pausing to chat to a lady behind him in the queue. Charlie drummed his fingers on the table impatiently whilst watching his friend trying his best to build up a connection with the lady.

After a while Cliff made his way back the table

'Bacon sandwich and coffee with two sugars as requested Charlie my mate.'

'Think I asked for hot coffee Cliff actually,' Charlie muttered in frustration.

'Sorry I got talking to a lady in the queue. I think I might have a chance there,' Cliff replied with a wink.

'I thought we were here to decide the best way forward in helping a friend of ours' Charlie said obviously annoyed. 'We need more information on Troy's movements and habits really. Some of the stories I'm hearing must be made up. They sound nothing like the Troy I know that's for sure,' Charlie continued.

'Yes, you are right. I apologize. You know I'm 100% behind our task with you and the others,' a chastened Cliff responded. 'Mind you I did get her phone number, so it was worth it,' he grinned.

Charlie looked suitably satisfied with Cliff's renewed focus now having, at least temporarily, returned from his amorous quest. 'I will tell you one thing though. When we've got Troy out, we need to do something about that bloody restaurant. This is my town. Even if it is in West Hartlepool, I'm not having those machete wielding thugs ruining my town with their bloody drugs.'

Cliff stopped mid slurp of his ever-cooling latte and looked at his friend, 'I totally agree but they are a dangerous bunch and we will have to live here in the future. Once we've helped Troy, we can decide what's the best course of action.'

Charlie nodded his agreement and turned his attention to his now lukewarm breakfast. Before they left, he arranged with Cliff to meet up again after he finished work at the ground. There was still work to be done and no time to waste.

....

Being a widower didn't stop Cliff from enjoying the company of women. Having been totally loyal to his wife he now had decided that there was still a limited amount of time to sample a "different cuisine". Like the others in his walking group the Headland was the centre of his life but thanks to his bus pass and senior citizens railcard he was able to pursue this more amorous side of his life up to once a week.

The Headland is a small close-knit community, and everybody knows each other's business. Betty, his wife, had been very popular in the community and her friends were incredibly protective of her memory. As one of the best singers on the Headland a few of her karaoke classics had even been retired after her death. To Cliff's horror a few local widows had been selected as possible replacements, after a suitable time of course, but Cliff, in his strong desire for freedom and not to be tied down, told everyone that Betty could never be replaced.

Cliff's monthly timetable was now a routine. On the first Monday of every month, he would go line dancing in Sunderland with Amanda, a petite, bespectacled blonde -on her head anyway - who lived in a semi-detached house close to the bus station. Her energy lasted way beyond the line dancing, and he was often grateful that the buses ran every twenty minutes because he could easily be convinced to stay after the departure time of his normal bus home. For the moment, at least, he was quite grateful for a rest the following Tuesday which was when his pottery class took place in Middlesbrough, a short hop on the Train. His regular extra-curricular companion, Gracie, was in the middle of a 3 month visit to Perth, Australia, where she was seeing her grandson for the first time. Gracie, prior to the trip, had been getting a little serious, despite Cliff's open and frank declaration that he wasn't looking for anything serious nor a life partner.

This hiatus, therefore, was giving him some much-needed time to reassess things. As much as he liked pottery, the pieces he had made were ideal as cheap presents, he wondered whether this element of his life needed to be binned.

On a random day during the last week of the month he often felt some pangs of guilt. This was because he would be seeing a married woman whose husband was a long-distance lorry driver. This was an affair, and it was purely physical with no time for small talk. It didn't really sit well with Cliff that as the husband, who out of necessity due to a gambling debt, was sleeping at least twice a week in his cab in a lorry park near the Daventry International Rail Freight Terminal (DIRFT), his wife was spending over half of the money he earned on their trysts in the Wolviston Premier Inn. Cliff was often surprised by how common it was that the woman, even if she didn't have a job, managed the finances for the household. In this case, however, given the circumstances it was certainly fortuitous.

Unless he fancied a second session of line dancing during the 3rd week of the month Cliff had that week off the love train. He'd let his libido, and his poor knees, decide.

Having separated from Charlie after their meeting in McDonalds Cliff walked with a purpose towards Church Street. This was an area close to the railway station which used to be the hub of Hartlepool's nightlife. Although it had been through a period of rejuvenation recently it was more a street for dining than drinking. However, Cliff surmised that, as it was an area within easy walking distance of Troy's marina apartment, it was worth spending a few hours of investigation there.

Being an all-day establishment the Ward Jackson, the local Wetherspoons, was an obvious place to start. It was too early for alcohol, so Cliff opted for a non-alcoholic cider, Wild Berries. As Cliff sipped on, what he considered, a slightly too sweet beverage for this early in the morning he looked around.

In the corner he recognised an old friend from his grammar school.

'Jesus!' thought Cliff. 'What has happened to Jamie?'

Deadly Circle/DC Poolie

His erstwhile best friend at school, well at least up to the sixth form where they parted ways, looked like he had hit rock bottom. He was wearing old and stained clothing which looked like it could stand up by itself and his face was so ravaged it made him look at least 10 years older than he really was. Cliff guessed that the real reason for his depressing appearance lay in the glasses, one nearly full and 2 empty, on the table in front of him.

'It's barely 10.30am,' thought Cliff, feeling really depressed and slightly sickened.

Cliff picked up his glass and walked over to join Jamie who instantly recognised his old friend. Cliff was thankful that Jamie wasn't in need of another drink as he didn't want to contribute to something that was obviously causing so much harm.

He briefly thought back to when they sat side by side in set 2 mathematics. Jamie was always so smart in his uniform, his mother wouldn't have let him leave home otherwise, and from an early age he had always been popular with the girls.

Cliff remembered hearing that Jamie's son had committed suicide, he wasn't sure of the details, and that Pat, Jamie's wife, had died soon after.

'Often happens like that,' was how the person who had related to the story to him had summed up the events. It clearly wouldn't benefit Jamie to reopen such raw wounds, so Cliff decided to tell him what he and the others were doing for Troy. Not expecting to get much, if any, information out of Jamie he showed him the photo really just using it as a prop for their chat. To his surprise Jamie took the photo from him and said, slurring many of the words for obvious reasons, 'That's the bugger who knocked my pint over. It was a full one too and he didn't even have the decency to offer to buy me another.'

'Are you sure?' asked Cliff leaning in.

'Yes, he and some other drunken arsehole were squaring up to each other.'

Pot and kettle sprang to Cliff's mind, but he was really interested now. 'When was this?'

'Last Thursday just before checking out time. I remember because I had won on the horses and that pint was bought with the last of my money. I bet Steve behind the bar there remembers.' He looked shattered as if he had accomplished the verbal equivalence of running a marathon.

Against his better judgement Cliff bought a pint for Jamie as he quizzed Steve about the incident. Steve had been working up the other end of the bar so hadn't served Troy himself, but he remembered that others in the bar had been surprised that the 'Pools new super star had been drinking pints of the 99p Porcupine special in a Wetherspoons.

'Porcupine?' Charlie had interrupted.

'Very popular amongst our regulars. Cheap and spiked,' he smiled.

'Was he involved in a fight?'

'Yes, apparently he got into a slanging match, hence Jamie's unhappiness,' he answered shooting a glance in the direction of Jamie. 'But then it turned nasty, and he threw a left hook followed by a knee to the bollocks. The other guy crumpled to the ground in pain.'

'What happened then?' Charlie needed the full details.

'Debbie the barmaid at that end was screaming so I ran around the bar chasing him out the door. He was way too quick

131

for me,' Steve added patting his ample belly, 'so I had no chance of catching him.'

'Which way did he go?' Charlie knew there were 2 possibilities.

'Back towards the centre.'

'Don't suppose you have any CCTV footage?' Charlie was more hopeful than expectant.

'Sorry it's wiped every 2 days.'

Cliff thanked Steve and gave Jamie his pint just as he was polishing off the previous one.

He sat down mulling over what he had just heard.

'There are 2 ways to get to the marina,' he thought. 'If he went that way ......'

He knew then what he was going to do next.

He jumped up and bade farewell to Jamie telling him not to be a stranger and to join them on their Headland walk sometime soon. 'It's great banter, fresh air and there is a lovely coffee van right on the promenade.'

Although Jamie said he definitely would, Cliff doubted he would see Jamie again, unless it was right where they were. In the pub.

Cliff's epiphany in the pub had led him to Bev who lived in the Headland but worked in West Hartlepool as a receptionist in the Travelodge. She had once told Cliff in the working men's club near where they both lived that, due to cost cutting, her shift didn't start until 3pm when check in commenced. He was due to meet Charlie at 4pm so he calculated that he just had enough time, particularly if he laid the groundwork first. Phone in hand Cliff called Bev on her mobile, catching her apparently in the Asda checkout queue.

Deadly Circle/DC Poolie

Bev had always had a soft spot for Cliff, and she was a United season ticket holder to boot.

'You will need a USB stick,' she said finishing their conversation.

Cliff had worked out that Troy's route home would have to take him past the Travelodge, which, due to its open access car park, had plenty of CCTV coverage. During the call Bev had confirmed that their footage, for insurance reasons, was kept for a week.

Having promised to take Bev to the Karaoke in Seaton Carew at the weekend Cliff left the Travelodge with the footage for the previous Thursday on his memory stick.

....

Dave, ever grateful for the loan of the company Mazda, wished he still had some influence with the company beyond the venue for the Christmas party which he still organised despite having retired. With age had come the desire to drive automatics and not manual cars. They were hard work and this one even had 6 gears for heaven's sake. He smiled as these thoughts, almost the polar opposite of mindfulness and meditation, entered his mind. 'When did I start to become a grumpy old man?' he mused.

The Newcastle United training centre is located in Darsley Park which is east of the city centre. Dave decided to take the most direct route of 33 miles in distance which meant travelling mainly on the A19, through the Tyne Tunnel and then onto the A191.

Deadly Circle/DC Poolie

It costs a mere £1.90 to use the crossing but, due to cost cutting and/or new technologies coming to the fore, you can't simply pay a man at a booth or chuck coins into a receptacle. No, you have to pay that massive sum online before the end of the following day.

'What a faff!' thought this new grumpy driver, Dave. 'And what idiot decides the road numbering? A19 and A191. Not confusing at all'.

Dave decided that his poor irritable demeanour was partly down to a lack of music, so he pulled over just after the tunnel to pair his android phone to the car. The rest of the 52-minute journey passed swiftly with Dave listening to his Americana Spotify playlist which he had downloaded after going to the annual music festival bearing the same name in Kilkenny, Ireland.

He had to drive around for a bit before locating the 'Café'. Had he not arrived with plenty of time to spare he might have got flustered circling the area of the training ground three times trying to spot 'the café down the road'. He was wondering what to do next when he spotted some big SUVs parked in a lay-by.

Dave thought this was worth investigating and drove into the lay-by. Sure, enough just beyond the row of cars, where the car park curved back towards the road, was a glorified portacabin with steam coming out of a small chimney.

'This must be it,' thought Dave. 'Not quite what I imagined but there isn't much else in this area.' As he got out of the car, after parking fifty yards away from the café, he was sure that he felt a few spots of rain. Those few spots quickly became a downpour, and he was glad that he reached the entrance before getting soaked.

Inside it was Tardis like, much bigger than it looked from the outside, and to Dave's relief it seemed very clean too. In fact, as he stood at the counter to order his mug of coffee he spotted the 5-star hygiene rating given to the establishment. They were clearly so proud of it that you would have to be blind to miss it. It was stuck on the wall right behind the till.

Despite there being 5 cars in the lay-by there were only two men eating in the café. They either didn't like, or they didn't know, each other. They were at opposite ends of the room.

'Now which one is Sid?' Dave looked at the two men. One was middle aged with a receding hairline and expanding girth. The other was much younger and eating a salad.

Dave picked up his drink and walked to the former. As he did so he could tell that the rain was getting heavier. He knew this because the sound of the rain hitting the metal roof of the portacabin was getting even louder.

'Excuse me, are you Sid?' Dave asked cautiously. He was aware that Sid, when he found him, wouldn't want everyone knowing that he passed on stories to @Talkingmagpies.

'Yes,' said the man looking up from his full English. 'Are you the Hartlepool fan? Alan told me that you might look in on me here.'

'Lovely to meet you,' Dave sat down opposite him, placing his mug on a coaster. 'I'm glad Alan prepared you for my visit.' Dave's face visibly relaxed.

Deadly Circle/DC Poolie

'As you know we are trying to help Troy and we want to find out if anything untoward happened while he was a Newcastle player,' Dave continued. 'For example, I've heard rumours of an incident on the night of the awards.'

Sid, knowing what this was about, had already thought long and hard about his dealings with Troy Harvey.

'Troy wasn't an angel. More the old school type of professional footballer with an eye for the booze and the birds.' In Sid's eyes there was almost a look of longing for the good old days of football when men were men and they both worked and played hard. 'He was a canny lad mind and only that once did I see him really step over the line.'

'Really. Can you tell me about that?' Dave couldn't hold back his enthusiasm.

'Well as you say it was the night of the awards. We were parked in a quiet area to the side of the hotel ready to pick up those who needed lifts home.'

Dave knew better than to interrupt and just leant forward eager to hear more.

'Anyway, I was to be Troy's driver. To clarify, that was for Troy and his, then, girlfriend Polly. Think they'd been an item for a few months. I saw them coming over, slightly the worse for wear, arm in arm. I didn't think anything of it until I saw another person, a man, coming out of the shadows from behind them. It was clear that he was trying to catch them up.'

Dave shifted in his seat desperate to ask questions but remained silent.

'I heard him call out to Troy. I don't think Troy heard him though as they just walked on. He called out again and I'm sure he called out "Roy" and not Troy. He really seemed agitated because they weren't reacting. I think he panicked trying to get their attention and reached out grabbing Polly's arm. Now this is where Troy became aware and went into full psycho mode and gave him a real beating. I dread to think whether he would have stopped or not, despite Polly screaming at him. It took me and 3 other drivers to pull him off the guy who was lying on the floor just taking the kicking. I'm sure he was just repeating "Why Roy?".

Anyway, we got Troy into the car. Polly insisted on being in the front with me and being dropped off at her flat. When she got out, she didn't even say goodbye to Troy who was spark out across the back seats. From what I hear she dumped him and wouldn't see him again.'

'Wow!' said Dave. 'The club did really well to keep that quiet.'

'They sure did,' replied Sid. 'Think it helped that the other guy must never have reported it.'

'Are you sure he said Roy and not Troy?' Dave asked.

'Yeah. One of the other drivers, Ted, said the same thing. Funny, isn't it?' Sid turned his attention back to the Cumberland sausage which he didn't want to go cold.

'Thanks for this,' Dave said appreciatively. 'Did anything else strike you?'

'Now you mention it,' said Sid, 'I couldn't understand how, given they were physically the same size, the other guy didn't fight back. He looked like he could handle himself.'

'Yes, that is strange,' said Dave, getting up and shaking Sid's hand.

....

Deadly Circle/DC Poolie

Later that day at 4pm Cliff and Charlie met up again and started off on the short walk towards the town centre. They were fairly sure the Twisted Bamboo restaurant would not yet be open, and they would be reasonably unlikely to encounter any of the people they had met the night before.

They made their way to the newsagents shop directly across the road from the Chinese Restaurant. This was the real reason for their return because when they left the previous evening, they had noticed a CCTV camera pointing from the newsagents towards the front door of the restaurant. They were keen to see whether there was any footage from the evening Troy had eaten there. They knew the date because it was on the receipt given to them by the very aggressive man the previous evening.

Cliff picked up a morning paper and a packet of mints and made his way over to the counter.

'Hello luv,' Cliff smiled at the girl behind the counter. 'How's business?'

'It's ok, I think. Steady going all day but very long hours though.'

'You may be able to help me if you will.'

'That would depend what kind of help you need.'

Cliff winked and grinned at the pretty shop assistant who smiled suggestively back at him. 'I'm sure you could help me in lots of ways, but all I need at the moment is a copy of your CCTV for a particular day.'

'You would have to see the owner for that. I couldn't let you borrow that without permission.'

Deadly Circle/DC Poolie

'Oh, that's ok I don't need to borrow anything. I have the date and approximate time so if I could just copy that onto my own memory stick it would only take a couple of minutes. I'm sure that won't be too much trouble nor get you into trouble. I won't tell anyone if you don't.' Cliff smiled again and looked straight into the young girl's eyes.

'Well, I suppose if you are quick it should be ok. The machine is just through in the back of the shop.'

After 10-15 mins Cliff emerged from the back shop waving the memory stick in his hand. He leaned across the counter and kissed the young assistant on the cheek making her blush with embarrassment.

'Thank you, my beautiful girl. I'll be back to see you soon and I'm sure we'll find lots of ways to help each other then.'

Charlie grimaced at his friend's spiel.

'What's the problem Charlie mate?' said Cliff, once outside the shop. 'It worked didn't it. And she was pretty you have to admit that.'

Charlie chose to say nothing.

'Good job we had the info from that bill from the Twisted Bamboo. We should really thank those heavies over the road some time. Not!' Cliff grinned.

This room is gloriously perpetually dark thanks to the blackout curtains stopping any light from ruining my gloom. Only the creaking of the old wooden rocking chair, which I picked up at the charity shop, breaks the nothingness that I

139

have created. By choice, I sit here in silence, with anger and hatred burning in my stomach. Why is life so unfair? I constantly think to myself. It can't be right that things just fall into place for some and go so wrong for others. People like you Roy, you bastard, seemingly can't do any wrong. Everything, up until now, seems to work out for you and you take it all for granted. I saw you, little brother, arriving at the football ground, chauffeur driven, in your fancy car. I've seen you going into that expensive Marina penthouse apartment with attractive girls on your arm. What you can do and enjoy with those girls is only because of what I did to Father. You swan around the local bars and restaurants without a care.

Well, your days living the high life will soon be over. Every time I leave this sweet, darkened sanctuary I chip away at your very existence. Soon you will find the foundations of your privileged life subsiding and you won't be able to do anything about it. You will be in free fall. And nobody will want to help.

Deadly Circle/DC Poolie

Chapter 9

Charlie and Barry had decided their next move should be to visit Troy in prison. This would enable them to confirm or deny some of the reports and sightings of him in various places. They had organized a slot to visit at 2pm that afternoon and would be soon on their way. Home House Prison was around a thirty-minute drive from Hartlepool. During the drive Charlie recounted the story of a previous visit he had made to Home House. It was during his time involved with a local Sunday morning team.

Apparently a relative of his worked for the prison service as a P.E instructor and they had arranged for the team to play a preseason game against the prisoners inside the jail. When they got there, they were about the strict rules for entry to the prison, what could be taken in and what was not allowed. As with most football teams at any level there is always one team member, usually nicknamed 'Trigger' or 'Chopper', who is not the sharpest tool in the drawer. This team, most definitely, had such a player.

They were explicitly told not to take in any tools or objects which could be used by prisoners to harm others or to help them escape. The players' bags were all searched thoroughly. All were ok apart from 'Trigger's', which on inspection, contained a screwdriver, some pliers and worst of all a Stanley knife. When challenged his reasoning was that he had no intention of harming anyone with them. They were to be used on his football boot studs. It took some serious negotiations to get him allowed into the prison to play in the game. Charlie even suggested they might want to keep him there for a while.

They parked in the visitor's car park and made their way towards the entrance of the prison. Although a comparatively recently built prison, it still had a bleak, oppressive air about it. After being led into the reception area and thoroughly searched they were led into the visitor's area and told to sit at a table and wait for the prisoner to be brought into the room. It was a totally different looking Troy who appeared handcuffed to a guard and with his head hanging down. The prison guard unlocked the handcuffs and told them that the visitors were permitted to stay for a maximum of thirty minutes, and nothing was allowed to be passed to the prisoner. He added, very clearly, that he would be always watching them.

'Hello Troy,' Charlie started. 'Barry and I are here to help if we can. We just need to check some things with you. Lots of people are with you and believe that you are innocent.'

'Is that right?' a very demoralised Troy replied. 'I've not heard or seen anyone since I was brought in here. It seems like everyone has just written me off and forgotten about me.'

'Only the Gaffer from the club has been to see me. And he just wished me all the best but said in his position, as manager, there was little he could do.'

'Well, that's not us.' Barry spoke up. 'I know I let you down at the hearing, but I am a lot better than I showed there. I believe we will find enough evidence to apply for bail again and ultimately prove your innocence.'

142

Deadly Circle/DC Poolie

Troy looked at the pair. 'Sorry Charlie I appreciate your backing and Barry I'm sure you are sincere in what you say but I saw you taken apart by that prosecution guy and I think this is just a step too far for you at the moment.'

'Troy, no one is queuing up to take your case. I am your best bet, and I can do it. You just need to be truthful with us and trust us to help you,' Barry pleaded.

Charlie told Troy about Cliff, Andy and Dave and what they were doing to help.

Troy thought for a moment and then lifted his head and said to the pair,

'Well, if good people like you and your mates are on my team how can I lose? Right then. What were these questions you wanted to ask?'

Charlie and Barry grinned at each other. Charlie opened his notes and said to Troy. 'Well, I most likely know the answer to this without asking but we have people reporting you coming back to the apartments obviously after a night around the bars and often with a lady on your arm.'

Troy laughed at this 'I would struggle to deny that, but I don't think that's a crime yet.'

'That's true,' Barry interjected, 'but the prosecution would use reports of that kind to build up a profile which is not going to help your case.'

'What about the night in question do you have anything you can tell us about that night?'

Troy's expression changed as he explained he has a recollection of being with a woman that night, and ever since he had been in custody, he had tried to remember the details but had found it impossible.

Deadly Circle/DC Poolie

Charlie took another look at his notebook and asked, 'There was an incident while you were with Newcastle United after the end of season awards ceremony, anything to say about that?'

'I regret that now. I overreacted then. In my defense this guy came charging out of the crowd toward me and my then girlfriend. I thought he was a threat to my girlfriend, and it was her safety foremost on my mind.'

Barry was writing notes as Troy was telling his story, but he stopped to ask, 'People around there said the guy was saying something about someone called Roy.'

I don't recall that at all,' said Troy, 'and I don't know anyone called Roy that's for sure.'

'Wetherspoons? Is that one of your favourite places for a drink? We have reports of you getting into trouble on occasion in there.'

'I have been in Wetherspoons but not for a very long time. It's never been a place I enjoyed visiting at all,' Troy replied. 'Cheap drinks and a rowdy crowd. Not my type of place.'

'The staff in the Twisted Bamboo Chinese restaurant recall you eating in there and leaving without paying the bill, obviously under the influence of alcohol.'

'And behaving badly to the female staff,' he added. Troy again looked baffled.

'Now that one I can completely deny. I have never set foot in there and most likely never will,' Troy responded. 'I never have liked Chinese food and can't see that changing now.'

Deadly Circle/DC Poolie

Charlie looked up from his notebook and commented to Barry, 'Think we have enough to work on there for now. Have you got anything else to ask Troy then Barry?'

'Just about the girl in the brothel on the marina who claims Troy knocked her about,' he said. Troy looked even more surprised at this statement.

'Well, I didn't even know there was a brothel on the marina and anyway I've never had to pay for sex yet and I don't believe I ever will.'

At this Barry and Charlie stood up to leave. Their thirty-minute slot had passed very quickly. They shook Troy's hand, wished him good luck and promised to visit again when they had more news.

Barry told Troy, 'I can't promise anything, but I do believe we have enough for a second bail hearing and then we can get you out of here.'

Troy thanked them both and asked them to pass his thanks to the others. 'I hope I get a chance to thank them in person very soon.

Deadly Circle/DC Poolie

There once was a young lad called Roy
Whose brother looked out for this boy
Instead of being a tiny bit grateful
He beat him in a manner so hateful
Now the world will implode for this Troy

Poetry that most certainly is not
But revenge you see is all that I've got
You've had a life so joyful and free
Would have been so dark if not for me
Even the sweetest will now go to rot

Mr Hedges, the teacher at the YDC, would be so proud.

'Billy Black, you have such potential,' he would always say. Probably because I was the only one who ever tried.

Well Roy/Troy or whatever you call yourself this week. To me you will always be little Roy.

I've had great fun running around in this dump of a town. I bet you think they worship you. Don't you?

The truth is Roy you are superficial in their lives. So superficial that the so-called Hartlepool fan I had a run in with didn't even know that it wasn't you he was scrapping with. You are nothing more than a man in a football kit or tracksuit. Suggestion always causes doubt to the truth. At least I think that is what my psychiatrist used to say to me when they suggested that you weren't in danger from Father.

Deadly Circle/DC Poolie

Well, this is not a suggestion. It is an undeniable truth.

PLAYTIME IS OVER NOW. YOUR DAY OF RECKONING IS COMING AND IT IS COMING VERY SOON.

Chapter 10

As it was another glorious autumn morning, they had decided to do their initial feedback on the Promenade. Charlie, feeling sorry for Barry for having to put his hand in his pocket all the time, had gone down in search of the coffee van having made it very clear, to Andy in particular, that there would only be liquid refreshment this time. Barry, Cliff and Dave had spread themselves out over 2 of the memorial benches facing the sea. Barry was amazed at how many benches there were and that everyone seemed to be commemorating the life of someone from the area.

Each of the benches had a wrought iron holder at one end and those people who tended to the benches either put fresh or artificial flowers in them. Barry wasn't sure what he thought was sadder, those where the fresh flowers had long since wilted and been left to rot or those which had no flowers at all and even the bench looked in disrepair.

'Maybe their relatives and friends have passed since too?' wondered Barry.

The bench he was sitting on was lovingly kept with fresh Calla Lilies and it commemorated the life of Jane Hutchinson who had died in 2020 at the rather young age of 43.

'Probably another sad victim of the pandemic,' Barry mused.

Deadly Circle/DC Poolie

Andy, who now was dressed again in his multi stained Jimmy Saville ensemble, was sitting astride his scooter facing the others but his uncanny sense of smell, or his perpetual search for self-promotion, caused him to turn and face up the promenade in the direction of the Gun Battery.

'Drinks up,' Andy announced, as he caught sight of Charlie returning carrying a tray of drinks. The smile disappeared from Andy's face when Charlie instructed him to return the tray to the van.

When Andy had returned and the drinks had been distributed, they relaxed for a few minutes watching old Henry who, nearby, had just started to serenade the passers-by with his guitar and tender voice. It was fascinating to see how he interacted with the passers-by with either a nod or a greeting, the latter was usually during a guitar solo. People would routinely stop and listen to the end of whatever song he was singing before getting on with their walk. The people of the Headland showed their generosity as well by throwing some coins, and even the odd note, into the bucket in front of Henry. Apparently, he was collecting for the local Hospice.

'Henry regularly helps out down there and puts on a show once a week for the patients and their visitors,' Dave shared proudly.

Charlie and Barry then started the informal meeting by thanking the others for giving up their time and doing such a good job of gathering some really interesting information.

'Having had the informal feedback from you all,' Barry started, 'Charlie and I went to visit Troy in prison to share our initial findings and to seek some clarification on some of the issues you had raised.'

Deadly Circle/DC Poolie

'He really seemed down to tell the truth,' Charlie continued. 'But he was really grateful to you three and said he hoped he would be able to show his appreciation when this dreadful thing is over.'

'I'm sorry Andy,' Barry chimed in. 'Troy, although cheered up by your exploits, doesn't agree with you that you can claim the Frontal Massage, shall we loosely call it, on expenses. Nice try though.'

This was the first that either Cliff or Dave had heard of this, and both turned their gaze, in looks of what can only be described as ones of incredulity but also with a touch of admiration, in the direction of Andy. To their surprise and joy Andy looked, for the first time ever, in their experience, red faced and a little embarrassed shifting slightly uncomfortably on his scooter seat.

Charlie cleared his throat to get things back on track.

'From the things you discovered, Troy, who due to either the drink or the drugs still can't remember everything, admits to picking up a few women and taking the odd one back to his apartment. 'He also,' Charlie was now referring to the notes he had taken when he was in the prison, 'says he was with a girl on the night of the murder but doesn't remember any more than that. This punch up, Dave, you found out about in Newcastle did happen and he regrets his overly violent outburst, even if he was protecting his girlfriend, but he doesn't recall hearing the guy say "Roy". Also, he doesn't know, or has ever known, a Roy.'

Charlie glanced across at Barry who took over. 'Troy does, however, flatly deny ever going to that Chinese restaurant, The Twisted Bamboo, and he didn't even know that

150

there was a brothel in the marina parade yet alone frequent it. In his words "I've never had to pay for it in my life".

He also says he hasn't recently been in the Wetherspoons and, even though his wages at Hartlepool are less than half what he used to get, he would never drink pints of Porcupine at 99p a pint. Now,' Charlie was getting excited now, 'this makes the CCTV evidence that Cliff and I gathered from the Newsagents and the Travelodge really interesting, and we need to study the footage carefully. Something doesn't sit right with me,' Charlie concluded.

'How are we going to do that?' Dave, being ever pragmatic, asked.

'Funny you should ask that,' Charlie smiled. 'I've had a word with my niece, Clare, who teaches Media Studies at the 6th Form College, and she has okayed it with her head teacher, who is a Hartlepool fan too, that we can use her media suite tomorrow after the college finishes as there are no evening classes then. She will even help us get set up. The caretaker will let us out at 10pm.'

Andy, whose face under his Russian hat flaps had returned to its normal pasty colour, suddenly brightened up. 'If we are going to work through the evening then we will need to be fed.'

'As long as it's not Chinese,' said Cliff, remembering the machete with its very sharp blade.

'There is a pizza place down the road,' Charlie laughed, also not wanting to risk another encounter with those 3 huge and intimidating gentlemen.

'It's settled then. We'll meet there tomorrow at 4pm outside the gates. We will need to get signed in.' Barry looked happy with the way things were going.

Dave spoke up again. 'I will have to give that a miss. I'm going to Birmingham tomorrow. Troy played for Villa before being transferred to Newcastle and I think it makes sense to investigate a little there too.'

The others nodded in agreement.

'Andy,' Dave turned to his long-time trusted friend, 'could you interview the other residents of the apartment block? There is something about that janitor I just don't trust, and he has been more than happy to paint Troy in a very poor light. I have a feeling he has influenced the police in a very negative way.'

'Bien sûr, mon ami,' Andy replied affecting quite a good French accent. 'That will merit some garlic bread to go with the pizza, je pense.'

As they all went their separate ways, they heard Henry finish off a unique version of "House of the Rising Sun" which received rapturous applause from a group of about 20 people which had gathered while the meeting had been taking place.

'Only on the Headland,' Charlie smiled, and headed in the direction of his car.

At 4.15pm Charlie, Barry, Cliff and Clare were still standing outside the entrance gates of the 6th Form College. Charlie was just about to apologise to his niece for the 3rd time when a symphony of car horns made them all turn and look down the road. Sure enough, the reason for their impatience was demonstrating his ability to annoy and frustrate the drivers of West Hartlepool's pre rush hour traffic as well. Had it been a dual carriageway the anger might have been tempered, but on this fairly narrow road Andy, and his scooter, were being followed by what looked like a never-ending traffic jam. The cars and vans just behind Andy were flashing their lights and tooting their horns and those further down the queue were just making as much noise as possible. Andy seemed oblivious to all that was going on behind him with his new hoodie over his Russian hat, both sound insulators. Andy had clearly decided that he could pretend to be unable to hear the complaints from behind. At least that is what he would say to any driver who confronted him by getting out of his or her car if Andy himself were to get held up. That was, without doubt, a whopper of a lie as the noise created was bringing people out of their houses and shops up to 50 yards ahead of him.

'Even a deaf person would surely feel some sort of vibration from that,' Cliff thought to himself.

As Andy drew level with them, he made an abrupt left turn without signalling, suddenly veering off in their direction. But instead of stopping he went past them through the gates and in through the door which led to the reception area. The white van, which had been tailgating him, screeched to a halt, having to skew slightly to the right as the driver, even at a mere 15 mph, slammed on his brakes. Fortunately, the cars immediately behind the van, although very frustrated by Andy's antics, had kept enough distance to brake safely.

Charlie grabbed Clare's arm and called to the others, 'Come on let's get inside before something ugly happens.'

By the time they were all standing in reception Andy had already put his scooter in a cleaner's cupboard and deigned to pull his hoodie down.

Deadly Circle/DC Poolie

'Some people have no concept of patience,' he smiled.

Clare sorted them all out some visitor lanyards and introduced them to Ken, the caretaker, who would see them out at 10pm.

'Drop by for some pizza later, Ken,' Barry called out, as they started to follow Clare through the maze of corridors.

'Maybe we should leave a trail of breadcrumbs so that we can find our way back?' Cliff suggested.

'Please don't,' Clare laughed. 'We haven't got enough cleaners to work these corridors as it is and there have been rumours of mice.'

As they entered the media suite there was a sharp intake of breath from Charlie.

'Bloody hell! Things have changed since my day when the highest tech the teachers had was a Banda machine.' The others nodded in agreement. Save Barry who, being so much younger, wanted to know what a Banda machine was.

Clare said, 'Uncle Charlie, I'm leaving you my laptop to use. Here are my login details. Please don't abuse this trust.' At this point she looked directly at Andy. 'There are strict parental controls, so any unsavoury sites are not accessible. It is hooked up to the projector so Cliff all you need to do to watch your CCTV footage is to put your flash drive in the USB slot there. I'm sure you can work it from there.'

Cliff who last year had taken a U3A computer skills course, ostensibly "to bring myself up to date with modern technology", but in reality, so that he could see how easy it was to meet women there, smiled confidently. 'No problem at all.'

Clare opened her desk drawer and took out a remote control. She pointed it at the projector and pressed the on/off button. All of a sudden, the screen on the wall that the projector was aiming at was filled with, at first, light, and then her laptop's wallpaper.

'Right, the screensaver will kick in if not used for 10 minutes. Now I must go. My child minder is only booked until 5pm.' Her uncle, who was standing by her, kissed her on the cheek and everyone else expressed their thanks.

Charlie, ever the organiser, pointed at some tables nested together and gestured for them all to sit there. 'Now we don't want to miss a thing and I think that we all should work together. I will order the pizza for our midway point, 7pm, and Andy you will have your extra garlic bread after you've given us a satisfactory report from your interviews at the apartment block today.'

Andy, to everybody's surprise, brought out his notebook and flicked back a few pages.

Clearing his throat first he began to read from his notes. 'Firstly, I focussed on those nearest to Troy's flats and those by the entrance and the lifts.'

'Flipping heck Andy! Sounds like all the repeats of Midsomer Murders you watch in the afternoon after our walks really has paid off,' joked Cliff, who was sitting next to his friend.

Andy looked like he ignored Cliff and kept going but Cliff was more than aware of a Dunlop Green Flash stamping on his foot.

'All in all, I interviewed the people in eight apartments. On Dave's suggestion I didn't revisit the couple he had already interviewed.'

'And?' Barry was starting to get impatient.

'Well, nobody had a bad word to say about Troy. Yes, some were aware he kept late hours and might bring home a guest now and then. As for him being noisy like the janitor says. Well, that is a downright lie. They, and that includes his neighbours, never heard him being louder than they would expect. What some did comment on was an altercation he had with the janitor very early on in his time there. Apparently, the janitor is a nosey so and so and is always interfering. Anyway, Troy took exception to this and told him to focus on doing his job. Others then commented how the janitor seemed to want to stir things up by asking them if they had had any run-ins or issues with Troy.'

Charlie grabbed hold of a marker pen and went to the flip board next to the desks. On it he wrote:

"Janitor has it in for Troy. His evidence has to be biased at best and could be fabricated."

'Is he married?' Cliff asked.

'According to Dave he isn't married and from my questions nobody has ever seen him with a woman,' Andy answered. 'Not surprising when you look at him. Right mess he is. I would never go out looking like that.'

The others stared at Andy wondering if he saw the irony in what he had just said but, to a man, none of them made a comment.

Charlie took the lid off the pen and wrote:

"Could he be the killer? He has keys, is a loner/sociopath. He hates Troy."

'Now that is an interesting start to the evening,' Barry chimed in. 'Andy, you have earned your garlic bread and you can have cheese on top if you like.'

Deadly Circle/DC Poolie

Andy sat there beaming accepting the approbation of the others.

Cliff wandered over to the laptop, key ring in hand.

'You don't need a key for it Cliff,' Andy called out. 'Clare gave us her password and stuff.'

Cliff turned around and, to Andy from the angle he was at, it looked like he was giving him the finger.

'This,' Cliff smiled pointing to what he, in fact, was holding between his thumb and forefinger, 'is a USB drive you old dinosaur. While your low brow form of detecting seems to involve you either getting your kit off or stuffing your face I prefer to live in the modern world of technology.'

Andy, instead of being offended, nodded his head in agreement as a smirk crossed his face. He was remembering both his experience with Sandra and the breakfast upgrade.

'Each to his own.' Andy replied enjoying his memories while waiting for Cliff to get on with it. They were soon all amazed with the confidence, competence and dexterity Cliff displayed and in no time at all a series of named files appeared on the screen.

'No offence Cliff but I'm surprised any of you would know their way around a computer,' Barry called out.

'Well, it helped sitting next to the ravishing Gloria in the U3A Computing class. She was the class swat and took a shine to me.'

'Give you a hand, did she?' Andy shifted in his chair, interested for the first time.

'Now that's for me to know and you to wonder,' Cliff replied. 'All I will say it that things did look bigger in her small hands.'

157

Deadly Circle/DC Poolie

'Enough of this side tracking. Let's start with the CCTV footage from the Newsagent's.' Charlie said, who had been with Cliff when they had retrieved it.

'Nice girl in the shop, wasn't she?' Cliff responded, as he clicked on one of the files near the bottom of the list. Almost immediately they all were watching surveillance video from the Newsagent's and there was, even more surprisingly, simultaneous dual footage from cameras facing away from, and in the direction of, the Twisted Bamboo.

'Charlie, do you have the receipt from the restaurant?' Cliff asked. 'It will have the time they printed out his bill and will give us a rough idea of when he was there.'

Charlie rummaged around in his pockets and brought out his wallet. From one of the compartments, he brought out a piece of paper which was folded in two. As he unfolded it he put on his reading glasses and said, 'This has a time date stamp of 8.49pm.'

Cliff dragged the cursor to the bottom of the screen and pressed play.

'I've estimated his time of arrival. Might as well see if we can see him arrive. We will have to watch carefully. Although the technology they use at the Newsagent's is good the resolution isn't great due to it being quite dark already.'

As they watched Andy, clearly now losing his concentration already, commented, 'This would be easier with a slice of pizza.' When the others said nothing, he added, 'Just saying.' Realising he wasn't winning Andy's focus went back to the screen.

'That might be him,' Barry called out. 'There. Coming in from the left wearing a hoodie.'

Deadly Circle/DC Poolie

'That person is certainly male and matches Troy's physique, but you can't really see his face.' Charlie said sounding rather disappointed.

As the figure entered the Twisted Bamboo Cliff spoke up again, 'Ok, let's fast forward to around the time he would have left.'

Ten minutes after they started watching the footage from later on a bowed figure, this time with the hood down, came running out the restaurant's front door. He stopped for an instant and turned around to throw something at a young Chinese girl who had obviously followed him out and, seemingly, had called out to him.

Annoyingly for those intently watching this scene play out on the left-hand screen he was facing away slightly from the camera so that, even with the hood down, they couldn't definitively identify the person as Troy. He turned to run and this time he was now suddenly in the footage from the other camera.

Obviously feeling confident that he wouldn't be caught, he stopped a second time to throw a second thing at the girl who was now, according to the left-hand screen, cowering in the doorway.

'I'm not sure what we hoped to discover but that really hasn't moved us on,' Charlie summed up the general feeling of disappointment that they were all feeling.

'Right,' said Barry trying to sound more positive than he really felt. 'Let's get that pizza ordered and we can talk things through whilst we are waiting.'

'Good idea,' said Andy. 'Don't forget the garlic bread. No cheese though. Can't stand the stuff'.

Deadly Circle/DC Poolie

While they were waiting for the food. Charlie once again took the lead and wrote this on the flip chart:

Nobody can definitely say that the person involved is Troy. Only that it looks like him. Discuss.

'It's certainly true in lots of these incidents,' Cliff chimed in. 'In those clips we couldn't say for sure it was him and people in the pub seemed to assume it was him because of what he was wearing and that he certainly had a resemblance.'

'I think that point counts against us in the end. I'm sure if enough people think that it is him that they saw doing these things then that would be good enough for a jury to believe. Sorry to bring a negative perspective but I'm thinking as a solicitor for the prosecution here.' Barry sounded so apologetic that the others couldn't argue with him.

Andy looking longingly at the door wishing that he could hear the delivery driver's knock spoke up, 'In the brothel the light is really rather dim, and they weren't sure either. Maybe I should have shown the picture to the bouncer, but I was too fearful for my health when I heard he was the boyfriend of the beaten-up girl. Bouncers are paid to pay attention and it was the girl I was with, and not the poor girl in question, who thought the punter was Troy.'

'We still need firmer evidence to back up these doubts if we want to get Troy out on bail,' Barry insisted.

'Cliff while we are waiting can we watch him leaving the restaurant again? There was something about the way he threw that looked funny.' Charlie asked.

Cliff replayed the clip.

'Stop!' Charlie cried. 'There look. He is throwing left-handed and the Troy I know is singularly right-handed. I often

160

comment on it to him because he can kick with both feet. Let's see the rest of the clip. I think in it he is throwing coins as well.'

'I think you are right,' Barry said, leaning forward.

'Bugger!' said Andy 'That second throw is right-handed.'

'No, it's not,' Cliff responded clearly excited, 'Look he is facing the same way but look at the wrist of the throwing hand. I noticed that in the first bit his sleeve rode up a bit revealing something shiny, a watch or bracelet, on his left arm. Now that shiny thing is still on his throwing arm but that looks like it's now his right arm. I think we are seeing his reflection, and not him, in the shop window opposite in this clip. Because of the angle he is just out of shot so we only see one image of him, the reflection.'

'Yes!' shouted Barry as Cliff played the clip of the first throw again. 'Look Cliff is right. I thought he might have a similar bracelet on each wrist but in each clip only one sleeve has ridden up the arm. That makes both throws left-handed.'

Everyone was now so excited that it was only Andy who heard the knock on the door.

The silence in the media suite would have been deafening had Andy not sounded like a masticating cow when eating his pepperoni pizza. With extra cheese and pepperoni of course.

Charlie had already written his next piece on the flip chart:

Is someone pretending to be Troy, if so why? (Left-handed)

Deadly Circle/DC Poolie

Cliff had, in between slices of pizza, found and started the CCTV clip from the Travelodge. It was running at 10x speed. All they were doing was stopping it every time somebody walked by on the path below to check whether it could be Troy going back to the apartment after the fracas in the Ward Jackson pub. They took it in turns to watch and had Cliff hit the pause button, rewinding if necessary, when they saw someone.

When Andy was doing that task Barry, who was still trying to absorb what they had found out so far, saw Charlie suddenly pick up the bill from the restaurant and bring it right up close to his spectacles.

'Bloody hell!' he exclaimed so loudly that Cliff instinctively paused the video and turned to look at him. 'How did I not see this before?'

'What is it?' asked Barry who had seen this whole scene unfold and was a step ahead of the others.

'Prawn curry,' said Charlie, as if he had found the answer to the question in the Hitchhiker's Guide to the Galaxy.

'Sorry mate we are going to need a bit more than that,' said Cliff smiling.

'Prawn curry.' Charlie repeated. 'Troy is allergic to shellfish. He was there on his own and would never order it. He would go into anaphylactic shock. He told me once that being in one was the worst experience of his life and he never wanted to experience it again.'

'Bloody hell! So, someone out there has been impersonating Troy.' Andy was gobsmacked.

Charlie went once again to the flip chart and wrote:

<u>Someone has been impersonating Troy, prawns, but WHO? And WHY?</u>

Buoyed by what was becoming a very successful evening they were all now back watching the Travelodge footage again when Barry heard the text message alert on his phone.

'It's from Dave,' he announced. 'He is staying in a Premier Inn in Birmingham tonight. He may have a lead but needs a picture of the victim to be sure.'

'Good man, Dave,' said Charlie. 'Barry, as Troy's solicitor, can you try to get one tomorrow morning?'

'Will do my best,' smiled Barry.

On the CCTV footage the dawn light of the following morning was now appearing.

'Well, we still haven't seen Troy go by. Could he have stayed out all night?' Cliff asked the others.

'Maybe, in the light of things that we just discovered, maybe that was the imposter in the pub as well,' suggested Barry. 'Anyway, let's keep going. Hold on who's that?'

There was a figure appearing but from the other direction.

'I'm certain that's Troy,' said Charlie. 'And unless he has magic powers he really wasn't in the pub.' Charlie walked one final time to the clipboard.

Since they had explored all the evidence, eaten all the food and were tired they decided to call it a night. Once they had tidied up and switched off Clare's lap top they went off in the search of Ken, the caretaker, shutting the door behind them.

In his hands Charlie had the folded A1 sheet from the flip chart. On it was the summary of that night's efforts.

Deadly Circle/DC Poolie

Deadly Circle/DC Poolie

Janitor has it in for Troy. His evidence has to be biased at best and could be fabricated.
Could he be the killer? He has keys, is a loner/sociopath. He hates Troy."
Nobody can definitely say that the person involved is Troy. Only that it looks like him, discuss.
Is someone pretending to be Troy, if so, why? (Left-handed)
Someone has been impersonating Troy at restaurant, prawns, but WHO? And WHY?
Someone also impersonated Troy in pub, CCTV evidence going in the other way.

Barry and Charlie now had enough evidence, maybe, for another bail hearing. They would decide that tomorrow, but Barry's first task was to get a picture of the victim for Dave. Andy could also go back to the marina area armed with that picture. Did anybody remember Troy with the woman in the picture? They all left with a spring in their step.

'Andy,' Cliff called out to him as Andy disappeared into to cleaner's cupboard, 'use the footpath. We want you alive tomorrow.'

165

Chapter 11

When Charlie, with Barry, last visited Home House Prison it was more out of hope and duty than optimism. The evidence the team had gathered by then was vague and tenuous, at the very best, and they had hoped that Troy's answers to their questions would give them some more leads to explore.

Unfortunately, due to Troy's still fuzzy memory, he hadn't really given them any positives just a few confirmed negatives: 'I didn't do that' or 'I never went there'.

This time Charlie, who was on his own as Barry had his own mission at the police station, went through the gates with optimism and enthusiasm. He was confident that after the previous night's work at the 6th form college that they would very soon get Troy out on bail.

Troy, who had looked so downcast during their previous visit, deserved to be kept in the loop and receive some good news.

As he sat at the table in the visiting room Charlie found himself glancing out of its one very small window and thinking how hard it must be to remain shut up inside with freedom being so tantalisingly close yet in reality so unattainable. This made Charlie even more determined to not only put on the most uplifting of fronts for Troy today, but to ensure that Troy need not spend a minute longer than necessary in this soul-destroying institution.

Charlie turned as he heard the door from the prison block open. He didn't know what he had expected to see but it certainly wasn't this. His jaw literally dropped, and he found himself rendered speechless. In front of him he saw not the mentally broken man from before, although that was still probably true on the inside, but a very obviously physically broken one. Troy had a black eye which looked even worse as the swelling made the eye look twice as big as its counterpart which was also red. Charlie had seen eyes like that in the past where the second eye wasn't injured. Its redness was due to crying because of unrelenting pain. There were also some other cuts and contusions on Troy's face. He now focussed on the sling Troy was wearing to support some issue with his right arm. Finally, if it wasn't enough already, there was the walking stick in his left hand.

'Left hand walking stick, right leg problem,' Charlie remembered this mantra a physio told him when he was recovering from a ligament injury during his playing days. Sure enough, Troy's ankle looked both swollen and slightly crook.

'What the fuck has happened to him?' Charlie started to rise from his chair. 'You have a duty of care to the people here. How did you let this happen?'

Charlie, despite being incandescent with rage, started to sit down again as the two accompanying prison guards gestured for him to maintain his distance.

Deadly Circle/DC Poolie

'It was an accident in the shower block. You can ask him yourself,' replied one of the guards. 'It looks a lot worse than it really is.'

'Yes,' continued the other guard, 'the doc has checked him over and isn't worried at all. The ankle is crook because he slipped where some other prisoner hadn't wiped the floor after showering. He fell into the mirror above the basin, smashing them both and as he fell one eye caught the sink full on. As he hit the ground he landed heavily on his shoulder.'

'Which fortunately isn't dislocated,' chimed in the first guard again. By now they had sat Troy in the chair opposite Charlie. Charlie, who knew that this was a total lie, decided to say nothing until he had spoken to Troy.

One of the guards left and the second one stood to the side clearly trying to remain in earshot.

'Tell me the truth,' Charlie said in a harsh whisper hoping to have the conversation without the guard hearing it, 'What happened? You didn't fall.'

Troy, refusing to look in Charlie's direction mumbled, 'It's like they said. I slipped and fell. Always have been clumsy.'

'That is rot Troy,' Charlie was now turning some of his anger towards Troy. 'Tell me what really happened.'

'I just have,' Troy said now looking at Charlie. 'Now leave it alone Charlie. I've got to live here.'

Well, that statement confirmed two things to Charlie. Firstly, that he hadn't fallen and secondly, he wouldn't get the truth from Troy by badgering him. So, he tried another tack and told Troy about their work and discoveries in the media suite. At first, he got no change out of Troy but as he told him

168

of the possibility that somebody had been impersonating him, he started to get a response. It was the 'prawn' evidence that finally elicited a comment.

'Wow!', he said. 'You guys really have gone that extra mile for me. It sounds like you all missed your true vocation and should have been Private Investigators.'

'Well to be truthful,' Charlie smiled, 'Andy already is a Private Dick. No scrap that. He already is a public dick. A complete public dick.'

Charlie was pleased that he had finally broken through with Troy.

'What's more,' he continued, 'Barry, after trying to get the picture of the poor victim, is going to the Prosecution Service to try to get another bail hearing. Barry thinks, although we have some evidence to show you are not a confirmed menace to society that we also need a change in circumstances to guarantee a second hearing.'

He looked Troy up and down. 'This, if you didn't really slip, could be your ticket to being let out on bail. Now what did really happen?'

'Do you think I'd get bail now?'

'I'm sure of it. And I will make certain that you are protected until you get out.' Charlie hoped that this would be true but, whether it was or wasn't, he had to keep Troy talking.

'Well, it did happen in the shower block but that is the only bit of the story that is true.' Charlie gestured for Troy to continue and sat back in his chair showing that he wouldn't interrupt.

'On the block there is this giant called Ossie Symonds, shaved head, tattoos and his biceps would make Arnold

Schwarzenegger look puny in comparison. Anyway, he is a massive Manchester United fan.' Charlie who was determined to just sit and listen had to stop himself from spitting on the ground. If there were one thing Charlie and the fellow Headlanders hated more than West Hartlepool it was Manchester United. 'Well do you remember the FA Cup final when I was playing for Villa against United?'

Charlie nodded not wanting to stop Troy's flow.

'Well apparently Ossie had put a big bet on United to win. A bet with some real heavyweight gangsters.' Troy paused long enough for it to sink in. 'And what did muggins here do? I scored twice in the last 5 minutes to win the match. To make it worse because United were winning with 15 minutes to go he doubled his stake.'

'I can see he might be a bit miffed with you.' Charlie was so surprised by the story that he had to say something.

'Anyway, he didn't have the money for the second bet. You see he thought he wouldn't need it. We are talking thousands of pounds here.' Charlie whistled. For him a £5 each way on the Grand National was his idea of being a high roller.

'They gave him a week to pay up or else. So, he tried to rob a Post Office and his robbing skills are clearly as poor as his gambling ones. He got caught trying to flee the scene and ended up in here doing 15 years minimum for armed robbery. The way he sees it is that he is in here because of me.'

'Bloody Hell! I'm not sure I agree with Ossie's logic. But what a story and what a coincidence. How do you know all this?' Charlie asked.

'Well, when I came in, he was on another wing and while he was trying to get transferred over he leaked the story bit by bit through some trustees who are in his wing but work over here too.'

'So, what did happen?'

'He came at me from behind, jumped on my ankle, shoved my head and shoulder into the basin and mirror so hard that they both smashed. Then he punched and kicked me for a while until he got bored. He said he could kill me anytime he feels like it, but he wants his money back first. He reckons that there are lots of 'faggots' in here who would 'pay plenty for a go at my arse'. I've asked him for some time to pay him back but judging by the look he gave I think he just really wants me to suffer.' Troy was shaking as he finished the story.

The guard in the room started to walk over.

'Right, you've had your thirty minutes,' he said.

'I ain't going nowhere and neither is Troy,' Charlie stood up to face the guard. 'He has just told what really happened. Now I want the warden to come here. If I don't get my way, I will go the newspapers and then to the police. I know that Troy, here, is at risk if he goes back to the cells. He is a celebrity in this small town and, believe me, you don't want all the negative reaction and attention you would get if the press were to find out.'

The guard turned away and spoke quietly into his walkie-talkie.

'We are to wait here,' he finally said.

'Well, we weren't planning on going anywhere,' Charlie replied. Troy had never seen him look so determined.

Ten minutes later a rather harassed and overweight man, clearly the warden, dressed in a slightly ill-fitting dark grey suit walked in accompanied by yet another guard. Charlie gave him the once over and quickly decided this guy, who was probably in his early forties, looked out of his depth in his current role.

Charlie wasted no time in taking the lead in the discussion that followed. He was right about the warden as he allowed this to happen without so much as a peep. Firstly, he explained what had actually taken place in the shower block, and then how Troy, who now was very likely to be out on bail in the near future, was still at risk if things didn't change. He didn't say it in so many words, but Charlie implied a cover up, stating how surprised everyone would be to hear all this happening without the warden, nor seemingly the prison's medical team, knowing what had really occurred.

'People are here to receive their punishment and I think that people on the outside would expect there to be a similar discipline system for any criminal acts which take place within the prison too.'

Charlie left the prison shortly after with a guarantee in writing, and signed by the warden, that Troy was to be assigned a 24-hour guard in the hospital wing of the prison.

'Now we need that bail hearing,' thought Charlie. He took out his phone and dialled Barry's mobile number.

. . . .

Junior Solicitor Barry Barnes was awake early and well prepared for what he knew would be an important day in Troy's case. Also, it was going to play a big part in convincing his new friends that he was the man to help them through the minefield that is the British legal system. Without doubt he knew, also, that he had to convince himself after his weak performance at the original hearing. He was sitting at his kitchen table having a last look through his notes when his mobile phone rang.

'Hello Barry, it's Cliff. I'm at a bit of a loose end here and wondered if I could tag along with you to the police station?'

Barry paused for a moment before answering.

'Of course, I'll be glad of the company I'll pick you up on the way. I'll be about thirty minutes. Will you be ready?'

'I'll be ready and waiting. Thanks Barry.'

. . . .

Mark Cross was sat in his car drumming his fingers on the steering wheel impatiently. He was outside DC Angela Hart's flat waiting for her to appear.

'Typical woman,' he thought to himself, 'Can never be on time for anything.' The fact that he was parked there five minutes before the arranged time would not have occurred to him. He was completely self-centred and motivated towards his career in the police.

Climbing the career ladder was really the most important factor for him. This attitude had cost him his marriage and his relationship with his kids. Everything had been pushed aside in his drive to be successful in his police career. It had also given him a reputation, amongst his work colleagues, of being surly and unfriendly.

Angela Hart was maybe the only person who saw him in a different light. She had always found him attractive and was delighted when given the chance to be working alongside him in the serious crimes section of the Hartlepool police force. He, on the other hand, was always of the opinion that he did not need people from his squad interfering with his superior detective processes. If anything needed doing, that involved mere leg work or research, then that was the job for those under him.

He tolerated the fact that he had to work closely with DC Hart, mainly because it would please his superiors, and rather than actively including her in the investigations he chose to carefully manage and monitor the task delegation. Angela Hart realised this very early in their time working together and was happy to go along with it in the hope that eventually things would improve and maybe a genuine relationship would be formed. She had hoped that the way she took an active role in the questioning of Troy Harvey would have made him change his mind, but she hadn't seen any perceivable change.

She emerged from the flats and made her way to the waiting car still one minute early.

'Good morning boss how are you this morning?' she asked.

'I'm fine, been here a while waiting for you,' he grumped.

DC Hart ignored the attitude. She was well used to it now and didn't let it bother her at all.

'We have a meeting first thing with that young solicitor representing Troy Harvey, wonder what he could want?' said DS Cross.

'He thinks they have some new evidence which casts doubt on Harvey's involvement in the murder, and maybe

174

enough to at least allow him to appeal against his remand verdict.'

'Very much doubt that. He did it I'm sure,' Cross snapped back. 'And the chances of that stuttering fool of a solicitor getting him off are nonexistent.'

DC Hart said nothing but had always been less than sure of Troy Harvey's guilt. Something had nagged away at her since they first turned up at the crime scene. They drove the ten-minute drive into the town centre where the police HQ was situated and made their way upstairs to DC Cross's office.

'Can I get you a coffee sir while we wait for our visitors?' DC Hart asked.

'Can if you like, but we won't be waiting long for them. It's just a waste of time if you want my opinion,' Cross replied.

'Maybe sir, but they sounded convinced on the phone, so worth hearing what they have to say don't you think boss?'

Cross didn't reply, just grunted and sat down in his chair behind his desk. She made her way back from the coffee machine with a white coffee with three sugars for the DS and a Latte, no sugar, for herself.

Cliff and Barry arrived shortly after, and both politely accepted the DC's offer of a coffee. Cliff was surprised when the newly confident and forceful Barry spoke first.

'You are aware that after our investigations and interviews with various members of the public we are confident that we now have enough information to cast doubts on Troy Harvey's involvement in this incident. Most certainly enough to allow a second hearing and hopefully we will get our client out on bail.'

175

Deadly Circle/DC Poolie

At this Barry produced a couple of A4 sheets outlining their findings:

1 Troy has never denied he enjoyed a drink and that he had often invited women back to his apartment. He has a vague recollection of being with a woman on the night of the murder but can't recall taking her back to his apartment.

He even admits to a fight outside of the Newcastle United awards night and regrets his overreaction, but in his defence he did think the man was attacking his then girlfriend.

2 Apart from these relatively minor incidents involving a relatively young man we can't find anyone who has a bad word to say about him and we have spoken to many people in the Marina Apartments where Troy lives. Apart from the janitor, no one has a bad word to say about him. The janitors report of noise and drunken behaviour was not confirmed by any of the other residents and many of the residents feel that the janitor has been trying to put words in their mouths about Troy's behavior. This attempt at character assassination has, however, fallen on deaf ears.

3 We have clear irrefutable evidence that somebody has been impersonating Troy probably in the hope of blackening his name. This has happened for example in a Chinese restaurant. He absolutely denies ever having been to the Twisted Bamboo and our evidence, including video footage, shows the person that they thought was Troy was left-handed, which he is not, and unlike Troy not allergic to shellfish. There are

claims he beat up a prostitute which Troy flatly denies. He was not aware that there is a brothel on the marina, and, he says that he has never paid for sex in his life. Looking at him I tend to believe that, especially given his apparent success with ladies in the bars. Then there was a fight in Wetherspoons. He does not deny being in Wetherspoons in the past but that was a long time ago long before the night of the fight. He, also, is not the sort of person to drink Porcupine beer at 99p a pint. Our CCTV footage, obtained from the Travelodge, shows that the figure fleeing the pub did not go in the direction of the Marina Apartments but in the morning, we do see him walking in the other direction.

'My officers will obviously check out the reports you have here, and indeed they may already have done so. Should we find anything useful in all this then we will consider it fully,' was DS Cross's abrupt reply.

'One thing which would really help us would be a photograph of the victim. Would it be possible to obtain one from here by any chance?' Barry spoke up again.

'No certainly not,' was DS Cross's sharp reply. 'This is an ongoing investigation, and the victim has not yet been identified.'

'If or, should I say, when we finally identify this unfortunate young lady it is for the police to inform her relatives.'

Barry noticed the DC's change of expression at this retort and wondered to himself what was behind that. They decided they had covered all that they had come here to do and left slightly crestfallen after the rebuff over the photograph.

Deadly Circle/DC Poolie

The pair left DS Cross's office and made their way out of the building.

'Well, that didn't seem to get us very far,' Cliff commented, 'and we certainly could have done with that photograph.'

'That's true enough,' Barry replied. 'He certainly has an attitude about him that DS Cross.'

'I've got something which may help you,' Barry and Cliff turned as they heard DC Hart's voice. 'It's a number for a guy called Quentin Booth. He works in the Crown Prosecution Service, and he may be able to give you some advice. Also, I have something else, but you must promise to keep any info gained from this confidential, as the girl has not yet been identified.'

Saying this she handed a copy of the victim's photograph to Barry.

Barry thought he should go to the CPS building alone, so he thanked Cliff who went off to catch a bus back to the Headland. He was going to seek out Andy who, at this time of the day, would be riding along the promenade chatting to everybody he knew and some he didn't. As he was about to leave the police station, he felt his mobile vibrating in his jacket pocket. Five minutes later Barry hung up from talking with Charlie. Things were really moving at pace now. Barry's first action was to use his mobile to take a picture of the victim's photo which he been given by Angela Hart. He forwarded it straight away to Charlie and Dave. He then phoned Dave explaining the conditions he had agreed with regards to the photo. Dave understood the sensitivity of the situation and said he would not mention why he was looking for this person and that he would assess the situation first before even showing somebody the picture. Charlie was going to forward the picture to the rest of the team, Cliff and Andy, but before he did, he was going to phone the two of them and pass on the same message that Barry was to give to Dave. He trusted both of them but, particularly in Andy's case, sensitivity wasn't always their strong suit.

With all that in hand Barry crossed the busy road, which separated the police station and the modern building which houses the Crown Prosecution Service and strode up to the reception where a rather smartly dressed young woman was on the phone. He waited patiently until the call was finished and, when she turned in his direction, he asked where he could find the office of Quentin Booth. Clearly doing what she always did with walk-ins, the receptionist asked him what it was concerning. Barry replied saying that he was hoping to expedite a bail hearing. When she started to dial Quentin's extension Barry added that Angela Hart had suggested he talk to Mr Booth on this issue.

'You are in luck,' she said. 'Apparently, he has 45 minutes free before he must go to court. His office is on the 3rd floor, room 321, and the lifts are over there.' She pointed to the corner of the foyer where two sets of lift doors stood next to one another.

Barry could have opted for the neighbouring stairs, had it been on the first floor, but feeling a bit tired after working so late the previous night chose to use the lift as advised.

A tall, handsome dark-haired man vaguely reminiscent of Colin Firth, but at least 15 years younger, was waiting to greet him.

179

'You know this seems slightly irregular but as soon as I heard Angela's name, I couldn't resist seeing what you have to say. How is she by the way?'

Barry noted that his whole face looked different, like there was a sadness or melancholy, when he spoke about DC Hart.

'She seems fine. I really warmed to her which is more than I can say about her DS. She is obviously a perceptive and focussed police officer, but she exudes a certain humanity too.' Barry surprised himself with the glowing recommendation he found himself giving her. As glowing as it was, she really had struck a chord with him and he meant every word of it.

'Yes, she is something special,' Barry could now see Quentin switch back to CPS mode as he changed topic. 'Now what is this all about?'

'I represent Troy Harvey.' Barry was about to reel off his pre-prepared argument but got stopped before he could get going.

'Sorry Barry, may I call you Barry?' Barry nodded. 'This isn't my case. It's my boss''.

'I know that, but I wanted your advice as he ran rings around me in court at the last bail hearing. I'm not asking you to be disloyal, but I don't want to go in ill prepared again.'

'I see,' replied Quentin. 'I will help you as long as, in my opinion, it doesn't undermine the case of the CPS.'

Barry thanked Quentin profusely and then went on to tell him about their detective activities which had made them confident, beyond any shadow of a doubt, that somebody had been impersonating Troy and that this person was trying to bring his name into disrepute.

180

Deadly Circle/DC Poolie

'I totally sympathise. In fact, even with the poor character evidence, which was presented in court, I felt it harsh that Troy, I mean Mr Harvey, be denied bail, but my boss has this thing about "entitled celebrities and their fancy Dan lawyers always finding loopholes for them that the poorer citizen doesn't have access to".' He stopped and smiled. 'He was ecstatic when he came back having got a remand judgement, although that euphoria was tempered by having "an open goal to shoot at". How did that bumbling schoolboy ever pass his exams? His words not mine.' Quentin made a gesture of sympathy towards Barry.

'No, don't apologise. I was less than useless.'

'Anyway, my point being,' Quentin was now back on point, 'that sort of evidence may help in a trial but I'm not sure it will overturn a remand judgement.'

Barry took out his phone and showed Quentin the 5 pictures Charlie had sent him which clearly documented Troy's injuries.

'These happened yesterday. He is not safe in prison, nor has he been convicted of anything. Even the police's first hypothesis was that he was a victim. All this, added to the evidence we have gathered, shows there has been a clear change in circumstances. This is what we need for bail to be given at a second hearing.'

Quentin, who had listened closely to all this, looked again at the pictures.

'I think even my boss would have to rethink his take on this. I mean it's not like, with those injuries, he is a menace to those around him. I doubt he will be able to do much more than hobble for a good few weeks. I'm certain we can find a

Deadly Circle/DC Poolie

BAIL401 form online. I will print it out and even help you fill it in. I certainly think my boss didn't see the true Barry in court.' Quentin slapped Barry on the shoulder. 'Do you think Angela might fancy a drink later?'

Chapter 12

Dave woke up and instinctively reached out behind him expecting to find the reassuring warmth of his wife, Kath. He was momentarily confused as his outstretched arm found nothing but duvet. He raised himself up onto his other elbow looking for his alarm clock, which had been the bane of his life when he was working but is now there as a joyous reminder of the fact that he is no longer governed by time. As one part of his brain realised that there was, in fact, no alarm clock there another part reminded him that he had just spent the night in the Premier Inn, Birmingham City – Aston. Satisfied that all the things he had just been confused by a TV in the bedroom - Kath would never allow that - and purple curtains also a no-no for Kath who preferred floral designs, now made sense so Dave snuggled back down under his duvet.

His night had not been quite as advertised by the aforementioned Hotel chain. Whilst he could not fault the quality of the Hypnos mattress, he certainly felt that the majority of the guests, or that at least those on his floor and the one above, did not adhere to the required night-time mantras of 'it's oh so quiet' and 'tiptoe please'. In fact at one point, it sounded like the elephant marching scene from the Jungle Book. The only difference being that instead of elephants trumpeting there had been raucous laughter. After that episode things had settled down for a while.

Deadly Circle/DC Poolie

Without having Kath's snoring, exacerbated by the nightly medicinal vodka, he had slept like a baby until the antics from the room directly next to his pillow had brought him back to full consciousness. The love making was symphony like, building up from an almost hushed murmuring of the wind section to the rhythmic bangs of the percussion ending up ultimately with the full orchestra, but, instead of canons being included like in the 1812 overture, it was a woman's aria.

Andy, don't stop.
Keep it just there.
More, more.
Yes, just like that.
Andy, you are wonderful.

Dave sat bolt upright as this memory flooded into his mind.

'Andy? Surely not here in Birmingham,' he thought. 'Note to self. Check to see if there is a mobility scooter plugged into a wall socket in the corridor.' He found his phone, which he had put on charge overnight and saw that he had just received an image from Charlie. He felt conflicted as he opened the attachment. Part of him felt like he had no right to be looking at this picture of the poor dead girl but, on the other hand, what he was doing could help Troy and maybe even get justice for her. He studied the photo closely and thought back to what he had seen the day before. It looked like it could be her, but her hair was certainly styled differently, and she looked like she had a different dress sense too. Checking his

184

phone again he realised that it was much later than he had thought.

He had arrived early in the afternoon the day before. The journey had been uneventful, and being Dave, he had tried to be as frugal as he could with the petrol consumption. He had headed straight for the area around Villa Park, the ground of Troy's former club Aston Villa.

Knowing that the football ground itself might not yield much information, let alone access, he parked right next to the Villa Shop on Trinity Road. He had wondered whether the training centre might have been a better option but as it was located at Bodymoor Heath, a leafy part of the affluent suburb of Sutton Coldfield, he felt it better to be somewhere where people would definitely be around to talk to him. And what could be better than the club's shop? Before entering the shop Dave decided to stretch his legs and walk around the area next to the ground.

Surprisingly, Dave's first impression was that it had a very student like feel. There were three streets parallel to one another (Jardine Rd, Nelson Rd and Endicott Road) which all looked rather neglected and were, in the main comprised he guessed, of multiple occupancy rental properties. Judging by the people who were leaving and entering the houses, and the decoration Dave could see through any curtain-less windows the inhabitants were, as Dave had originally surmised, very young and probably students.

Dave expected to see flyers advertising concerts or other events, maybe even political posters, but to Dave's shock and horror there were multiple posters of numerous girls who had gone missing. Some posters looked very old but there was

185

another one, which had been pasted to many of the walls and fences, of a brunette who had gone missing just under two weeks ago. All of them had one thing in common, at least according to the posters. They were all students at Aston University.

Dave walked back to the club shop and, this time, he went in. Inside there was only one shop assistant.

'I suppose it must be very different on match days,' Dave mused.

He went up to the counter and spoke to the bored looking young man who was sitting on a stall looking at the classified job adverts.

Fighting back the urge to ask him about job satisfaction Dave said, 'I wonder if you can help me?'

'Yes, of course.'

'My youngest daughter is applying to the Uni here and, as a football fan, wants to find some digs near the ground. I've just wandered around and I must say I'm quite concerned both with the standard of accommodation and the fact that there are so many girls who have seemingly gone missing.'

The young guy thought for a second and then replied, 'Yes, if I were you I'd get her to look nearer to the University. As you say the area doesn't really have much going for it apart from being a cheap area to live.'

'What about all those posters?'

'Well, some say that girls have vanished, and others say that it is an overreaction and the girls have just, without telling anyone, given up their studies and gone home.'

'There still seems to be lots of female students here,' Dave pressed.

Deadly Circle/DC Poolie

'Between you and me I think that there is almost a 'groupie' culture amongst some girls. They choose to live here in the hope of becoming a Villa WAG. I suppose it is a quicker way of becoming rich and less work than a degree.' The shop door signalled the entrance of a proper customer so Dave, feeling he had got all he would from this guy, thanked him and left.

Feeling a little peckish Dave located a pub near the ground. Judging by the interior décor the Holte Pub was totally dedicated to the football team. Every wall was covered with flags, scarves and other club memorabilia. The TVs were even showing old Villa matches, wins only of course, on a loop.

Whilst ordering a ploughman's lunch, Dave certainly loved his cheese, he asked the barman whether many players came into the pub.

'As a rule, no,' he answered. 'We sometimes have charity evenings which, because of the prizes, are very popular with the female fans. Some of the players usually attend those.'

'Really. Why do you say that about the female fans?' Dave asked.

'They love the signed pieces of used football kit. Even if it's dirty,' the barman grimaced. 'But the prizes they really want to win are one to one tours of the stadium, or even a meal, with a player.'

Dave enjoyed his food but couldn't shake from his mind the images of the girls on the posters. He made his way back to the car. It was time to check in at the hotel. He didn't want to be late as there was only a limited amount of parking spaces and you couldn't reserve one.

Deadly Circle/DC Poolie

He resolved to ask Charlie for a picture of the poor girl in Hartlepool. It was a gruesome thought, but she could be one of the girls on a poster.

....

Dave left his hotel room and was relieved to find no mobility scooter blocking his way in the corridor. Having checked out, he took another look at the poor girl's picture before getting into the car for what he felt was an unnecessary first journey of the day. He was still cursing himself for not having had the foresight, the day before, to take photos of the flyers documenting the missing students when he was parking the car in Nelson Road. Returning to the area brought a cloud of doom back down over Dave. He couldn't help but wonder what fate had befallen these young women.

The first thing he did was to find the flyer of the girl he thought might be the victim. He found the photo, sent by Charlie, and held it up next to the one of the girl in the flyer. It was her. He was sure. Although her eyes were shut and there was no youthful smile in the forensic photo which Charlie had accessed Dave could see a perfect match in the facial structure of each image. Dave was both elated and, at the same time, deflated.

'You poor thing,' he spoke these words quietly but wanted her to hear him. 'Hopefully we can find some closure for you and your loved ones.' He took a picture of the flyer and then meticulously took one of all of the other different missing girls. He didn't want to make the same mistake again by forgetting to gather some evidence which later on could have been useful. As he did this he was struck by the fact that the murdered girl looked slightly older than the others.

When he finished taking the photos, he opened up his message app and texted Charlie.

'I've found her! I have some more things to do. Will tell you more later.'

As he started his car his phone beeped telling him he had received a reply.

'Bloody hell Dave! Really? We will have to tell the police. Do what you have to do but we will have to tell them by this evening.'

'Agreed.' Dave put the car in gear and drove off.

Dave, who never really liked driving in unfamiliar city centres, gave a silent thanks to the car's satnav as he pulled into the last remaining car parking space which was situated directly in front of Aston University's Student Union Building. According to the blue sign next to the space he had 45 minutes free parking. That meant he needed to get a wriggle on or he might end up with a ticket which would go directly to the electrical company and not him. Even though the people at the firm loved him they wouldn't be impressed by that. Inside the building Dave saw an unmanned reception and thought that would be a good place to start. When he got closer he saw that copies of the very same flyers he'd seen earlier, by the Villa ground, took pride of place on the wall display behind. They sat beneath a very poignant and unambiguous message,

'2 IS BOTH FOR COMPANY AND PROTECTION. DON'T GO IT ALONE!'

Dave was brought back from his thoughts by a voice from behind.

Deadly Circle/DC Poolie

'Can I help you?' Dave turned to see a crop haired young woman smiling at him. For a second Dave hesitated, mesmerised for some reason by her. Then he realised why she had had such an effect on him. She reminded him so much of a young Kath. The Kath who had captured his heart and held it safe for so long. It was her eyes. Those sparkling eyes, beautiful and engaging.

'I hope you can,' he stuttered, 'but you are going to have to trust my intentions. Can I buy you a coffee?' Dave had noticed a Costa machine in front of some informal seating. He knew that she would be more relaxed, and hopefully more willing to divulge information, if they stayed somewhere familiar and she felt safer.

Rather embarrassed Dave was sitting, two minutes later, watching his new companion using his credit card to purchase them a latte each.

'Why are these machines so complicated? And why am I such a technophobe at times?' Dave tried not to let such experiences get to him, but it really was annoying.

As it turned out this technological vulnerability enabled Natasha Phillips, so her lanyard claimed, to relax with him. Sensing this positive atmosphere Dave, aware of his time constraints, decided to jump in and asked her straight away about the pictures by the reception. He pointed out the one of the victim and said that finding out more about her may help a friend of his who is in a spot of bother. He said that he may also be able to locate her and, by doing so, clear up the mystery surrounding her disappearance at least. Natasha told him that her name is Zoe Young but then seemed a little reluctant to divulge any more. Dave's strength is his interpersonal skills and so he changed the subject knowing that he would only find out some more if Natasha could fully trust him.

The next ten minutes were taken up with Natasha seeing a string of Dave's family photos followed by a discussion of life as a modern-day student who has to start off their working life already facing a huge student loan debt. Much relieved, as this latest topic isn't one he is that up to speed on, Dave's heard Natasha change the topic back to Zoe.

'Do you think you can locate her?' Natasha asked. 'Only the police seem incapable of doing so.'

'I really think I can,' he replied sincerely. He wished he could tell her the truth now but remembered Charlie's warning of the need to be both sensitive and respect confidentiality.

'I've only known her since she came back to restart her studies,' Natasha was opening up now.

'Restart?'

'Yes, there was an incident, a violent one, and she took a 2-year break. As the gap was so long she had to repeat the first year. I remember her saying one weird thing though.'

Dave nodded for her to continue.

'She said that she had only come back when it was safe for her to come back.'

'Safe? In what way?' Dave was really intrigued by this.

'All I know is that she had digs by the Villa ground and that this guy she was seeing got really out of control.' Natasha sat back up in her seat and took a measured sip of her, now cooling, latte.

Dave pressed, 'Wish I could find out more. This could really help my friend.'

191

Deadly Circle/DC Poolie

Natasha thought for a second and then spoke again, 'I know someone, a PHD student, who was her best friend. Give me a minute.' With that she stood up and walked over to the reception.

Dave saw her making a call. After putting the phone back in her pocket, she walked over to him.

'Meet me at 1.30pm in the Holte pub. She will be there too and if she thinks you are ok then she will join us.'

Dave made sure that he arrived ahead of time. He wasn't sure how busy the pub would be, and he knew that a quiet table away from the attention of other people would be best. He ordered a non-alcoholic cider and sat at a chair which afforded him a view of both entrances. Just before 1.30 Natasha entered the pub on her own. Although she wasn't striking in her beauty, somehow, she gained admiring looks from both the men and women in the bar.

'She is just like Kath,' Dave thought. 'She captivates everyone without even trying.'

As she looked around the bar Dave managed to catch her eye and he stood up, leaving his coat on the back of the chair, to go and buy her a drink.

'What can I get you?' Dave asked, pulling out his wallet.

'Just a Diet Coke, thanks. You'd better get Nancy something too. She likes Coke as well but the full fat version. It will save you from having to keep coming up to the bar.'

'So, you think she will talk to me?'

'Why don't you ask her yourself,' she answered looking past Dave to the barmaid.

Deadly Circle/DC Poolie

'He seems nice enough,' said the barmaid as she opened the bar flap to allow her to join them on the customer side of the bar. 'Thanks for the drink.'

'I thought you were a PHD student,' Dave sounded a little confused as he followed the two ladies to the table.

'I am,' she smiled turning around to look at him, 'Even academic greats have to eat.'

At the table the topic quickly turned to Nancy's friendship with Zoe and their fraternising with the Villa players.

Nancy's explanation of their lifestyle choice was unashamedly forthright and logical.

'We had to choose between acne pocked faces, greasy unkempt hair and cold pizza or hard chiselled bodies, haute couture and a chance to escape from the norm. Do you want to go to parties with cheap cider or Champagne?'

Dave nodded showing that he understood the allure of such a lifestyle.

'For a group of us,' she continued, 'there was no contest. That first year, where the exams seemed a lifetime away, was one big party. Nobody took it really seriously. We all scrubbed up quite well and the footballer's lifestyle meant that they had both time and money for us. We didn't even mind if they were playing away.'

Nancy looked at Dave to see if he had picked up on her play on words alluding to infidelity. Dave's involuntary twisting of his wedding ring showed that he had.

'How about Zoe?' Dave asked.

'She started out like the rest of us. She drifted from one guy to another at first but then we started to see less of her as she became embroiled with one of the players. She had become much more secretive, so we didn't really know who it was. What we did know is that she was really happy to start off with.'

'So that happiness didn't last?' Dave enquired.

'We noticed that she started to wear sunglasses, both indoors and outside. That made us a little concerned, but we were genuinely worried when she wore only long-sleeved dresses, even on warm spring days. For someone so naturally pretty the amount of make-up she was applying was also tell tale of her covering things up. We couldn't let this slide, so we confronted her.'

'What did she say?' Dave's face showed both interest and concern. He could never hit anyone, let alone a woman.

'Her answer was that of a classic victim of abuse. If that is a real word. He didn't mean it. He was going through a stressful time.'

'Poor thing,' Natasha chimed in. 'Sometimes the girls even blame themselves.'

Nancy shook her head to show that such things, although commonplace, shouldn't happen.

'Just as we were about to intervene, she disappeared, and we didn't see her for two years.'

'Any idea why?' Dave's role, it seemed, was to ask short and slightly inane questions.

'No, she never really spoke of it when she returned. It was like an episode of her past that she didn't want to revisit.'

'The one time the topic came up,' Natasha said feeling that she had something to contribute. 'She called it a major wakeup call and she said that she had finally come to her senses. I didn't push her, and she left it at that.'

'I hate incomplete stories,' Dave said taking a sip of his cider. 'I wish we could fill in the gaps.'

While they had been talking Dave had noticed a young man, in an Iron Maiden Sweatshirt, watching them from another table nearer the bar. Every time Dave glanced in that direction the young man, who was staring directly at the three of them, averted his gaze and it had really started to make Dave feel uncomfortable. He was on the point of saying something to the two women when Natasha gestured towards him making it clear that he should join them.

"This is Cole Parker,' she said by means of explanation. 'He helps on our support line. Cole, tell Dave about the call you received.'

'Yes, I was on duty last Friday and this person, a female probably in her 20s or 30s, rang the hotline to say that she had some info about the missing girl, Zoe Young. She went on to say that it was something from a few years ago but that, given the nature of what she had seen, it might be very important.'

The other three at the table merely listened giving Cole their full attention.

'Can I just pre-empt this by saying that this is, as far as I can remember, exactly what she said. Personally, I found it very uncomfortable to listen to and I think you will too. If I were to sugar-coat it though then the extreme nature of this event might be lost,' he paused to gauge their assent.

'Go on.' Dave urged.

'She explained that, as a newly married mother, she couldn't come forward officially. Apparently, at that time, she had met a guy with similar interests online and together they had gone to a S&M club in Solihull called 50 Shades of Pain. And it was there that she saw Zoe with some guy. He was basically trying to get the other men there to treat her as a sex toy. The rougher the better. He had suspended her in a sling and made sure that the handcuffs and the feet bracelets were done up really tight to ensure that she was totally at the mercy of the men who were now surrounding her. At first it was all quite gentle, and she seemed compliant, but this angered her guy, and he was ordering the other men to be more extreme causing her to bleed and be penetrated in every orifice. She became very agitated and started to writhe and scream. The men, thinking she was enjoying it, just hit harder and pushed everything further in. Fortunately for her he hadn't used a ball gag on her mouth, so she was able to call out the club's safe word. The guys immediately backed away, but her man became even more incensed, and he went apeshit.'

Cole paused for a second. 'Her exact words on the call. Not mine. Apparently this guy picked up a bull whip and lashed her across the body and face and he was just about to penetrate her anally with the handle when he was pulled off her by the other guys. The lady making the call said that she, and a few other women, freed Zoe from the sling and tended to her the best they could. That was the last time the woman saw either of them there. However, the guy she had gone there with told her that the man 'who had lost it' was a Villa player. As he was more into bondage than football he didn't actually know the player's name.'

Deadly Circle/DC Poolie

'Wow! That was some story. It must have been difficult for you to tell. Thanks Cole.' Nancy's face had taken a real ashen tone.

'When was this?' Dave asked.

'Six years ago, in May. She said she could never forget the look on that poor woman's face so when she saw the poster she knew that she had to say something.'

'Six years ago,' Dave thought to himself, 'Troy joined the year after.'

Dave bought them all another drink and while at the bar he phoned Charlie to update him.

'Charlie, we might have some more suspects. How many people at Hartlepool United had ties with Villa six years ago?'

Chapter 13

As the kit man/groundsman at Hartlepool football club, Charlie Green knew he had a full day ahead of him. Because of the financial situation there he had been asked to take on more than one job. He was happy to do this because of his love for his hometown club. With the help of one or two dedicated volunteers he was proud of the work they did to keep the ground looking spic and span.

He was awake and up out of bed earlier than normal and showered and shaved before his bedside alarm had even sounded. Talk Sport was playing on the radio with two ex-premier league players talking about the pressures of top-level football. This brought a smile to his face.

'Try playing your football at this level boys,' he spoke to the radio 'when your livelihood and career is on the line, that's real pressure.'

With his regular breakfast of tea, toast and cereal finished he was on his way to the ground an hour earlier than normal. It was around a forty-minute walk from his home to the football ground. This, he thought, would give him time to sort out in his head what he would need to do once he had got to the ground.

It was a home game so all the usual match day tasks would need to be seen to first before any investigations to benefit Troy. Match days were always a joy for Charlie whose whole life was built around football and this club.

Deadly Circle/DC Poolie

Firstly, he went into the away team dressing room and showers, checking everything was clean and ready. The home dressing room and shower areas also were spotless and warm, with the strips laid out in order on the benches. He made his way outside and spoke to one of the volunteer helpers at the ground. Graham Young was one of Charlie's regular volunteers and the one who had worked with Charlie the longest.

'Graham, can you give the pitch a last once over with the grass cutter?' Charlie asked.

'Will do Charlie, won't take me long. The pitch looks almost perfect,' Graham replied.

'Almost doesn't do it for me you know that.' Charlie answered, with a wink.

'Yes boss, I know that boss I'm onto it now,' Graham laughed as he answered.

Corner flags were positioned, goal nets checked, and sprinklers switched on and then Charlie was happy that everything was ready for the game.

He then walked into the office block where he found the Secretary, Joan Blackford.

'Any chance of a coffee Joan?' enquired Charlie.

'Of course,' she replied, 'as long as you make it yourself and get me one while you are at it.'

Charlie shrugged his shoulders and made his way to the kettle and mugs which were on a table in the corner.'

'Any news on the Troy Harvey situation Charlie?' Joan asked. 'Have you been up to see him at all?'

'Really, he is just how you would expect I think. Very down and wondering how he got into this mess at all.'

199

Deadly Circle/DC Poolie

'It's very sad. He seemed a nice guy on the odd occasion I got to speak to him,' said Joan.

'He is a nice guy, Joan. He has just found himself in a very bad place. Some mates and I are trying to see if we can help him out in any way. You may be able to help too, actually. Would you know if any people at the club would have been at Aston Villa when Troy was there or maybe even just before his time, Joan?'

The Secretary thought for a while. 'Well, the Gaffer was definitely there at the time. It was his connection which helped to get Troy signed here again.'

'Why would you be asking that though? What would that have to do with Troy's problem?' she continued.

'Probably nothing,' Charlie replied. 'Just trying to explore every avenue really.'

'I think it's best if you make an official request for any further information of that kind though Charlie. I don't want to get into any bother.'

'Ok Joan, understood. Thanks for your help anyway.'

Next, Charlie made his way under the stand to the Supporters Club Bar

He was surprised to walk into the Corner Flag Bar to find a bigger crowd than usual inside. As a rule, people wouldn't turn up until at least a couple of hours before kick-off. The reason for the turn out soon became apparent. Local singer/musician Henry Frost was putting on a fund-raising day for the football club. Henry, of course, was a good friend of Charlie and his mates from the Headland promenade. Charlie headed over to talk to him.

'Great to see you here Henry. Thanks for doing this.'

200

Deadly Circle/DC Poolie

'No problem, mate. You know I love playing in front of a crowd and looks like we may get a good turn out here and make a few quid for the football club,' Henry replied.

'Any chance of you singing in tune though?' Charlie said with a smile.

'You know me mate, I'll play and sing them anyway. If they are in tune that's a bonus,' was Henry's reply. 'Anyway, we have karaoke after the game. If you fancy showing your vocal talents, you are welcome.'

Charlie sidestepped that invitation and asked, 'Seen anything of Cliff and the others around?'

'Yes, Cliff is sat with Andy in their usual corner.'

'Ah yes I can see them now. Not used to this many people in here this early,' remarked Charlie.

'Must be my good looks and talent that's attracting them in mate,' Henry suggested.

'More likely the cheap beer and free pies I would think,' grinned Charlie ducking to avoid a friendly slap across the head from the singer.

'The bar is over there my friend if you feel the need to buy me a beer.'

'I'll give it some thought and let you know sometime in the future,' was Charlie's reply.

He made his way through the growing crowd in the bar and was lucky to find a seat next to Andy and Cliff.

'Hello boys how are things going?' he asked. 'Can I get the pair of you a drink?'

Andy's ears pricked up at this. 'Aye thanks,' he said. 'Cliff likes a lager and a pint of bitter for me. Cheers.'

Deadly Circle/DC Poolie

Charlie and Cliff glanced at each other and grinned at this totally typical Andy response. Charlie made his way to the bar and ordered the drinks including one for Henry which he passed onto the singer with a wink.

He sat back down with Andy and Cliff, and they began running through what they had found out and planning their next moves.

'I need to find out if any people connected to the club would have been at Aston Villa when Troy was there. Or maybe in the period just before.'

'Well Bob Scott, our manager, played for Villa and I'm sure Troy's time there would have overlapped. As far as any others maybe 'the professor' over there Arnie Power could help.'

At seventy-eight years of age pensioner Arnie Power really was the historian of the football club. His whole life had been built around the club and he had certainly experienced the highs and lows of following a team at this level. Charlie knew him as a gentleman, quietly spoken but fiercely proud of his hometown football club.

Charlie made his way over to speak to him just as Henry started his act with a rousing sing-along version of the John Denver song Country Roads. He sat down next to Arnie and waited till Henry's song was finished.

'Hello Arnie, I was hoping you would be able to help me out with something.'

'Of course, always happy to help if I can,' Arnie replied. 'What is it that you need?'

'Some information on connections between our club and Aston Villa, you know the sort of things. Player transfers either way. Back-room staff. Anything really.'

'Don't think Villa have ever been a club we have had a close relationship with. How far back are you wanting to look at?'

'This is to do with the Troy Harvey case, and I need to know if there are any people here now who would have been at Villa while Troy was there. Or maybe a few years before.'

'Oh, I see now,' said Arnie. 'If this information will help get to the bottom of this case good luck. I'm not sure myself whether Troy is guilty or not, but I hope he is proved innocent and released.'

Just then the volume in the Corner Flag bar went up a notch or two as Henry led the crowd into a raucous version of Sweet Caroline and Charlie and Arnie were reduced to their own version of sign language. They had to admit Henry knew how to work a crowd and everyone seemed to be singing along and having a great time. Eventually the pair gave up on the sign language and Arnie pulled a pen from his jacket pocket and wrote on a beer mat.

203

HOPE THIS HELPS

MANAGER BOB SCOTT .... player at villa for around 10yrs and may have played for a short time whilst Troy was there.

FIRST TEAM COACH

HARRY GARSIDE... Academy coach while Troy was at Villa. He left to be coach here when BOB SCOTT got the manager's job.

JIMMY DUNNE.... player at Villa and lost his place here when Troy was signed.

BRAD PICKEN ... reserve goalkeeper at Villa when Troy signed.

All of these will have spent time at Villa with Troy or left just before he signed.

Good luck
ARNIE

Charlie stood up and shook Arnie's hand and thanked him for his help. He made his way back to Cliff and Andy just as Hi Ho Silver Lining threatened to take the roof off the bar. Henry was in his element playing to a crowd like this and he was certainly making the most of it.

'Was Arnie able to help you then?' Cliff asked.

'Yes he was, all these little pieces of information help to build a case to cast doubts on Troy's involvement in this crime.'

Deadly Circle/DC Poolie

'Nice pint they sell in here,' chimed in Andy. 'I'd have another if my dodgy knee was up to fighting my way to the bar.'

'Ok I can take a hint. I'll get you another round in. You just sit on your rear and rest your ever so dodgy knee,' laughed Charlie.

'Maybe one of Matty's free steak pies would help as well' Andy remarked.

'The pies Matty brings in Andy as you know he pays for himself. Most people will buy him a drink or drop something in the collection box for the football club.' Charlie tried to sound as serious as he could.

'Yes, Charlie that's right, I almost forgot about that. I'm sure he drinks bitter. Best get him a pint as well.'

Charlie shook his head in frustration and made his way to the bar.

Chapter 14

Barry, who hadn't gone with Charlie to the prison before the weekend, had seen pictures of Troy's injuries but seeing them in person took his breath away.

Charlie had grown to like Barry since their first meeting in the café after the previous bail hearing and seeing the look on Barry's face he raised a finger to his mouth. He knew how guilty Barry still felt about his abject performance the last time he had represented Troy and he also knew that Barry's reaction to seeing Troy in this state would be to apologise again. That would, to Charlie's mind, be unnecessary. They were, thanks a lot to Barry's planning and visit to the CPS, well past any situation where recriminations were still needed.

Today, Charlie was sure, would be a really positive day with Troy being released on bail. The bail hearing had been fast tracked into being the first case of the week. Quentin had been true to his word and convinced his boss, who had finally overcome his prejudice against the 'privileged few', to expedite things and give Troy Harvey a second chance at being released subject to wearing an electronic tag. Of course, these machinations could only get Troy back into court. It would be down to the Magistrate on duty that day as to whether Troy would actually be released on bail.

They had arrived thirty minutes early in Barry's new car. He had previously swung by the Marina Apartments to pick up

Deadly Circle/DC Poolie

Charlie who was there to select an appropriate suit for Troy for the court appearance. Not having seen Charlie outside the entrance, as planned, Barry had gone up in the elevator to the flat in an effort to hurry Charlie along.

As the lift door opened he could see that the front door of Troy's penthouse was wide open and, much to his surprise, Barry heard laughter, female laughter, emanating from inside. There were at least two or three distinct laughs. Actually, raucous cackling may have been a more apt description. As he stepped inside he saw a whirlwind of activity as, what could only be described as a cleaning gang, five women sprayed, wiped, hoovered, dusted and washed every surface and item in the flat. In the corner Charlie sat on an armchair smiling at the many saucy comments made by these cleaning dervishes. He seemed to take particular delight at those directly aimed at him.

He waved as he saw Barry entering the flat and at the same time bent down to pick up a suit carrier.

'What's going on?' Barry asked. 'Who are these women?'

'Even you should be able to work that out Barry me boy,' he replied. 'Me and the girls from the club's canteen are getting the place all sorted for Troy's return. He doesn't want to return to somewhere that looks like a grisly set from CSI Miami. I cleared it with the club and the manager, Bob Scott, even allowed young Tony Marsh to drive them over here. He is coming back after training to collect them so they can prepare the lads' lunches.'

'You're confident aren't you?' Barry smiled.

Deadly Circle/DC Poolie

'So should you be after all our work and what happened to poor Troy in jail.' He started moving as if to leave. 'Thanks girls. See you later.'

'Don't forget you owe us all a cuddle at least for this. You know we all fancy you.' a rather suggestive look crossed the face of an elderly woman with a blue rinse as she said this.

To Barry's joy and amazement, he saw the checks of his new friend go a deep red.

'Right. Let's get out of here before I'm molested,' said Charlie, now almost at sprint speed.

Troy, because of his shoulder and other injuries, arrived not in chains but handcuffed to a prison guard. They discussed leaving him dressed as he was but unanimously thought it worth the pain to change him into his suit for the hearing.

'We don't want our sincerity in today's procedure to be misconstrued,' was Barry's argument which summed up their approach to the situation. Troy was obviously still an emotional mess and the mental scars, although not as visible as his physical ones, were laying heavy on him. His dialogue was almost monosyllabic, and he appeared to lack any spark of life.

Charlie, realising that a more coherent Troy would be needed upstairs, placed a hand on Troy's good shoulder and looked him straight in the eyes.

'Come on Troy. We are almost there. On top of what we had before we now know who the victim is and that you have no previous link to her. We are even investigating others who may well be the real murderer.' Charlie paused for a second before going on, 'We need you to play your part in there.'

'Yes,' interjected Barry, 'your injuries speak for themselves, but you must be able look the magistrate in the eye and agree to any caveat he or she may come up with. Do you understand?'

Troy was clearly lifted by this news. He visibly pulled himself together and smiled. 'I'm ready,' he said.

. . . .

'Wow!' Charlie was beaming from ear to ear as he put a large macchiato in front of Barry, 'You were awesome.' They were sitting at the same table, in the café across from the courthouse, as a few weeks earlier. But this time the misery previously etched on their faces had been replaced with jubilance.

'Come on Charlie,' Barry replied sheepishly. 'It was laid on a plate for me. They couldn't deny him bail this time. Particularly, after the beating he had received.'

Charlie wasn't standing for any humility, 'You were so eloquent. You stated our case clearly and precisely and the way you got them to concede a fairer curfew was skilfully done my friend.'

'Yes, I think the Magistrate was more than fair,' Barry ceded. 'Even the CPS didn't object.'

'They couldn't really. Could they?'

'How long do you think this electronic tagging process takes?' Charlie was obviously keen to get Troy home as soon as possible.

'Not too long, but long enough for you to get me a blueberry muffin. We can go and collect Troy after I've had a much-needed snack.'

Deadly Circle/DC Poolie

....

DS Mark Cross was sitting at his desk. He was leaning forward trying to control his rage.

'Well thanks to you Troy Harvey has just been released on bail,' he almost spat out the words.

The object of this bilious verbal attack, DC Angela Hart, was seated on the other side of his desk.

'You needn't deny it,' he continued. 'I know that misfit of a solicitor, Barry something, went straight from here across to the CPS and right into your ex-lover's office. You think you can go behind my back young woman? Well, you can't. I have my sources over there too. On top of that you were seen passing him an envelope. I didn't believe it at first but thanks to the wonders of modern technology your attempt at playing at being a spy was caught on our very own CCTV. Thank God I still have friends in this building because I can't trust those I work with in my own team.'

He was now incandescent with rage.

'Firstly, I doubt it's thanks to me to be honest,' Angela was not going to allow such bullying antics from this man. 'Troy's friends are the ones who were prepared to go the extra mile to gather evidence that, at the very least, casts doubt over his guilt. Secondly, we are here to punish those who commit the crimes. How do my actions prevent justice from being done?'

'But if you hadn't disobeyed me and gave them a copy of that photo, he would still be in jail now,' Cross roared.

'Exactly! Surely our job is to find the ones guilty of crimes and not just lock up anyone who we think may be involved. Thanks to them making that extra effort the victim has now been identified and her family will be notified.'

'Very true,' a voice boomed from the doorway as Chief Constable Coates came into the office. 'I hope you have learned something about teamwork from DC Hart's actions. Only through people working together can we get the results we all hope for.'

'The information has been passed on to the Birmingham Force and, based on what we have told them, they have reopened cases for missing women around that area,' the Chief Constable continued. 'And furthermore, your work over the last twelve months has not gone unnoticed by me and others around here, so I'm pleased to tell you I have today expedited your name for your promotion and have no reason to think it will not be confirmed. After all you passed your sergeant's exams 6 months ago and have been waiting for a position to open up. Your work is exemplary, and you will be found a position where your skills are best utilised and appreciated.'

Knowing that DS Cross was obviously furious with this praise of his colleague the Chief Constable paused for a second and then turned his focus towards Cross.

'Well deserved don't you think Cross?' Chief Constable Coates knew that Cross was in no position to contradict these opinions and was enjoying asking him this question. The subsequent grunted reply said it all and brought a smile to the face of Coates who winked at DC Hart before turning and leaving the room. 'I expect my teams to function as a team and that ethos starts at the top,' he spoke this loudly, without looking back, so that all those in the outer office were also made aware of his feelings about the situation.

211

Deadly Circle/DC Poolie

....

'Yuk! Not exactly a chic fashion accessory are they,' Charlie was staring at Troy's newly acquired ankle bracelet. Barry and Charlie had driven Troy home in Barry's car and together they had waited for the technicians to arrive to set everything up. Once they had entered the apartment they had been both swift and efficient in their work.

'Obviously they are well practised at doing this,' Charlie had mused.

'Apparently I'm now the 545th inhabitant of Hartlepool to be actively wearing one of these at the moment,' chipped in Troy, who was already visibly more relaxed by being at home. Even if it was the site of a brutal killing.

'Blimey! And I thought Hartlepool was a sleepy little coastal town,' retorted Charlie looking genuinely shocked. 'I wonder what the other 544 people did.'

Located at the phone socket the technicians had set up a monitoring unit. Troy, who had elected to wear a loose-fitting tracksuit, then had the bracelet fitted to his one healthy ankle. Somehow, unlike Andy, he really suited a tracksuit and didn't look like he was going to go to the park and expose himself anytime soon.

'Apparently they transmit a radio signal every 60 seconds and during my hours of curfew I must be within 40 metres of the base unit.' Troy was telling the others this almost as much to remind himself of the restrictions as to give them the basic information. 'I can shower with it on too but shouldn't really swim or use hot tubs. Apparently, that could bugger up the signal.'

Charlie and Barry, who had already been fully briefed by Quentin, both nodded feigning the receipt of new information.

'How about drinking? Are you allowed to drink alcohol?' Charlie asked even though he was aware of this stipulation too.

'As I was intoxicated and had Rohypnol in my system at the time of the murder I have been asked to wear a sobriety tag.' Troy's response was almost robotic in its delivery. It was like he was recalling a fact, word for word, to pass a test, 'It cleverly tests my sweat and analyses its contents for alcohol.'

'There are some people I know where it'd be beeping all day,' smiled Charlie.

'It might be a bind but at least you are safe here and out of prison,' Barry said, trying to be practical. 'And to be fair it's not like you're in any fit state to go out gallivanting anyway.'

Troy looked past his two companions and surveyed the flat.

'I haven't been here long, but I was just getting used to calling this home. After the last few weeks, it feels as much a sanctuary as a home. Thanks guys for all your efforts. And Barry sorry I doubted you. You have gone above and beyond.'

Barry's face reddened with embarrassment. He really hadn't expected to hear this.

As tender a moment as it was Charlie decided to change the topic. After all, only half the job was done. They still had to clear Troy's name by getting him a not guilty verdict.

'The girls from the canteen really have done a fantastic job cleaning up the apartment. It looks like you could eat off every surface. A real 5-star hotel feel.'

213

Deadly Circle/DC Poolie

'Yes, I must thank the girls tomorrow personally. Maybe we could stop by the florists on the way? I may still be accused of this horrible thing but I'm not going to hide myself away,' Troy replied stoically.

'Of course, we can,' Charlie was full of pride and admiration for his young friend. 'Does it feel weird at all being back here?'

'Weird certainly,' Troy put his hand across his mouth. This was a mannerism Charlie had frequently observed whenever Troy was contemplating something. 'I suppose deep down I know I didn't do this, nor would I ever have harmed that poor woman. You know me Charlie. I have my fun with women, but I put them on a pedestal. I worship them and even if my relationships are eventually screwed up, for one reason or another, I have never laid a finger on any woman. In a way if a part of her spirit still resides here then I will be her companion. I may have some demons, like drink, in my life but I have nothing to fear from the consequences of that night.'

'Flipping heck Troy! Did you swallow a dictionary when you were in the hospital ward?' Charlie was laughing. 'That is the longest sentence I've ever heard you say.'

'Yes, it's plum worn me out,' Troy smiled and settled back into the corner of the sofa. 'How about a video? You guys can join me for my first evening in curfew.'

'Good idea,' said Barry, 'I could do with some down time. Something light and fun would be good.'

'It just so happens,' said Charlie reaching into a carrier bag, 'I have just the film.'

Troy and Barry both looked in anticipation and then laughed as one when they saw the title.

Deadly Circle/DC Poolie

'Escape to Victory,' chuckled Charlie, 'I saw it on my shelf this morning and I thought it really apt.'

He gave Barry the DVD to put in the machine. Troy needed to rest his injuries so he shouldn't have to move any more than necessary.

'I put some non-alcoholic drinks in the fridge,' he added, getting up and walking to the kitchen area of the open plan living area. 'And we have some nibbles in the cupboards too.'

Just over two hours later, having all had their first relaxing evening for a long time, Charlie and Barry bade farewell to Troy and his electronic monitor.

'It's only just after 9 o'clock and it is already pitch-black outside,' said Barry. 'That bracelet shouldn't need charging for at least 72 hours so don't worry about that.'

Troy stood at the window as he watched his two friends, Barry was indeed now a true friend, get into the car. As the bright red of the rear lights dwindled and finally disappeared Troy tried to ignore the slight sinking feeling in his stomach. Had he known that there was a pair of eyes down there staring unblinkingly up at him, and that those eyes had been focussed on his flat since the moment he arrived earlier, then that feeling in the pit of his stomach would have grown out of all proportion.

Little did he know that his first evening back in the apartment would be so marked with violence and death.

Chapter 15

Alan Tubbs, the surly janitor, returned to his live-in apartment on the ground floor next to the main entrance with an angry look on his face. He was so flustered that his, normally dexterous fingers, struggled to find the correct key. Had any unsuspecting resident happened by, at that moment, to ask for help with a particular problem then they would have encountered a totally different response to the usual 'Uriah Heap' one which Alan affected to hide his contempt for those he was paid to serve. This time they would get a real insight into his persona. One which portrayed the, almost perpetual, anger living within the visually repulsive janitor.

He had spent the last few hours watching the return of Troy from prison and then had seen him 'having fun' with his friends up in the penthouse when he had snuck up to one of his many regular spy holes, one which afforded him a clear view into the open plan space of Troy's apartment. One which, if discovered, would give him a good excuse for being there. The problem with the electrics on the balcony of the empty, adjacent apartment had given him the appropriate cover he needed ever since Troy had moved in.

'Why the bloody hell have they let him out?' Alan asked himself. 'I thought I'd done enough to ensure he was put away for a long time. I can't let him get away with this.'

216

Deadly Circle/DC Poolie

He rather noisily shut the door to his home behind him. Normally he tried to avoid being both heard and seen but this time his mood was out of control, and he just didn't care what anyone thought. On that balcony, watching Troy relaxing and wallowing in his freedom with his friends, he had formulated a plan of attack. With that in mind he made his way over to the freezer and carefully took out his weapon of choice.

As he still had a few hours to kill, a rather ironic play on words, he made himself a cup of strong tea and sat down at the small kitchen table contemplating the pain he was going to inflict on Troy. His favourite chair always had him facing his one true treasure in this soulless and sparsely decorated dwelling. That treasure was a cheaply framed picture of him, as a youth, with an older rather unkempt man.

Alan's mind drifted back into the past. He had been brought up in a rather run down council estate, on the outskirts of Middlesbrough, by his mother. He had never met, nor even seen a picture of, his father. In fact, his mother just quickly changed the subject whenever he asked questions about his father. Over time his romantic notions that he was the son of royalty changed. Given the vast number of new, short term, uncles he was introduced to he had decided by the time of her death that she probably didn't even know for certain whose cock it was that had shot him into life.

His time at school had been like hell on earth. All he really wanted was to have friends and to feel included but no matter what he did he was always an outcast. Someone the other kids enjoyed taunting and bullying. One verbal attack that he still remembered was from a kid who lived down the road.

Deadly Circle/DC Poolie

'Looking at you your dad must be fucking ugly. I mean I'd give your mum one cos she is hot,' he continued with a final parting shot. 'Mind you my dad says the same, but he's scared he'd catch something off her. He called her a right slag.'

Alan hadn't done any better with girls either. At primary school they all had a game where they would run away feigning horror anytime he came within two yards of them on the playground. They tried to do it in lessons but here the teacher, who was also repulsed by his physical appearance, soon squashed any such antics. He soon learnt to stand over by the fence during playtimes and lunchtimes. Although the teacher was, overtly, on his side even she placed him slightly away from any girl in the classroom. Two weeks after starting secondary school he thought things had changed for the better when a rather pretty and popular girl said she'd like to go to the pictures with him. She said she'd meet him at the playground near the cinema and that she'd even snog him if he brought her some flowers. He wanted to really impress the girl with some red roses. He'd seen that they were meant to be romantic when watching an advert on TV. The florist in the local precinct had some red roses but what little pocket money he got wouldn't buy him even one rose. His mother had just gone upstairs with an 'uncle', so he knew that he had time to take some money from his mother's hiding place. She thought he didn't know that she kept her 'earnings' in a vase on the mantelpiece. Alan may have been needy and ugly, but he certainly wasn't thick, so he took just enough for the roses and maybe an ice cream for each of them. He chose a crumpled old £5 note and left before his mum came back downstairs. He hadn't been sure what to wear so he put on his school trousers and a white

218

collared shirt. He decided a tie might be too much, but he knew to try to make the best of his normally greasy, tousled hair. To that end he had combed it across and applied some Brylcream, often used by his uncles when they were about to leave, to hold it in place. At the florists he bought three red roses, 'one for each of us and one for luck,' was the line he had practised.

He then went and sat on the agreed bench ten minutes early. As time ticked by, he noticed a few familiar faces start to gather around the park. He thought it a bit odd, but it was the local park he supposed. She was now twenty minutes late and the film would start soon. Alan started to panic a little looking around as even more kids from school were appearing. Really confused Alan sat there for almost another ten minutes. The faces around him were growing in number and closing in on the bench. Suddenly, Craig James, the school football team captain and well-known hard nut, pushed his way through the crowd and approached Alan.

'Did you really think Janine would want to go out with you?' Craig was speaking loudly for the ever-enclosing crowd. 'She only asked you out for a bet. It's me she fancies. Not you you pocked stained arsehole.'

He was really enjoying himself and was now standing squarely in front of Alan who had remained seated out of fear for his safety.

'I couldn't afford the flowers she likes so we thought we'd get you to buy them.' he looked at the flowers, 'Only three. We bet you'd bring six you stingy sod.'

All around the crowd were laughing and yelling "Fight, Fight!"

219

Deadly Circle/DC Poolie

'Now give them to me and I will only give you a slap. If you don't I will give you a good kicking.'

Alan bowed his head forward and handed over the flowers. Craig took them and passed them to his lieutenant, an equally violent kid called Stevie, saying, 'Stand up then.'

Alan slowly stood up knowing that flight, given the size of the baying crowd, was not an option. His head jerked back as the first punch arrived. Craig did not stick to his word and proceeded, much to the enjoyment of those watching, to hit him continuously until Alan fell to the floor. At which point Craig showed the crowd how hard the school team's captain could kick. He finally turned away, much to the approbation of the onlookers and walked off hand in hand with Janine towards the cinema.

'We'd better not have missed the start,' he called back laughing. Alan could hear Janine laughing too.

When he got home he was horrified to see his mother holding up the vase and staring accusingly at him. His hand went to his pocket and brought out the £1.50 he had left for the never to be acquired ice creams. As his mother snatched the money from him she raised her other hand and brought it sharply down on his face.

'Do you know what I put myself through to earn that money you worthless piece of shit?' And with that she struck him again.

Betrayed by those two women on that monumental day in his life. That really had left a scar in his psyche. Since then, he decided that he'd use and abuse women and even pay to get exactly what he wanted. He'd never let women control or hurt him again.

220

Deadly Circle/DC Poolie

His thoughts were brought back into the present by his cat, Cleo, who had jumped onto the table and was staring directly at him. He had chosen wisely when he had found Cleo at the cat rescue shelter. She was a Sphynx cat. One of those ugly, hairless cats. Pointless in the extreme. In Cleo he had found someone, or something, even uglier than him and that made him smile. He poured some milk into the bowl and returned to his chair. The picture again caught his attention and his mind drifted back to the day of his mother's funeral. His neighbour, an occasional uncle but also the only friend Alan had ever had, Jim Grimthorpe had sat next to him and told him that if he wanted he'd let Alan board with him and even give him a job as his assistant. For Alan, who knew that Jim was a handyman who got his work by word of mouth and recommendation, it was a godsend. He had just done his GCSEs and therefore could leave school whenever he wanted, and this offer gave him the chance of a new life.

The next 5 years were the happiest Alan had ever known. Jim was an excellent teacher and genuinely cared for Alan. Under Jim's tutelage Alan became a very competent handyman acquiring skills in a wide range of practical areas. Jim, also not a very good-looking man, even educated Alan in the ways of women. Well in the ways of women of the night.

The world fell in for Alan when Jim died unexpectedly during a rather adventurous threesome.

'I tried to tell him that he might be too old,' BJ Betty said knowingly to Alan at his cremation. 'But at least he died happy with his boots off and a condom on,' added the 3rd participant of the ménage, Jizzy Jess. Alan had hoped he'd continue to do the same job but with him as boss. However, it soon became clear that Jim had been the perfect buffer between the customer and Alan. Without that buffer Alan's lack of interpersonal skills soon drove the customers away and he found himself needing to look for another job.

After drifting for a year or two he saw the advert for the job of janitor in the Hartlepool Echo. As it turned out the anti-social hours and low pay meant that he was the only qualified applicant. Initially, Alan was excited by the nature of the job. He thought he would have day to day interaction with the residents and might even make friends. How wrong he was. Instead of friendly interaction he got indifference or, even worse, was blanked. They saw him as an employee rather than a human being and only wanted anything to do with him when they needed a problem to be resolved. He soon began to hate them.

Troy's arrival, although initially interesting because of his celebrity status, brought all the unhappiness and hatred to a head. He was the epitome of all that he had come to despise. Despite having everything that anyone could want Troy never showed Alan any empathy nor kindness and even seemed to go out of his way to annoy and upset Alan. That was why Alan had been driven to do what he had done. Alan glanced at the clock on the wall. It was almost time to make Troy pay for being back in Alan's life.

Alan's meticulous observations of the residents and their lifestyle told him that all would be quiet after 12.15, particularly early in the week. The adrenalin was coursing through his veins as he checked all was ready in the holdall, which he had carefully placed by the door. He didn't want any last-minute panic trying to find it.

Deadly Circle/DC Poolie

Having shut the door, this time quietly, and given Cleo some cat snacks to keep her company he made his way to the control room. It was really a combination of a stock room and utility control room, but the latter sounded more important. Knowing that there would now be nobody about he found the control switch he needed and turned it to the OFF setting. Now when he went into any public area the automatic lights would not come on and he could remain hidden in the dark. The stairwell was conveniently located next to the control room, and he would use the stairs to reach the penthouse floor. He couldn't use the lifts as they would be noisy, and their light system was on a different circuit.

Not being as fit as someone his age should, he paused when he reached the landing of the top floor. Not only would this short break allow him to get his breath back it would also give him a chance to sort things out before going into the apartment. His eyes had become accustomed enough to the darkness that he could open the hold-all and remove the all-important shopping bag. Feeling rested and extremely motivated he prepared himself to move on. In his right hand he held the shopping bag and his set of master keys and in his left hand he had the holdall.

'What do we have here then?' He froze as he heard these words coming from the dark corner behind him. As he tried to make sense of what was going on he felt his right shoulder being grabbed causing him to slightly lose his balance in the dark. Almost simultaneously there was a sharp, burning sensation coming from his throat. The life drained instantly from his body as a shadowy figure, wearing a gimp mask, drew a Stanley knife from right to left in a quick and practised move

223

across his jugular. He certainly didn't hear the sound of the resulting arterial spray hitting the glass panel of the door he had, moments before, been going to walk through. Nor did he hear the carrier bag full of the fetid fish heads hit the floor. They had been bought earlier at Hartlepool's fish market with the intention of, once having been placed in Troy's heating duct, trying to cause a real stink in Troy's life.

The shadowy figure stepped over the fallen body and prised the master keys from its clenched hands.

'Messy bugger,' he laughed to himself as, with gloved hands, he pushed the door open making sure that he didn't get any blood splatter on his gloves. 'At least you won't have to clean it up in the morning.' And with that he slipped through the door and turned left towards Troy's apartment.

He walked slowly along the corridor towards Troy's apartment in the darkness, careful not to make a noise. He was well familiar with the surroundings as he had lived in the same apartment block previously. Now that he had the janitor's master key in his hand entry to the penthouse would be easy. His ear pressed firmly against the door told him all was quiet inside and Troy was most likely asleep. He took a last look around the corridor now that his eyes had adjusted to the darkness and then he turned the key and slowly entered the apartment. The first thing he noticed was that there was a table lamp left on in the lounge area.

'Very kind of you Troy, leaving a light on for me like that. Wouldn't want to trip over anything would I?' he whispered under his breath.

He took a minute to look around the plush penthouse apartment and shook his head.

'How could a bastard like you think you deserved all this? Well now it's time to pay and pay you will.' He spat out the words with his anger rising by the second.

He made his way silently to the master bedroom where he knew his target would be sleeping. Pulling a wooden cosh from under his coat he opened the bedroom door. Troy lay asleep on his back, snoring contentedly it seemed.

'Payback time Troy, Wakey Wakey!' he shouted loudly.

Troy woke startled, but before he had time to grasp his situation, he was knocked unconscious by a vicious and well-aimed blow across his forehead. His assailant then dragged him off the bed and along the floor into the living area. He dropped Troy's listless body to the floor and moved a dining chair into the centre of the room. He pulled Troy up onto the chair and, removing a bundle of cable ties from his pocket, he fastened him securely to the chair. A snap of gaffer tape around his mouth would stop him from calling out with just enough gap around his nose to allow him to breath. He then got a bowl of cold water and splashed it liberally on his face. This brought Troy back to consciousness. Troy tried to focus on his assailant who he could now see was wearing a rubber face mask.

'Glad you are back with us now boy. I want you to enjoy as much as possible of your last day on earth.'

He was certain he recognised the muffled voice behind the mask, but he couldn't gather his thoughts coherently enough to make sense of what was happening to him.

'Thought you had come back home to be the local hero did you? Well, that was never going to be the case. No one can treat me as you did and not expect a response. That bitch from

225

Birmingham found that out sure enough. Just like the others did.'

Troy felt himself beginning to drift out of consciousness again until his attacker's voice screamed at him.

'Stay awake you twat, this is your last day, and you don't want to miss a second of the fun.'

With that he brought the cosh down hard across the back of Troy's hand. The pain was excruciating, and he cried out as much as he could given the constraints of the gaffer tape. He wriggled and struggled to free himself from the ties but to no avail. His eyes were now wide open showing his fear and pain.

'Who was this?' he thought, and what had he ever done to him to cause such hatred. Then suddenly he felt more pain as the cosh was smashed across his left knee.

'Try playing football now my friend. Don't worry a comeback is not an option for you since you won't be around much longer.'

'I was going to have you looking like you had thrown yourself off the balcony just like I did with her from Birmingham. Stupid bitch. Then I decided that was too quick for you. I intend to enjoy myself with you first.' He paused for a second savouring the moment, 'When we first met, I looked after you like a brother. Little did I know what a backstabbing bastard you are! But you are going to pay for that now I promise.'

Troy tried to speak but it was impossible behind the gaffer tape.

'Okay you've got something to say. Have you? Well, I swear if you scream or shout out your life will be over before you finish the first word.'

Deadly Circle/DC Poolie

He moved closer to Troy with an evil looking blade in his hand. He then ran the blade across Troy's neck and laughed loudly.

'Maybe I should just slit your throat now? Or maybe you could lose an eyeball or your tongue even. That's not much use to you at the moment is it?'

He ran the blade along the line of Troy's mouth with enough force to make a slit just enough so that he could make himself understood. A trickle of blood started to run down from the corner of Troy's mouth. Seconds later that trickle seemed more like a constant flow as the cut opened up.

'Oh dear, I seem to have nicked you and made you bleed. Such a shame. Still, I think that is the least of your worries at the moment.'

He took two steps back and sat on the sofa directly in front of Troy. Troy stared at his assailant trying to unscramble his thoughts.

The intruder was dressed in fairly loose-fitting clothes. His black trousers were probably elasticated joggers and above the waist he wore a warm fleecy type of jacket of the same colour. He seemed relaxed sitting there with his legs uncrossed and his cosh resting on his left thigh. The already nightmarish image of this sick individual was emphasised by the fact that he was not wearing a ski mask, or something similar as might be expected, but a leather gimp mask with a zip for a mouth. Troy's sphincter contracted involuntarily at the thought of there being a sexual element to this attack as well. Surely not. He'd only just escaped such a fate back in prison.

'Come on then Superstar. Speak up. I thought you had something to say. Something to ask.'

227

Deadly Circle/DC Poolie

Troy, whose brain was receiving messages of pain from all over his body, tried to ignore the agony emanating from his latest wound. The so-called nick was in fact a sizeable gash to the side of his mouth caused deliberately by the final flourish the bastard had performed when dragging the Stanley knife across the tape. He knew he needed to try to communicate but was worried about the amount of blood he could feel coming out of that wound. Almost mimicking the actions, or so he presumed, of a ventriloquist he constricted the muscles on the damaged side of the mouth and at the same time relaxed them on the other side in the hope that it would allow him to speak without opening the wound even more.

The attacker leaned forward in an exasperated fashion pretending he couldn't understand Troy.

'What was that you said, you bastard?' He then made some mumbling sounds, obviously mimicking Troy's efforts at speech, to try to make Troy believe he had been incoherent. He was in control and Troy needed to be continually reminded of this.

Troy, however, knew this wasn't in fact true when the attacker continued, 'Come on boy speak up. I bet you were asking who I was and why I was doing this.'

Troy realised that the man had heard him well enough. He hadn't implied that Troy had pleaded for his life like most would do. He had just simply paraphrased Troy's two questions. Questions that most people in Troy's situation wouldn't ask. They'd just want to get out of this safely and knowing the identity of the assailant certainly could be hindrance to that happening.

Deadly Circle/DC Poolie

'I tell you what. I will give you clues to my identity. Each time you can't guess who I am my cosh will come out to play again. Does that sound fair?' he paused for a second not really waiting for an answer, 'Actually I love the sound of this game. We will play it anyway.'

He got up and, because of Troy being seated, loomed like the Grim Reaper over him.

'I've known you for years and years,' he started.

Troy shook his head in reply. Almost immediately he felt the cosh hit his damaged ankle and the sound of a muffled scream escaped through the narrow slit in the tape.

'I looked after you when you came into my life.'

Troy searched his brain for an answer. He didn't want another blow from the cosh.

'Tom Collins,' he called out knowing this wasn't true.

The bastard had now gone around behind him, and he felt another sharp pain, this on the back of his neck, as the cosh found a new target.

'Did you say Tom Collins? Your first manager as a schoolboy. You sad fuck! If he were alive he'd be at least 90.' With that his neck received another blow. 'New rule. No guess or a crap one means you get hit twice for being such a loser.'

He appeared once more, but now to Troy's left.

'I lost my job in the team because of you. Come on I will give you 5 seconds. And yes I am in the football industry too.'

Troy knew he'd been given a lifeline and plucked a more recent name from the air,

'Jimmy Dunne,' he said hopefully.

This time the blow came first before the sarcastic put down. His inner thigh was the latest location for a searing pain, but Troy knew that if this twat had hit the intended target then any potential future would have involved singing soprano in a choir and no chance of progeny either. He let out a continuous high-pitched squeal and rolled, as best he could, from to side to side to fool the attacker that the very worst had indeed been done.

'What that loser? He hasn't the brains to do something as intelligent as this.'

Seemingly satisfied the assailant stepped back once more to be centre stage in Troy's soon to be ended life.

'Not being an arse man, well with men that is, I think that pain will be the most I can give you for a while.' He stopped talking again clearly planning his next move.

'I tell you what. I will make it easy for you. You got me transferred and with that my chance of playing for England disappeared.'

Troy blinked suddenly in realisation. 'Surely it can't be?'

'I brought you here to end your football career like you did mine.'

As he was saying this he was removing the gimp mask. Had it not been a case of life and death the sight of a psychopath struggling to get a sweaty leather piece of bondage clothing off would have been comical.

'Think I've read somewhere that you should use talcum powder to help with that,' Troy snidely remarked, 'Bob!'

With a final tug the mask came off and flew across the room and there in front of Troy stood Bob Scott. Erstwhile Aston Villa player, until Troy took his place, and now incumbent Hartlepool United manager who, supposedly, had thrown Troy a footballing lifeline by recruiting him.

Deadly Circle/DC Poolie

'That's better,' Bob said, leaning in towards Troy in a menacing way. 'I suppose I will have to finish off what I've started.'

He looked around the living area as if seeking inspiration. When he finally turned back to Troy an evil smile crossed his face, 'I don't know why I said that. I was always going to kill you.'

Chapter 16

Troy's imagination was working overtime. One part of his brain was being analytical and trying to assess and understand all that had transpired whilst the other part was freewheeling into abject panic. He needed to try to calm Bob down. To try to gain some semblance of control in this seemingly hopeless situation. While that one part of his brain was coming up with possible solutions, 'Keep him talking' and 'Get him to remember the good times' the other part was giving in, accepting that life, in this current form was coming to an end. A gruesome, painful and very unpleasant end.

'No!', he thought as the positive part of the brain took over once more, 'You can't just give up. You're a fighter. You always have been. You have got to try.'

'Yes and die trying. Maybe in an even more sadistic way,' chimed in the negative part.

Troy spoke slowly and passionately. Or at least he was trying to put in as much passion as the slit in the tape around his mouth would allow.

'Bob, you don't have to do this.' No response.

'We were, we are, friends.' Bob was seemingly paying no attention to his pleading.

'I won't tell anyone. You need help and I will get it for you.'

232

Deadly Circle/DC Poolie

This last argument had the exact opposite reaction to the one Troy had hoped for. He turned around looking even more angry and manic than before, if that were possible, with one hand thrust into his jacket pocket.

'You! You help me?' his voice quavered with rage, 'You destroyed me. You took away my hopes and dreams. You set my life on a downward spiral.'

Troy needed to say something. To somehow contradict this.

'No, I didn't. I was your teammate.'

Even as this last word was coming out of Troy's mouth Bob was holding up his hand telling him to shut up.

'I heard you. You see.' His face was reddening with anger as he recalled the string of events, 'After training I heard you in the ear of the manager. "I could be much more use to the team if I were to play in the middle of the pitch",' Bob affected a wheedling, cloying voice trying to mock Troy. '"I would create and score more goals than we currently are. I could get us higher up the table". You bastard you were slagging me off to the manager and trying to muscle your way in. I had helped you. Been supportive of you and here you were throwing me under the bus.'

Troy's body visibly lost energy as he, too, remembered that conversation. One that he had kept hidden, until then, in the very depths of his memory. It certainly wasn't his finest hour in his life. On the other hand, it also wasn't anywhere near the worst thing he had done.

'I've hated you from that moment on,' Bob continued. 'I was grateful to the manager for not listening to you but then I had that slight calf injury, and you were given your chance.

233

Deadly Circle/DC Poolie

One you relished and made the most of. You bastard! After each game during my injury I heard, or my mates also told me that they heard, you were sticking the knife into my back. Saying to anyone that mattered that you made the team better by playing in that position. That Bob Scott was a has-been.'

Troy just stared at Bob. Knowing now the justification for this hatred. Knowing that he wasn't going to be able to change things. Knowing that he was going to die.

'From being on the cusp of playing for my country I found myself on the scrap heap and was sold down a division in the next transfer window. I had been a confident player until then but your actions, somehow, took that all away from me and here I am now managing a team with no real future. Sid Hackett almost had a heart attack when I suggested blowing all of our budget on one player, you. But I insisted. I realised, you understand, that this was my last shot at getting revenge. And boy did I want that.'

With that Bob pulled something, not quite recognisable to Troy, from his jacket pocket and approached Troy once more. Troy was trying to focus on this new object, this new weapon of destruction, when he was struck with extreme force on the side of his head by the cosh which was still in Bob's other hand. He lost consciousness for a moment or two and when he came round he could feel a wetness hitting his body. Bob was shaking, no squirting, something at him. In blind panic he realised that the liquid hitting was coming from a can of lighter fuel. Any doubt that he might have had was dispelled when the unmistakable smell of fuel became undeniable.

'My career went down in flames,' Bob leered at the distressed man sitting tied in front of him. 'Now I will end yours the same way. I will watch you burn. I will make you squirm. And I will see the panic, pain and then resolution in your eyes.'

With that he snapped off another bit of gaffer tape a fastened it over the original piece.

'You will die to the sound of your own screams, and I will watch it happen. Don't worry once you're dead I will put out the fire. I don't want anyone else to suffer. After all I'm not a mad man.'

He put his hand back into his jacket pocket and pulled out a lighter.

'It almost feels a shame that this must end so soon.'

Troy heard this sentence followed by a click and the lighter produced a bright yellow flame. A flame that he knew could extinguish his own.

Troy shut his eyes. He had hated fire for as long as he could remember. When he had just started secondary school his next-door neighbours' house had been engulfed by flames when a chip pan fire had got out of control. With his eyes shut he was back there watching his best friend's father run back into the flames to save the pet Labrador. The human inhabitants, once they realised, they could do nothing to stop the spread of the fire, had evacuated themselves into the back garden.

From his vantage point in his bedroom, at the back of his detached house, he looked down on a family losing everything they had in the world. And through his window he could hear his friend shouting the name of his beloved pet. He was struggling violently in the arms of his much bigger brother who was trying to prevent him from rushing back into the house to get the dog. His father, much more reluctantly, had gone in instead. No matter how long Troy continued to stare at the back door neither the father nor the dog came out. The memories of a family's life ruined by fire caused Troy to open his eyes again and his stared at the naked flame of the lighter.

There was a loud, sudden noise and a whoosh of air which caused the flame to flicker. The front door had burst open, and another figure also dressed in dark colours had come rushing in.

Troy wondered for a moment whether he was hallucinating or having a weird sci-fiction dream where he was seeing himself, but from another dimension. Because the physique and the face, from what he could see in the confusion, looked just like Troy.

Something similar must have been going through Bob's mind because his reaction was to look at the intruder and then quickly back at Troy as if to make sure that he was still there.

Troy got a better look as the new guy, Alternative Troy as we shall call him for the moment, bundled into Bob, knocking him to the floor sending the lighter, with the flame still glowing, out of his hand so that it landed just a few feet from Troy. Troy watched on, incapable of anything apart from spectating, as the two well matched figures rolled around the floor taking it in turn to try to land a painful punch, kick or knee. It soon became apparent that Alternative Troy was getting the upper hand. Initially he was landing blows, and more solid ones, in the ratio of 2:1 and then it became 3:1. He seemed also to have more stamina for such a fight and when Troy caught a glimpse of their eyes, he could see a fire and determination in those belonging to Alternative Troy that, to

236

Deadly Circle/DC Poolie

Troy's satisfaction, was missing from Bob's. In fact, Bob seemed to have given up and was trying to work himself free of Alternative Troy's clutches. His focus seemed to be on the balcony. That was not a sensible means of escape in Troy's, now hopeful, eyes. That hope soon faded when he became aware of smoke and then small flames emanating from the edge of the white rug on which Troy's chair was situated.

Realising the danger of the situation, with him still doused in lighter fuel, he started to make as loud a noise as possible to try and summon help, but they didn't, or couldn't, hear him. He knew that Bob would have been pleased to see him in such a predicament but hoped that Alternative Troy, who looked similar and slightly older than him, would try to help him. On the other side of the room, they were now having more of a stand-up fight next to the unlocked balcony doors.

Alternative Troy was still in the ascendancy, and it looked like he would soon be victorious but then his left foot slipped on the door mat by the windows and suddenly Bob was free. Alternative Troy was still between him and the door leading to the penthouse landing and Bob, who clearly didn't feel he could overpower the other guy, opened the balcony windows and made straight for the railing.

Alternative Troy was getting back to his feet to follow when he heard a bang and saw that Troy, who in trying to get away from the fire, had toppled the chair over. He was lying prostrate on top of his chair with quite large flames closing in. He looked out to the balcony and saw Bob clambering over the railing. Alternative Troy looked back at Troy and then out to the balcony once more. Clearly, he was deciding what to do.

237

Deadly Circle/DC Poolie

He ran to where Troy was and pulled Troy and the chair clear of the rug. He then went over to the sink and filled the washing up bowl with cold water. It took three return visits to the sink before he thought he'd got the fire under control. To be certain that there were no lingering embers of the fire he took his jacket off and placed it over where the fire had been. Having done what looked like an attempt at a flamenco dance to stamp out any residual fire he picked it up and went to the balcony and looked down.

It has been slow going for Bob. He wasn't as young, nor as fit, as he'd once been. He had used all his core strength to trapeze down, balcony by balcony, to the 2nd floor and he was shattered. His desire for self-preservation made him persevere and he was hanging from the floor of the 2nd balcony, just about to perform another trapeze movement down to the first-floor balcony, when he was distracted by a loud yell from above.

Tiredness and that distraction caused him to lose the purchase of the grip of his right hand and he found himself dangling one handed. And that hand was slipping too. He looked below and saw a turfed area with some flowers.

'Better to try to control it,' he thought. So, he used what little purchase he still had in the left hand, combined with all the remaining core strength he could summon, to swing out slightly before letting go and falling the final two floors.

He experienced a split second's elation as he felt his feet hit their desired soft grassy landing. However, that was very short lived as his right knee crashed into a terracotta plant pot. One he hadn't seen when hanging up there. He let out a massive yell and, after checking he hadn't suffered a broken bone, he got very gingerly to his feet and limped very painfully over to the garden gate. Having opened it he looked left and then right.

'Which way?' Bob mused. To the right was the marina and loads of sailing boats. That was quite near but where could he go to from there? To the left was the town. That made more sense. Just as he started to hobble in that direction, he became aware of a car coming from that direction and with its lights on. If he went that way he would be exposed. It was a single carriageway, brightly lit for night-time security, and there would be nowhere to hide. He knew that, now he was injured, he couldn't win a foot race so he reluctantly turned around and set off, as quickly as his injury and the accompanying excruciating pain would allow, in the direction of the marina.

Seconds later the car parked outside the entrance of the building and the front doors were already opening. It was all done so quickly that the driver had taken up almost three parking spaces.

Alternative Troy had been watching things progress. The fight had taken more out of him than he realised, and his energy levels had really fallen once the danger was over. He had seen Bob's descent and his subsequent flight and now he was watching Charlie and Dave get out of Dave's company Mazda.

They instinctively made to go into the apartments but were stopped in their tracks by a yell from above. They looked up and saw Troy. At least it looked like Troy but when the person called down to them again Charlie was sure that it wasn't him. Same accent different tone.

239

Deadly Circle/DC Poolie

'I'm the one who called you,' the person on the balcony yelled. 'Roy is quite badly hurt but safe. The real killer is Bob Scott, and he's just got away.'

'Did he say, Roy?' Dave enquired of Charlie.

'I think so but that's irrelevant,' Charlie replied in an irritated voice. 'We need to find Bob Scott. That's what we must do now.' He looked up and called to the balcony. 'Which way did he go?'

'He's gone off in the direction of the marina. He fell from the 2nd floor and has injured his leg. He was limping badly and won't be able to go very far, or fast, on foot. You go after him I will look after Roy.'

'You see he did say Roy,' Dave mused. Charlie just shook his head and took out his mobile.

First he called WPC Angela Hart.

'Angela things have moved on a pace here. Bob Scott has attacked Troy in his apartment he is on the run somewhere around the marina area here. Could do with your assistance.'

'I'm in Middlesbrough at the moment taking a bit of down time, but I want to be involved with this. I'll organise the troops and I'll be with you as soon as possible.'

Chapter 17

Charlie called Cliff to check his and Andy's location. Cliff stopped riding his pristine looking electric bike and got off it. The bike was actually two years old, but he hadn't used it much recently. It was, in reality, a purchase made out of desperation. He had been desperate to get his leg over but, a bike, wasn't the object of this desire.

In fact. it was his first attempt to find a woman in his life after his wife had died. It was towards the end of lockdown, when restrictions were being relaxed a bit, and when he was out walking with the guys he had become enthralled by this pretty petite woman who flew past them every day on the promenade.

Having ensured that she had no rings on her left hand he made his excuses to the guys one day and tried to intercept her. His plan was to ask her if he could ride along. The spanner in the works of this plan was that the only bike available to him was his poor dead wife's three speeder with a large basket on the front.

Two days on the trot he funnelled in behind her but each time he was quickly outpaced and left behind. A TV advert for an electric bike came to his rescue and he made an expensive online purchase fifteen minutes later. It took three weeks, not only were lockdown prices high but supply was far exceeded by demand, for the bike to arrive.

Deadly Circle/DC Poolie

After two days of practice, he was ready and went off to execute the plan. Unfortunately, she wasn't alone. Her new cycling companion was a youngish and annoyingly handsome man wearing lycra shorts, which appeared very well filled with, what Cliff hoped was, just comfort padding. To make matters worse when he overtook the two of them, which was now easy thanks to the electrical back up, he saw that she was now wearing a diamond engagement ring.

After that the bike had lost its allure. Having got off his bike he carefully leant 'the white elephant', as he had dubbed it, against his hip. He could see that the caller was Charlie, so he took the call.

'Whereabouts are you two now Cliff? Troy's been attacked in his apartment, think he's in a bad way.'

'Attacked by who?' Cliff asked in surprise. 'We are approaching the marina arcade from the other side just like you asked us to. We are about 50 yards from the start of the arcade.'

'Everything's confused over here but it seems it was Bob Scott.'

'What the fuck! Bob Scott! I know he was on that list of ex Villa personnel, but I would never have suspected him.'

'Neither would I but he is definitely in the frame now. He's done a runner from the apartment block and is probably around this area still. He has hurt his leg or ankle jumping from one of the balconies to escape so he won't be moving very fast.'

'If you and Andy could check around the marina area for him that would be great. Don't think he will have got far.'

'Of course, will do. Hope Troy's going to be ok.'

Deadly Circle/DC Poolie

Cliff turned to where he expected to find Andy but wasn't particularly surprised when he wasn't there. He craned his neck first one way and then the other. He had almost done a full 360 search when he spied the mobility scooter parked to the side of the brothel.

In the doorway he could just about make out two figures engaged in conversation. The smaller one on the right, who looked like he had basset hound ears, was Andy in his disgusting Russian hat.

As he got closer to the building Andy saw him and called out, 'I was just explaining things to Norman. We got off on the wrong foot last time. I've told him that we know that Troy wasn't the attacker and that we are close to find the bastard who did it.'

'Aye that's right,' added Norman. 'Me and Andy are sweet now and I've told him that he can get a special members' card at a discount if he sorts this out.'

Andy looked like he'd won the lottery and shook Norman's hand.

'Come on Andy, you randy old goat, we have a job to do, fire up that scooter and let's find Troy's attacker,' Cliff said, as he straddled his electric bike.

Cliff spent the next couple of minutes filling in a bemused Andy on what he knew so far.

They had gone about 30 yards when Cliff spoke again, 'Where to start looking that's the thing? What would you do in his shoes Andy?'

'Don't think I'd want to be in them shoes, but I'm pretty sure I wouldn't be moving along the front of these bars. It may be late, but some bars are still open and plenty of folk can clock you. He is the manager of the local football team after all and as such quite well known.'

'Andy. Let's go round the back. If he's still around here, it's more likely he will be hiding or moving along where it's less populated.'

The pair made their way to the end of the parade and around the back of the buildings. The difference between the front and back of the bars was startling. Bright lights and loud music replaced by darkness and dustbins. It took a while for the pair to adjust their eyes to be able to see even a few feet in front. The headlights on Andy's mobility scooter and Cliff's electric pedal bike helped somewhat, but still they had to be careful to avoid the potholes and broken glass which were everywhere.

'Not much chance of seeing anyone around here, a few streetlamps or security lights would help,' offered Andy.

'Think you are right their pal,' said Cliff. 'We'll make our way along. You never know we might get lucky.'

A sudden movement, probably a cat or a rat, fired into life the one working security light in the area much to the annoyance of a young guy and a woman getting very friendly at the back of one of the bars.

'Not as lucky as some it seems,' Andy chuckled. 'Better than watching those internet porn shows. Brings back a few memories don't you think mate.'

'Behave yourself you horny get. We have an important job to do here. Anyway, you do alright in that department for your age I reckon.'

'I have my moments my friend but not as many as I would like. Not as many as you my old mate. Do you think we

Deadly Circle/DC Poolie

don't know what you get up to when you're not with us? We've heard things.' Andy's reply came with a barely hidden chuckle.

The pair, now with Cliff sporting a reddening face, moved along checking every dark corner and alcove they could identity as a potential hiding place. However, they hadn't noticed, just around fifty feet or so ahead of them, the dark figure hiding behind an industrial size waste skip which was moving slowly so as not to be seen.

Bob Scott was intent on keeping himself in front of the two hunters. He had not wanted any CCTV security cameras capturing him or his car around Troy's apartment, so he had parked well away from there. Now that his plan had gone wrong, and he was in real pain with his injured leg, he was cursing himself for not having a backup plan as well.

He just couldn't understand why everyone seemed to think highly of Troy. Couldn't they see what a backstabbing piece of shit he was. His hatred for Troy Harvey was reaching new heights as the pain in his leg increased. And now these two old bastards were on his case. If he were fit he'd simply kill the bastards, but he had no weapons and couldn't put any real weight on his damaged leg. He'd be crap in a fight even against Compo and Foggy. No, the dark was his friend and stealth were the nearest thing he had to a weapon. As he sat in the darkness his thoughts drifted back to the night of the murder.

He had been very proud of the plan he had come up with and he was sure that nothing could go wrong. His revenge on Troy Harvey, and Zoe Young, would soon be complete. For weeks he

245

Deadly Circle/DC Poolie

had been shadowing Troy and making notes and observations about his behaviour. Finally, he felt he was ready to implement his plan, and, in truth, it went better than he expected.

He had chosen the night of the Stockport match. He knew that he had infuriated many of the team by showing Troy special treatment. However, Troy played in that game he knew that was going to substitute him and that Troy would react badly to this. Before the match he left team coach, Harry Garside, to take the team talk and warm up session while he headed down to the marina and to Troy's apartment.

Scott had kept a key for the apartment since the time when he lived there during his first months in Hartlepool. He knew where the CCTV cameras were and avoided them as he made his way into Troy's home. Knowing, from his time at Villa, that Troy always drank milk from the bottle to line his stomach before a heavy session, he headed straight for the large American fridge in the corner. He took out an open bottle of milk and added to it a dose of the drug Rohypnol. More than enough to render Troy unconscious for a significant amount of time.

Troy's overreaction, by storming home when substituted, was perfect. He knew that when he slipped back to the apartment after the team debrief Troy would already be incapacitated. After gently knocking he let himself in and made sure that Troy was dead to the world. He had heard Charlie talking to Troy about their texting exchanges and sought out Troy's phone. Now he was ready for phase 2.

With his official club tracksuit on and his hoodie pulled over his head he could easily be taken for Troy at a quick glance. Even more so when he donned Troy's expensive sunglasses.

This time when he left the apartment, he didn't hide himself fully from the CCTV. It was too early for chatting to Charlie so, having used Troy's right thumb to biometrically access his phone, he needed to make sure that the phone didn't lock itself again.

This soon became a burden but fortunately, because of Troy's antics earlier, Charlie soon texted him. He took great pleasure in pretending to slag himself off and once the conversation finished he went to a bar to find a young lady. One similar to the one mentioned in the final text and who could be mistaken for the bitch Zoe.

Although he left with her, as his plan required, he made up an excuse and headed towards his car which was parked near, but out of sight of, Troy's apartment. Zoe Young, the cow who had caused him so much grief in Birmingham, was lying drugged in the boot of the car.

It had been so easy to abduct her the day before even in broad daylight. She deserved what she had coming to her. Getting her up to the apartment had been annoying but uneventful and he knew that CCTV would make it look like Troy had taken her up.

Once in the apartment he knew he was going to succeed. He had time to enjoy himself and as the coroner's report would say he did that both roughly and in her every orifice. He took great pleasure in causing her as much pain as possible. The only tricky bit was when he had to manipulate her so that she could scratch Troy. Troy's other injuries he delighted in causing himself.

247

Deadly Circle/DC Poolie

Before the final act he planted the Rohypnol in the toilet cistern and trashed the apartment. Finally, under the cover of darkness he dragged her out onto the balcony, hoisted her limp body above his head and threw her to her death. He then took one risk and used Troy's torch app on the phone to see what had happened to her.

He felt a rush of adrenaline a surge of pure joy when he saw that she had landed on the railing below and that it pierced through her chest. His final job, before leaving the apartment, was to place the phone back next to Troy who he had left lying face down on his bed. As he shut the apartment door he smiled thinking of what was to come for Troy.

Those wonderful memories gave him a renewed energy and he started to think of what he needed to do to get out of the mess he now found himself in.

. . . .

The conquering hero had come back into the living area from the balcony. The first thing he did was to hoist Troy, together with the attached chair, back into the upright position. He needed time to think so he stood back for a second to assess what to do first. There were some obvious contusions and what might be broken bones caused by the cosh. He had seen it lying on the floor next to the sofa. Bob had dropped it when he had burst in and fortunately, for him, Bob had not got hold of it during the ensuing fight. Even though the second layer of tape masked any clear evidence, as to the scope of the damage, it was clear from the blood trail, down one side of the mouth which then continued in a thick pattern onto Troy's, once

248

white, sweatshirt that Troy had already lost a lot of blood. He picked up the Stanley knife, this time left by Bob on the table when he had taken the lighter out and cut the zip ties which bound Troy to the chair. He then helped Troy, taking 90 percent of Troy's weight for him, over to the sofa.

For the moment he left the tape bound and went once more back to the sink area and selected what looked like the cleanest of the washing up towels, which were hanging in a neat row. He could now repeat the the slit cut which Bob had made. However, he ensured that his cut stopped well before it reached any flesh. With his other hand he swiftly placed the towel over where he thought the cut was. He didn't want Troy to lose any more blood. Seeing no evidence of blood escaping he carefully lifted Troy's hand so that he was now in control of the towel.

Troy, now able to try to communicate spoke, 'Thank you. Who are you? Why do you look so much like me?'

'All in good time, little one. I need to make sure I get you taken care of first,' came the reply as he turned his back on Troy. Troy was even more perplexed when he thought he heard his hero say. 'Just like I always have.'

Before he could follow this up he heard that same voice on the phone.

'Yes, we need an ambulance urgently. There's been an assault at 48 Waterside Apartments in the marina complex,' he paused to listen and then added. 'There has been an attack with a heavy cosh. Looks like all over the body, including the head, and there is at least one knife wound. Please get here as soon as you can.' After another pause he continued. 'Also, there is a dead body in the stairwell on the top floor. I think the police are aware.' With that he hung up and turned back to Troy. 'While we are waiting we can try to get a little liquid into you down the good side of your mouth. You must be really dehydrated. I'll put the kettle on.'

Meanwhile Charlie and Dave decided to make their way from the apartment block and toward the marina bar area. As it was now so late some of the bars and restaurants had closed for the night. However, some of the places with late licenses remained open and there were a good number of people congregating both inside and outside of them.

Between the pair and the start of the built-up commercial area was a large patch of waste ground. On this were placed two forty-foot yachts which had been lifted out of the water for repairs or paintwork, a large mound of builder's rubble and an electricity substation. Plenty of places for someone to stay out of sight especially in the total darkness which surrounded them.

'I can hardly see you in this darkness Dave. Not much chance of seeing someone who doesn't want to be seen.'

'Can't disagree with you there Charlie boy, but a sudden thought has just occurred to your very useful friend,' Dave said.

'Who is this very useful friend, and how do you know he has had this sudden thought?' mocked Charlie.

'Because it's me stupid! I am about to save the day with my miraculous feat of forward thinking and planning.'

'Well can you get your miraculous feet moving and let's get searching,' a frustrated Charlie shouted.

'Just give me two minutes while I go back to the car and when I return all will be revealed. Literally.'

Deadly Circle/DC Poolie

Dave jogged back to his borrowed company car and returned carrying a medium sized cardboard box.

'These my buddy are the latest thing in led hand-lamps. The MT14 gives you 1000lumens of light and has an incredible beam range of over 300 metres. Used officially by the US army and ……..'

'For fucks sake Dave you are not trying to sell me one. We just need them to work,' Charlie was getting more and more frustrated with his ex-salesman friend and felt no compunction in cutting him short.

'OK OK,' Dave responded.

He pressed the button and Charlie had to admit it was impressive. The beam lit up a good portion of the waste-ground and beyond.

'For once your salesman bullshit and reality have collided and came up with the truth. These are very good. I have to agree,' Charlie conceded.

'Now let's use them and find the bastard who has caused all this trouble and hurt lots of good people,' said Charlie.

'I'm with you my mate, but while we are discussing various degrees of night vision, would you know which creature has the greatest degree of night vision?'

'For Christ's sake Dave! You can be so fucking annoying. I was not aware we were discussing various degrees of night vision and no, I don't know and at this moment I don't bloody care. I'm looking for a killer.'

'Well since you asked so politely, I'll tell you. The answer is the owl. So, you know now. One day you may be grateful for that information.'

Deadly Circle/DC Poolie

'Well, I can't fucking wait for that day. Now stick your fascinating facts up your arse and let's find Bob Scott,' Charlie fumed.

'Charming,' Dave grinned at his mate and received a friendly clip around the ear for his trouble.

The pair of old friends made their way across to the two yachts, each climbed on board one of the vessels and searched around the deck. There was nothing unusual to be seen on the decks and the cabin doors were both securely locked.

With their powerful hand-lamps leading the way they searched around the enormous pile of rubble and the substation and were happy that, wherever Bob Scott was, he was not hiding anywhere on this piece of waste ground.

....

'Billy. I don't get it. You are my big brother, and I don't remember you at all. Was it so bad that I pushed you and those dreadful people out of my life forever?' Troy was talking to the back of Billy's head as he was replacing the tea mug onto the table. 'How is that even possible?'

'Well to be fair it was only Father who was a bastard. Mummy had her heart in the right place and I'm sure she didn't really know what was going on.' Billy was now back looking at his younger brother.

'You killed to protect me though,' Troy said incredulously. 'And the thanks you got was prison and loneliness.'

'And eventually a beating.'

'A beating? Who from?'

252

Deadly Circle/DC Poolie

Even though his face was swollen, with tape hiding his mouth shape, Billy could clearly see Troy's genuine concern.

He looked down knowing the pain his next statement would cause his brother, 'From you.' He then reminded Troy of the incident in Newcastle.

'That was you. I'm so sorry. I was drunk and fearing for my girlfriend. That must have really upset you.'

'Troy, I've been a messed-up fuck since Father did what he did to me. All that kept me going was reuniting with you. When I couldn't find you I drifted here and there living the life of a real screw up. Then I found you. I was so excited.' Troy was focusing on his older brother soaking up this tragic story and not wanting to interrupt, 'When you did that to me something snapped in me.'

He went on to explain his recent actions and that he was even pleased that Troy was in prison. That Troy was experiencing something of the life he himself had had to endure when he was younger.

Troy knew he couldn't even try to understand what Billy had been through, but he resolved there and then that his life's goal, from now on, would be to have Billy close and to help him have as good a life as possible. There was one thing nagging at him though, 'Why did you come here tonight?'

'Well, I realised, when I saw you had been released, that maybe we had another chance and I got here early in the evening hoping to chat to you. In prison you learn to be patient and how to kill time, so I just waited,' Troy smiled, and thought how true that was. And he had only been inside for a few weeks, 'Well I saw the comings and goings of your friends. Then I saw the janitor loitering around. He was a real strange guy. I was worried for you.'

'Was?' interrupted Troy.

'Yes, He's dead. I found his body in the stairwell,' Troy cursed himself for not asking sooner. He had heard what Billy had said to the ambulance people. 'A real bloody death I think. Thank God it was dark, and I couldn't see properly. Bob must have taken that knife to him.'

'I didn't like him much, but nobody deserves that,' mused Troy. 'Go on with your story.'

'Well then I saw this guy arrive, didn't see him clearly, and he put on that gimp mask. He went up the stairs first. I was really scared. He looked like he meant to do real harm. I was about to follow when the janitor reappeared and went up the same set of stairs. I didn't know what to do then so I waited ten minutes and slowly followed.'

'I'm so grateful you did,' said Troy.

'When I found the body I knew you were in trouble. I remembered I had picked up one of you mate's flyers in the pub, so I called him on the number he had put on the poster. I wasn't going to call the police for help, and I knew I might fail on my own.'

In the distance Billy heard the sound of sirens and went out onto the balcony to check. The night sky was awash with blue lights. As well as the ambulance which was turning into the road there were at least five police cars approaching from all corners of Hartlepool. For seemingly the first time in his life Billy realised that he had no fear of such a strong police presence.

Deadly Circle/DC Poolie

…………

Cliff and Andy were carefully making their way on their vehicles, headlights shining into the dark corners and alcoves, but no luck so far at finding their quarry. The fugitive meanwhile was shuffling his way along keeping himself a distance in front of his hunters. His injured leg was incredibly painful, but he knew there was no future in letting it slow him down too much. He had to get to that walkway on top of the lock gate. He had given up hope of getting away in his car on this side of the lock. The old gits had cut him off from that escape route. He had to find another way.

'What do you reckon Cliff? We are almost at the walkway and still no sign. Have we missed him, or has he used another route?' Andy asked.

'No way to know that. All we can do is our best and see where that gets us.' Cliff replied.

Bob Scott heard this exchange as he worked his way along and allowed himself a wry smile.

'These amateurs are no match for me,' he thought. 'I'd be embarrassed to be caught by these grandads.' He could see the lock bridge around 50 metres ahead 'Not far to go now,' he told himself, trying to summon up more energy. The Harbour Master's office was just ahead and below that was the all-important walkway.

Suddenly he heard Andy's mobility scooter picking up speed and stopping directly level with his hiding place behind a stack of empty beer casks. Andy turned the scooter headlight and shone it into the darkness but saw nothing untoward. He then moved off towards the Harbour Masters Office and climbed the exterior stairs to Tim Bentham's office.

Bob Scott saw this as his opportunity to make his escape. Cliff was only yards behind. Andy had now disappeared up into Tim's office. This was his last chance to get away. He gathered his strength and moved out of the shadows and headed as quickly as he could towards the single-track lock bridge.

Cliff spotted him instantly and yelled at him to stop although he knew that it was never going to happen. He held his finger down on the horn on his electric bike to attract Andy's attention.

Scott head down, fighting the pain in his leg, was forcing himself to keep going across the bridge. A shaft of light danced in front of him on the bridge attracting his attention. He looked up to see Charlie and Dave shining their MT14 led 1000 lumen torches directly at him and just about to step onto the far end of the walkway. All he could do now was turn around and hope for the best. Turn around he did but hope was not enough for him today.

The Harbour Master shone the massive spotlight directly at him, blinding him temporarily. He tried to make his way back across the walkway, once his sight recovered. But he saw Cliff coming towards him. He twisted, looking in desperation for a way out, but only succeeded in making his damaged leg give way causing him to stumble against the fence rope.

As that happened Andy, who now had a flare gun in his hand, fired a flare aiming directly at Bob's head. Andy missed by his target by yards, but the shock of this action caused, the already off balance, Bob to tumble headfirst into the dock water.

Up in the Dock Master's office Andy was enjoying himself and he fired a second flare up into the night sky directly above the dock where the stricken killer was thrashing about in the murky water.

Cliff grabbed a life belt from the walkway and threw it into the water.

Andy was down on the bridge now; he too had a lifebelt in his hand which he threw more at Scott than to him it seemed.

'Games up now, you bastard. You will be spending the rest of your life in jail. And you deserve it,' Andy yelled at him.

The flare had attracted Angela Hart and her police squad towards that part of the marina. Blue lights and sirens came from all sides, and they soon had Scott out of the water handcuffed. He was unceremoniously bundled into the back of a police car and whisked off to the station where he was formally arrested and charged.

The four friends hugged each other and congratulated themselves on a job well done.

'Well lads we should all be proud of what we have done here, and I'm sure no one will be more grateful than Troy,' Charlie remarked.

'Will he be grateful enough to stand us a pint would you think? Very thirsty work this detective lark,' Andy chimed in.

'Only you Andy would come out with a statement like that. Okay a good drink is in order, but it will have to be at my place as the pubs are all shutting now,' Charlie laughed, and thought to himself that they may be an odd bunch of friends. But they were definitely a great bunch of friends.

It had seemed to take ages for the paramedics to appear out of the lift on the penthouse floor. Apparently, in accordance with the Health and Safety procedure where violence had taken place, they needed to wait for a police presence to accompany them into a potentially hazardous situation.

Troy had been triaged and assessed and he was now now lying on a gurney with a blanket over him. As they made to leave Billy sat back down on the sofa knowing that Troy was in good hands.

'Oi Billy,' Troy called from the gurney. 'You're not getting away with it that easy big brother. You are family and family are allowed to come in the ambulance. Get one of my warm jackets from my wardrobe and shift your arse into gear.'

Billy smiled and jumped to his feet. They were finally back together again.

Chapter 18

Not a word was being spoken. The only sounds were the crisp crack of the delicious fish batter being broken by jaw pressure; the loud slurps of builder's tea being swigged down; the murmurs of delight and contentment and Andy's Richter scale rated belches.

'Bloody Hell Andy!' Charlie exclaimed, voicing the thoughts of everyone else around the table. 'Can't you control that disgusting body of yours? We were all enjoying a moment here.'

'If we were Bedouins, I would be being praised for showing my appreciation of the great food,' replied Andy indignantly as he wiped the dribble of mushy peas with the back of his hand, even though he had a serviette on the table.

The table in question was situated outside Verrills fish and chip shop on the Headland. He ignored the serviette once more when he then proceeded to transfer the green slime, now on the back of his hand, onto the left ear flap of his disgusting brown Russian hat.

'You really are a dirty get!' exclaimed Dave. 'I sometimes wonder why we put up with you. Now Angela, you asked us all here to give us an update. Thanks for treating us to this delicious meal.'

Deadly Circle/DC Poolie

As Angela was opening her mouth to speak Andy felt contrary enough to mutter, 'For my great company and witty repartee.'

'Well guys,' Angela started, looking around the gathered group of Barry, Charlie, Dave, Cliff and lastly Andy, 'Dave is quite right. Not only do I want to update you I have some exciting news for you.'

Angela then went on to update them on the Bob Scott case, 'Well as you know he was remanded in custody and sent to prison after admitting to the murder of Zoe Young.'

Everyone around the table, even Andy, was leaning forward and listening transfixed, 'Well the latest news is that he is seeking to do a deal. A sort of plea bargain.'

'Cheeky bastard!' Cliff couldn't hide his contempt. He hated violence, particularly violence against women.

Angela acknowledged this outburst and went on, 'He has admitted to committing six other murders. Please remember I'm telling you this in confidence, but you guys deserve to know this because we wouldn't have any of this without you.'

'You have our word,' said Charlie, 'Our lips are sealed. Aren't they guys?' Although he was speaking to them all, they knew he was really only saying this for the benefit of one person. Poor old Andy was beginning to feel picked on. Nothing new there.

'These six murders were of female students living in the Aston area of Birmingham,' she paused again to let this news sink in.

'Those poor girls. What a tragic waste.' Dave was thinking of all the posters he had seen stuck forlornly too many of the walls and fences near the Villa ground.

Deadly Circle/DC Poolie

'He is currently on his way to Birmingham. He has agreed to take the detectives, who are working these cases there, to where he has buried the bodies. He wanted to negotiate a reduced sentence but given the heinous nature and large number of murders he won't get that.'

'Thank God!' Barry had been silent up till now and had to express his relief that criminals like Bob couldn't hold justice to ransom.

'What will he get then?' Andy asked, thinking that he'd never give something away for nothing in return.

'He will get slightly better conditions in jail. For example, a slightly bigger cell and maybe his own TV.' Angela sounded slightly bitter at even these concessions, 'More importantly, for him, they will keep him out of harm's way. He will be a marked man in there and plenty wouldn't think twice about killing him.'

'He won't be in an open prison will he?' Dave asked, horrified at the thought.

'No,' Barry chimed in, 'He will still be in a maximum-security prison but probably in a special wing for more vulnerable prisoners.'

'He only offered this after he tried to plead insanity,' Angela sounded angry now. 'Fortunately, the psych evaluations of the three independent psychologists each concluded that he wasn't insane. Just a narcissistic psychopath.'

'Is it wrong for me to hope that his life is made Hell every single day he draws breath?' Dave was still thinking of those poor girls. Nobody around the table contradicted him.

Deadly Circle/DC Poolie

'I'm slightly afraid to ask,' began Charlie. 'You said you had other news?'

'Well last night, thanks to information you passed on, I was part of a raid at the Twisted Bamboo. All this will be released to the press later today. You will be glad to know,' she added, looking directly at Cliff and Charlie, 'that Machete Man resisted arrest and will get extra jail time for doing so with a deadly weapon.'

'A bloody big deadly weapon,' said Charlie, shivering at the thought.

'We recovered £10 million of heroin. That's street value of course.'

'That's great,' said Cliff.

'Anyway, there is more.' Angela was smiling now. 'Because of all your help you all have been put forward for the King's Gallantry Medal and there is talk of a financial reward.'

Dave's reply was something Angela hadn't expected, 'Please don't. We want to remain anonymous. We don't want a target on our backs. I mean you can't be sure you got everyone concerned. Even if you did they probably have friends in other gangs or towns.'

The others, who were initially surprised by Dave's response were now starting to nod in agreement. You could always rely on Dave to think things through. 'And any financial reward could be directed towards something useful. The Headland's Community Centre is in dire need of restoration for example.'

Andy who had perked up at the mention of a reward had to ask, 'Please tell me that you're not shutting down the brothel. I've just bought my gold card membership. I'm hoping to get a free upgrade to platinum.'

Angela was grinning from ear to ear, 'You guys are incredible. Dave I will sort that out for you. And Andy fear not. We have just asked them to maintain a slightly lower profile.'

Barry audibly cleared his throat to get everyone's full attention. 'I have some news too,' he was looking very pleased with himself, 'I have handed in my notice.'

'What? Why?' Charlie was looking perplexed. He had grown very fond of Barry.

'Don't worry Charlie,' Barry patted the shoulder of his concerned friend. 'I was really unhappy with Mr Broadbent's treatment of Troy. And of me for that matter. He left both of us in the lurch and distanced himself from the whole process. I can't work in a corporate system which treats its clients and employees like that. So, I told him so.'

'Good for you,' said Cliff, 'What are you going to do? We've just got used to you. As we are on this topic we might as well address the elephant in the room. Who are you? And what have you done with our Barry?'

Gone was Barry's regular dark 3-piece suit. The white shirt and the usual colourful tie were gone as well. Instead, Barry was wearing beige chinos held up by a black leather belt and underneath his sand-coloured linen jacket he was wearing a dark blue open neck shirt. On his feet his usual shiny brogues had been replaced by some matt black slip-on shoes. Even his hair seemed more casual somehow.

This whole new persona screamed self-confidence and independence. This was no longer line toeing Barry they had first met. 'I'm not going anywhere Cliff. I love it up here. In fact, I'm getting even closer to you lot.'

'How so?'

'Well, I have had this inheritance from my grandfather for a while now. I've sat on it trying to find my path. As you can see I'm going to be myself from now on.'

'Very Zen,' said Dave, pleased with this reference.

'I've just signed the rental documents. I've found some offices just over there.' He jerked his thumb in the direction of the rows of shops below. 'And I'm going to set up a private practice here on the Headland. During this case I've built up relationships with the Police, the Court and the CPS. That's not a bad base to start from.'

'Not a lucrative area my boy,' Charlie was obviously pleased but still concerned whether Barry had thought this fully through.

'I'm not going to turn anyone away. I love this place and the people. People will pay me what they can. I have my inheritance and I have put feelers out on how I can get some more support. One final thing,' he paused for effect. 'I'm going to use you lot as my investigators. That is if you want to. It won't pay much but will be interesting.'

'You try and stop us, and we will do it for expenses only. Welcome to the Headland.'

Cliff, Charlie and Dave couldn't believe that these words had come out of Andy's mouth.

Dave was first to respond, 'Before our mate Andy over commits us all can I just say something about my own plans,' Dave now had the attention of the full group, 'After what has been a very full-on period for us all, my priority is to get a couple of weeks away with the wife. Somewhere nice and warm ideally. I know she has been pushed into the background lately with all that's been going on. After that Barry I'll be happy to do what I can to help you build up your business and, at the same time, help some local people in need.'

'Of course, we all understand that, and it fits in with my plans perfectly. As it stands it will take at least 3 weeks for me to get things fully up and running,' Barry replied. 'You guys surpassed all expectations with the way you have acquitted yourselves these past days and I've been working on how the three of you could become even better at the roles I have planned for you. These days there are many courses for all facets of the field of investigation,' he then looked directly at Cliff, 'There is one I thought would suit you, Cliff. You are our charmer. Our undercover man. It's a conversational Swedish course, ideal for learning how to adapt language according to any situation. It's run by a young Swedish friend of mine, Ingrid. We could also corner the fairly local Scandinavian market. But, on reflection, common sense then set in and I thought that maybe that was too much of a niche market.' The others smiled as they could see that Barry was ribbing Cliff about his amorous nature. However, the faraway look in Cliff's eyes showed that he had not seen the wind-up nature of this suggestion and that his imagination was in full flow.

'A better one,' continued Barry, 'would be a course on psychological profiling which would I'm sure prove very useful to you.'

'Yes I'd love to have a go at that. It sounds very interesting and right up my street,' Cliff paused for a second, 'But I tell you what. Give me the number for Ingrid, your

Swedish friend. I'm sure she would be able to teach me some very useful things as well. And there might be some legs in that first idea of yours too.'

'Sounds like you're really ready to give one, I'm mean take one, for the team,' laughed Andy.

Barry now turned his attention to Andy. 'For you there is a surveillance course which would demonstrate how to follow and track suspects, on the ground, without being seen yourself. It would focus on using all of the traditional methods combined with any modern gadgets which are available now. There is also a Health and Beauty course, but I think it would be unlikely you would pass that one,' Barry laughed as he spoke, 'Still the surveillance role means you will have to lose that dirty bloody hat, and that questionable tracksuit, from time to time.'

'A right cheeky bastard you're getting cockney boy. I'm beginning to regret all the nice things I said earlier. I'll have you know I scrub up very well when the occasion demands it.' Andy feigned indignation but it didn't fool anybody.

'And for you Dave. When you return from your sunshine holiday, I had a logistics and planning course in mind. You are our natural leader, and this might help in that area. As the only driver amongst us there will be a company car available for you to do any extra travelling, which may become necessary. It will also be ideal to help with stakeouts and the like. I'd like you all to do an Audio-Visual course as well. That's one area where I think we all could do with some training. What do you think guys?'

'I do have one useful thought, Mister Cockney Boy, how about the company buys us all a beer and we celebrate our success and the beginning of our future together?' Andy was already revving up his mobility scooter. 'Race you all to the pub.'

And with that off he went.

. . . .

The two brothers were sitting in a car outside what used to be their home.

Billy turned to his younger sibling, 'You still can't remember anything?'

They had just got back from having a walk around the block.

'No, thank God. It's still a blank to me. There is absolutely nothing familiar about any of this.'

'I was relieved to see somebody had taken down that old shed,' Billy was staring at the wall behind which lay their childhood garden. 'I think that would have brought back too strong a memory.' They sat in silence until Billy spoke again, 'You know I'm going to call you Roy from now on.'

'That's fine by me Billy,' Roy turned smiling at his older brother. It was such a weird, yet wonderful, experience to not only to have a brother in his life but also to have reclaimed his real-life history. 'If it's the name that our real parents chose for me then it is my name. Apparently the Harveys, my adoptive parents who did a great job in bringing me up, thought Roy was old fashioned. They named me Troy so as to be both modern and not a confusing transition.'

Billy smiled, 'I think people do similar things with the names of dogs they get from rescue centres.'

Deadly Circle/DC Poolie

Roy's response was to playfully punch his brother, 'Very funny. Woof! Woof!'

'In those days we lived here as Billy and Roy and now we sit in this car as Billy and Roy again,' Billy said wistfully.

'Yes, we've come full circle.'

'Sadly, more a deadly circle looking back on things.'

Billy changed the topic, 'Are you happy to become the new Hartlepool United manager? After all its all happened so quickly.'

He looked down at Roy's still badly swollen knees knowing the prognosis was that Roy could never play competitive football again.

'You know what? I am ready. After all it's a logical next step for a footballer who comes to the end of his career. I've just taken it a few years earlier than I'd planned.'

'Yes, I can see that. It's still a massive change though,' countered Billy.

'It's much easier to do with you here with me. Charlie is dedicating his final few years at the club to training you up so that you will then be ready to take over from him. I couldn't think of anyone better to help my brother.' There was real emotion in Roy's voice. An emotion, until now, he hadn't felt capable of feeling.

'I know. I'm so grateful.'

'No. You deserve it after all you went through to keep me safe. And to make sure we make this work long term it is certainly best that we don't live together. I want you close but not that close.'

'Good job that the neighbouring apartment was still available,' mused Billy.

Deadly Circle/DC Poolie

'Yes it certainly was. A good investment for me all around.'

Deadly Circle/DC Poolie

Final Thoughts

I came to Hartlepool with no hope in my heart. A heart, which was full of anger and carrying a huge sense of injustice. I'm not proud of who I was and certainly regret so many of my actions over the years. I can try to justify them starting with the undeniable abuse I suffered at the hands of that evil man, but all actions and decisions have their consequences. I must be man enough to accept blame for mine.

Unlike many I've met, both inside and outside of institutions, I now have a real chance at turning things around and I'm determined not to blow it. It almost seems wrong that, as an adult, I have more support than I did in those dark times. Roy has been a rock for me and has helped me find a counsellor to navigate these next few difficult months. I know the road may be rocky but with Roy and the counsellor I feel they will be my steamroller breaking down any boulders into stones of a manageable size.

To embrace the future, I need to accept my past mistakes. A lot of my bad behaviour in Hartlepool was minor and inconsequential but my violent outburst and subsequent attack on that poor girl was neither of those things.

Roy has been down to the brothel and, hopefully, paved a way for me to seek forgiveness. I need to work out how I can make it up to her. Fortunately, they will not be involving the police. I am very grateful to her, and her boyfriend, for that.

Deadly Circle/DC Poolie

Once I have done that I will feel able to address the future, more or less, guilt free.
Wish me luck.

Acknowledgements

Dave and Cliff would like to acknowledge the inspiration provided by our dearly departed friend, Harry Marsh. A wonderful charismatic character well known to all the inhabitants of the Headland. Elements of his unique personality live on in some of the key characters of this book.

Putting our ideas down on paper has turned out to be the easy part. We would like to thank Andy, Charles and Paul for giving us their time, enthusiasm and insight while either proof reading or test reading.